OLYMPUS
AT WAR

Also by Kate O'Hearn

The Flame of Olympus

The New Olympians

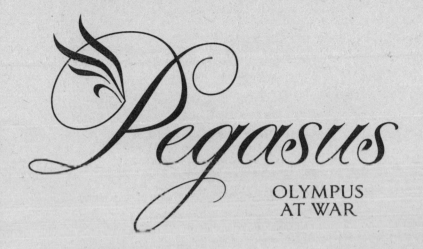

Pegasus

OLYMPUS
AT WAR

KATE O'HEARN

Aladdin

NEW YORK LONDON TORONTO SYDNEY NEW DELHI

ALADDIN

An imprint of Simon & Schuster Children's Publishing Division
1230 Avenue of the Americas, New York, NY 10020
First Aladdin paperback edition January 2014
Text copyright © 2013 by Kate O'Hearn
Cover illustration copyright © 2013 by Jason Chan
All rights reserved, including the right of reproduction in whole or in part in any form.
ALADDIN is a trademark of Simon & Schuster, Inc., and related logo
is a registered trademark of Simon & Schuster, Inc.
Also available in an Aladdin hardcover edition.
For information about special discounts for bulk purchases, please contact
Simon & Schuster Special Sales at 1-866-506-1949 or business@simonandschuster.com.
The Simon & Schuster Speakers Bureau can bring authors to your live event.
For more information or to book an event contact the Simon & Schuster Speakers Bureau
at 1-866-248-3049 or visit our website at www.simonspeakers.com.
Designed by Karin Paprocki
The text of this book was set in Adobe Garamond.
Manufactured in the United States of America 0215 OFF
4 6 8 10 9 7 5 3
The Library of Congress has cataloged the hardcover edition as follows:
Kate O'Hearn.
[Olympus at war]
Pegasus / by Kate O'Hearn.—First Aladdin hardcover ed.
p.cm.
Summary: Reborn as the Flame, thirteen-year-old Emily has saved Olympus from destruction, but when the gruesome Nirads begin a new invasion, Emily and her friends become entangled in the conflict as old grudges are unearthed and new enemies are discovered.
978-1-4424-4412-6 (hc)
[1. Pegasus (Greek mythology)—Fiction. 2. Diana (Roman deity)—Fiction. 3. Monsters—Fiction. 4. Mythology, Roman—Fiction. 5. Fantasy.] 1. Title.
PZ7.O4137Peg 2012
[Fic] dc23
2011052026
ISBN 978-1-4424-4413-3 (pbk)
ISBN 978-1-4424-4414-0 (eBook)

OLYMPUS
AT WAR

OLYMPUS WAS UNLIKE ANYWHERE EMILY had ever been before. It was a magical fantasyland filled with people and creatures beyond imagination. A place where rain didn't fall but the lush green gardens never wilted. Flowers bloomed constantly, filling the air with their intoxicating fragrances. The air itself seemed alive. It was honey sweet and warm and enveloped you in a blanket of peace; it was rich with the sounds of singing birds and filled with insects that never stung. If a bee landed on you, it was only because it wanted to be petted.

The buildings in Olympus were as beautiful and unique as the land itself. Most were made of smooth white marble with tall, intricately carved pillars reaching high into the clear blue sky. There were open theaters where the Muses danced and sang for the entertainment of all.

The wide cobbled streets were lined with statues of the strongest fighters and heroes. There were no cars or trucks pumping pollution into the air. The Olympians walked or flew wherever they needed to go. Occasionally they would ride in a chariot drawn by magnificent horses.

Then there were the libraries, more than Emily could count, containing the texts from the many worlds the Olympians visited and guarded. Some of her favorite books were in the library at Jupiter's palace, brought in especially for her.

Emily could never have imagined a more perfect place.

But living in Olympus, amid all this splendor, Emily was miserable.

She missed her father. She spent every waking moment thinking and worrying about him. He was back in her world, a prisoner of the Central Research Unit. The CRU was a secret government agency obsessed with capturing aliens and anything out of the ordinary to use as weapons. She had been their prisoner for a short time and knew how single-minded and cruel they were. But they still had her father. What were they doing to him? Were they punishing him because of her escape? Had they killed him? So many fears and unanswered questions tore at her heart that she could never be completely happy or stop worrying about him.

Even spending time with Pegasus didn't ease the pain. Emily was desperate to get back to New York to find her father, but Jupiter wouldn't let her go. He insisted her place was here among the other Olympians. And with the invading warrior race of Nirads still posing a threat to Olympus, Jupiter couldn't risk sending any of his fighters to Emily's world on a rescue mission. No matter how much she pleaded with the god, he refused to allow her to leave.

Emily paused as she walked through the gardens of Jupiter's palace. She raised her face to the sun and felt its warm rays streaming down on her. Was this the same sun that shone in her world? Was her father allowed to see it? From her own experience as a prisoner in the CRU's deep underground facility, she doubted it.

Emily felt even more determined. If Jupiter wouldn't let her go, she had no choice but to run away and rescue her father herself. Walking along the stream that coursed through Olympus, she saw a group of beautiful water nymphs splashing on the shore. They waved and called their strange greeting. Moments later they slipped beneath the surface, and the water calmed as if they'd never been there.

Lost in thought, Emily wasn't paying attention to where she was walking and tripped over a small rock. She cursed and righted herself. On top of everything else, she was still getting used to the new gold leg brace that Vulcan, the armorer of Olympus, had made for her. He had constructed it using the same gold as Pegasus's bridle. A very special gold that was lethal to Nirads. With one brief touch they were badly poisoned. Longer contact proved fatal to the ferocious warriors. With this brace Emily could not only defend herself against the invaders, she could walk and run once again.

But learning to get around with the strange device had taken time and effort. Now she could almost move as well as she had before her leg was permanently damaged by the Nirads in New York.

She walked toward Jupiter's maze, a large labyrinth built in the middle of a garden and consisting of tall green bushes grown in complicated patterns. It took a lot of practice to navigate it, but Emily and her friends had discovered that the maze was the perfect place to hold private conversations.

Emily found her way through the labyrinth, where Pegasus was waiting for her beside the pedestal at the center. The magnificent winged stallion always stole her breath. Standing quietly in the dark of the trees, he glowed brilliant white. His head was high and proud, and his coat shiny and well groomed. There wasn't a feather out of place on his neatly folded wings.

When Pegasus saw her, he whinnied excitedly and nodded his head.

Beside the winged horse stood Emily's best friend from New York, Joel. Joel's Roman features, black hair, and warm brown eyes always reminded her of the classic Italian paintings she'd seen in the art museum. He was no longer the violent, angry boy she had first met. Spending time in Olympus had softened his outer shell of rage and hurt due to the loss of his family. Now he let others see that he had a deeply caring heart and a ready laugh. Joel spent his days working with Vulcan in the Olympus armory. He had even helped design the brace on Emily's leg.

Emily looked around. "Where's Paelen?"

"He'll be here in a few minutes. He had something to pick up." Joel reached for her elbow. "Em, you're absolutely sure you want to do this?"

"What choice have I got?" Emily answered. "Joel, all I think about is saving my dad. There's nothing else I can do. We wouldn't have to sneak around like this if Jupiter would help!" She threw her hands up in frustration. As she brought them down, brilliant flames flashed from her fingertips, hit the edge of her good foot, and scorched the ground around it. Emily howled and hopped in pain.

"Emily, calm down!" Joel warned. "You know it gets worse when you're upset."

"Nuts!" she cried. "Being the Flame of Olympus is one thing. But constantly setting myself on fire is another!"

"You've got to calm down," Joel insisted. "Remember what Vesta taught you. You can control the Flame if you remain calm."

"That's easier said than done," Emily complained as she sat down and rubbed her singed foot. Ever since she emerged from the Temple of the Flame, she was discovering powers she couldn't control. Powers that continually set things alight.

Joel sat down beside her. "We'll get your dad out of there. I promise. But you can't help him if you can't control the Flame."

"Joel's right." Paelen emerged from the trees behind them. In contrast to Joel, he was small and wiry, and he was able to get into the tiniest of spaces. Paelen had a notorious habit of getting into trouble, but with his crooked grin and dark, sparkling eyes, he always found a way to make Emily smile. "And if I were you, I would lower your voices. Half the maze can hear your conversation." He sat down beside Emily and gave her a playful shove. "Set yourself on fire again I see."

"No, I tripped," Emily answered, shoving him back.

Paelen smiled his crooked smile. "Of course you

did; which is why your sandal is charcoal and still smoldering."

In the time they'd spent in Olympus, Emily had really grown to like Paelen. Between him and Joel, she couldn't have asked for better friends. Paelen was also one of the few Olympians who understood what they'd been through as prisoners of the CRU on Governors Island.

"Speaking of sandals"—Emily changed the subject—"you didn't steal Mercury's again, did you?" She noticed the winged sandals on his feet.

"Me? Of course not," Paelen said in mock horror. "You know I'm no longer a thief. Mercury just gave them to me. He is having another set made for himself." Paelen paused and frowned. "He said the sandals prefer to stay with me. I do not understand what he means, but I'm not going to say no to such a useful gift." He petted the tiny wings on the sandals. "These flying sandals saved our lives in your world and helped us escape the CRU. There is no telling what else they can do." He leaned closer to Emily and eagerly rubbed his hands together. "So, tell me. When do we leave for New York?"

Pegasus stepped forward and started to nicker.

Paelen nodded and translated for the others. "Pegasus heard Jupiter, Mars, and Hercules talking. They are going on an expedition to see if they can discover how the Nirads entered Olympus in such large numbers without being seen. Until they know and can secure the route, we are still in danger. Pegasus suggests if we are going to go to New York to rescue your father, we should leave once they're gone."

Emily rose and kissed the stallion on his soft muzzle. "Thank you, Pegasus. That's a great idea." She turned to Joel and Paelen. "It's settled, then. The moment Jupiter leaves, we're out of here!"

Quietly they discussed their plans as they strolled through the maze. Emily rested her hand on Pegasus's neck as he walked beside her.

"We'll need some human clothes," Joel mused aloud. "We can't arrive back in New York dressed like this."

"What is wrong with these?" Paelen looked down at his tunic. "I have always dressed this way."

"You're kidding, right?" Joel smirked. "Paelen,

we look like rejects from a gladiator movie! Look at me—I'm wearing a dress!"

"It's a tunic," Emily corrected him, "and I think it suits you." She looked down at her own beautiful gown made from fine white embroidered silk with an intricate braided gold belt at her waist. The material ended above the golden brace on her damaged left leg, leaving it exposed. Emily had never felt embarrassed revealing the deep, angry scars from the Nirad wounds while she was on Olympus. The Olympians regarded them as a badge of honor. She had earned them in the service of Olympus, and she had learned to be proud of them. But as she gazed down at her leg now, she realized that the deep scars and leg brace wouldn't be viewed as positively in her world.

"Joel's right," she agreed. "I can't go back there like this either. We've got to hide this brace."

Pegasus started to neigh, and Paelen translated. "If anyone should try to steal it from you, Pegasus would defend you, as would Joel and I." A playful twinkle returned to his eyes. "Of course, should that fail, you could always set yourself on fire again. That would surely scare off any attackers!"

"Thanks, Paelen," Emily teased as she shoved him lightly. Then she patted Pegasus on the neck. "And thank you, Pegs. But I still think we will need to find other clothing."

"Other clothing for what?"

Emily looked up at the owner of the new voice. Despite all the time they'd spent in Olympus, she still couldn't get over the sight of Cupid. Seeing Pegasus's wings had been strange at the beginning. But somehow they suited him. She couldn't imagine him without them. But looking at a teenager with colorful, pheasantlike feathered wings on his back was something else.

Cupid pulled in his wings and landed neatly in the maze before them. "So, where are you going that you need new clothing?" he asked.

"None of your business," Joel shot back. "Didn't your mother ever teach you any manners? It's not polite to listen in on other people's conversation."

"Of course," Cupid said. "But she also taught me that when humans and Olympians mix, there is always trouble. And what do I see before my curious eyes? Humans mixing with Olympians."

Cupid smiled radiantly at Emily, and it set her heart fluttering. She had a terrible crush on him, and he knew it. He was the most beautiful Olympian she had ever met, with fine features, light sandy blond hair, sapphire blue eyes that sparkled, and skin like polished marble. Though Cupid was very old, he looked no more than sixteen or seventeen.

Emily stole a glance at Joel and saw his temper starting to flare. The way Cupid pronounced the word "humans" was always meant as an insult. "Get out of here, Cupid," Joel warned. "This is a private conversation, and you are *not* welcome."

"Is this true?" Cupid said slyly to Emily. "Do you really wish me to go?"

The intensity of his stare kept the words from forming on her lips. Everything about him was trouble. Joel had told her some of the myths concerning Cupid. She knew that, like a coward, he had fled the area when the Nirads first attacked and had stayed away until the danger had gone. Yet despite all this, she couldn't tell him to go.

Before the moment became awkward, Pegasus stepped forward and snorted loudly.

"Trouble?" Cupid repeated as he turned and feigned innocence to the stallion. "I am not causing trouble. I just wanted to speak with the Flame."

"Her name is Emily," Paelen said defensively. He moved to stand in front of Emily to block her from Cupid. "Do not call her Flame."

"And I told you to leave," Joel added, taking position beside Paelen and crossing his arms over his chest.

"Or what?" Cupid challenged. "What will you do to me, human?"

Once again Pegasus snorted, and he pounded the ground with a golden hoof. There was no mistaking the warning. Emily saw fear rise in Cupid's eyes. Even Paelen took a cautious step back from the stallion.

"There is no need to lose your temper, Pegasus." Cupid held up his hands in surrender. "I shall go."

His wings opened as he prepared to fly. But before leaving, Cupid plucked a colorful feather from his right wing and placed it in Emily's hair. "Something to put under your pillow to remember me by," he said as he jumped into the air and flapped his large wings. "See you later, Flame!"

Pegasus reared on his hind legs, opened his own huge wings, and shrieked into the sky after him.

As Cupid escaped, he turned and waved back at her, laughing as he went.

"I came this close to hitting him!" Joel said, balling his hands into fists.

"Me too," Paelen said.

Pegasus gently nudged Emily and nickered softly.

"You must stay away from Cupid," Paelen explained. "Pegasus says he is trouble. Even more than— What?" Paelen turned sharply to the stallion. "Me? Pegasus, how can you compare Cupid to me? We are nothing alike. I may have been a thief, but Cupid is a troublemaking coward, and I resent being compared to him. And what about you?" Paelen turned to Emily. He pulled the feather from her hair and tossed it to the ground. "You should have told him to go. Cupid would think nothing of handing you over to the Nirads if it meant saving his own skin and feathers. Stay away from him!"

Emily watched in complete confusion as Paelen stormed off into the maze and disappeared. Paelen had never shown any trace of anger or raised his voice to her before. "What did I do?"

Joel looked at her in surprise. "You really don't know?"

When she shook her head, he said, "Never mind. We've got bigger things to worry about. You must learn to control those powers of yours before we leave. You've got your training session with Vesta. Keep it and learn as much as you can."

As Joel walked away, Emily turned to Pegasus and shook her head. "You know something, Pegs? The older I get, the more confused I get. Can you please tell me what just happened here?"

Pegasus gently nudged her and led her back toward Jupiter's palace to find Vesta.

Emily spent a long afternoon back in the Temple of the Flame struggling to learn how to master her powers. Vesta tried to teach her, but every time Emily summoned the powers, they became uncontrollable.

Vesta patiently explained how to pull back the Flame, to control it. But every time Emily tried, she failed, and flames shot wildly from her hands and around the temple.

"I can't do it," Emily complained, defeated.

"Child, you must focus," Vesta scolded. "I can see your mind is elsewhere. If you are not careful, you will lose control of your powers completely and hurt yourself as you did earlier today."

Emily's eyes shot over to where Pegasus stood at the entrance of the temple. He lowered his head guiltily.

"Thanks, Pegs," she muttered.

"Do not blame Pegasus for telling me what happened," Vesta said. "He cares about you and does not wish to see you harmed." Vesta rested her hands on Emily's shoulders. "Emily, you must understand. You are the Living Flame of Olympus. Your power feeds the Flame here in this temple, and it keeps us alive. Countless generations ago, I took the heart of the Flame to your world and hid it in a child. It has passed from girl to girl throughout the ages until it finally reached you. You were born with this power. I am sorry that we have had to summon it from within you to save Olympus. But the moment you sacrificed yourself in this temple you changed. Emily, you carry the power of the sun deep within you. If you do not harness these powers soon, you may do yourself and everyone around you a great harm."

Emily looked down at her burned sandal. She already knew how dangerous her powers were. She had accidentally burned up enough items in her quarters to prove it. It was reaching the point where she was running out of secret hiding places for the singed victims of her powers.

"I'm sorry," she finally said. "I'll try harder."

Turning back to the plinth, she looked into the brightly burning flames. They were fed by her and were the only things in Olympus her powers couldn't damage.

"All right," Vesta said patiently. "Look into the flames. I want you to focus on what you intend to do. Visualize yourself doing it. Then concentrate and carefully release the power within yourself."

Emily lifted both her hands and concentrated. She imagined that she was a giant blowtorch turning on the gases. She felt prickles start in her stomach and flow up her spine and flood down her raised arms toward her hands. "Come on, Em," she muttered to herself. "You can do it."

Suddenly a wide, wild stream of fire shot out of her fingertips.

"Very good. Now concentrate," Vesta instructed. "Control the stream, Emily. Make it tighter."

Emily held her breath as the raging flames shot out of her hands. Concentrating as Vesta taught her, she pulled back and refined them until they became a narrow beam of red light. But the tighter she pulled back, the more intense it became.

The beam of light shot through the flames in the plinth and across the temple until it hit the far wall. It did not stop. It burned a narrow hole right through the thick white marble and continued out into the sky over Olympus.

"Cut if off now, Emily," Vesta warned. "Just think 'stop'!"

In her head, Emily imagined shutting off the gases to the blowtorch. But nothing happened. She mentally turned all the dials and flicked all the switches that controlled her powers. But once again, the beam would not stop.

"Cut it off, Emily," Vesta cried. "You must make it obey you!"

Emily tried again and again, but nothing happened. As her panic increased, so did the intensity of the laserlike Flame. It pulsated as it tore through the skies over Olympus.

"I CAN'T STOP IT!"

A sudden blow from behind sent her tumbling forward, and she fell to the floor. With her concentration broken, the red beam stopped. She panted heavily and studied her hands. No burns, blemishes, or pain. She looked up, and what she saw made her suck in her breath. Pegasus's whole face and neck were burned bright red. Worst of all, his soft white muzzle was black and blistering. It was Pegasus who had knocked her over and stopped the flames. But when he touched her, her power had singed his beautiful skin.

"Pegasus!" Emily ran over to him. "I'm so sorry. I swear I didn't mean to do it!"

She felt sick as she inspected his wounds. She had done this to him. "Please, forgive me!" Without thinking, Emily reached forward and gently stroked his burned face. At her touch the skin started to heal. Soon Pegasus was completely restored.

"I can't do this, Pegs." Emily sobbed as she stepped away from him. "I just can't. I hurt you. What if I'd killed you? I'm just too dangerous to be around."

Emily dashed out of the temple. Tears rose to her eyes as she ran down the tall steps. She cringed as she replayed what happened and, worse still, what could have happened.

At the base of the steps, she looked up and saw Pegasus and Vesta emerging from the temple.

"Emily, stop!" Vesta called.

Emily turned and ran farther away. She couldn't face Pegasus again, knowing she had almost killed him. She ran past other Olympians on the street, ignoring their curious stares and concerned queries. She had to get away. Away from Pegasus and anyone else her powers could hurt. She was just too dangerous to be allowed in public.

Emily finally ran into the open amphitheater. The Muses weren't performing that day, so the thousands of seats sat empty and alone. The perfect place for someone dangerous. She ran down the steps, toward the center stage, and threw herself to the ground. It was over. Her life was over. There would be no trip back to New York, no rescue of her father.

All there was now was pain.

Sobs escaped her as she finally realized all the things she'd lost. She wished she'd never emerged from the flames at the temple. Olympus and Pegasus would have been better off without her.

Tears blinded Emily as she looked around in misery at the beautiful marble theater encircling her. She wiped them furiously away. As she flicked the tears off her fingers, there was a blinding flash and a terrible explosion.

Her world went black.

EMILY AWOKE IN HER BED. FOR AN INSTANT she feared she was back at the CRU facility on Governors Island. But as her eyes slowly focused, she saw that she was in her beautiful room at Jupiter's palace. All the windows were open, and the sheer curtains were blowing gently in the sweet, warm breeze.

"Welcome back."

The Great Hunter, Diana, was standing beside her bed. The two had formed a tight bond after their time together in New York. She was the daughter of Jupiter and everything Emily hoped to grow up to be like. Diana was strong, brave, and caring. She went to New York and risked her life to save Pegasus.

The tall woman took a seat on the edge of the bed

and lightly stroked Emily's forehead. "That was quite a shock for us."

Emily frowned. She was stiff and sore, with a pounding headache. She knew something big had happened—she just couldn't remember what. Finally she recalled the events at the temple. "I hurt Pegasus," she whispered miserably. "I burned him."

"Pegasus is fine," Diana assured. "You are the one we are all worried about."

Emily raised her head and looked around the room. They were alone. No Joel, no Paelen—and no Pegasus. Her friends were keeping away from her because she was dangerous. Her powers were uncontrollable, and now she had to be locked up.

"What happens now?" she asked softly, unable to face Diana. "Where are you going to lock me away?"

Diana frowned. "Lock you away? Child, why would we do that?"

Emily's emotions welled up. "Because I'm dangerous and I hurt Pegasus."

"Oh, Emily," Diana pulled her into a tight embrace. "No one is going to imprison you. Your powers got away from you, that's all. It has happened to all of us. We just did not expect to find your tears quite so potent."

"My tears?" Emily sniffed. "I don't understand."

Diana explained that the amphitheater caretaker had watched Emily run to the stage and saw how the flick of her tears had caused an explosion that shook all of Olympus. He was far enough away to be hurt, not killed. However, the blast did destroy the theater and create a huge crater. Pegasus finally found her suspended high in a tree several miles away.

"I-I don't understand," Emily said. "My tears caused an explosion?"

Diana nodded. "We do not really understand either. When the Flame emerged from you, Vesta said its full powers would be released. But she never expected them to be this potent. Even your tears are filled with the power of the sun."

She couldn't even cry without hurting herself or everyone around her! Every day was getting worse and worse. She was no longer a person, a girl with a bright future ahead of her. She had become a nuclear bomb waiting to go off.

"I don't want it," she finally said in a whisper. "I

don't want any of these powers. I didn't ask for them. I just want my old life back with my dad."

"I am sorry, but you do not have a choice," Diana said. "You were born with the Flame. It is part of you. But I promise, you can learn to control it. Do not fight your powers, Emily. Embrace them and accept them as your ally, not your enemy."

"And if I can't learn?" Emily asked.

"You must," Diana said as she stood and crossed to the door. "Rest now. You will feel better soon."

Emily doubted she would ever feel good again. She climbed stiffly from her bed and walked over to one of the windows. She sat on the ledge and quietly watched the activity below, just like she used to do in her apartment in New York.

But this wasn't Manhattan she was looking out over with its heavy traffic, police sirens, crowds, and shops. It was Olympus. The light breeze blowing through her hair was sweet and warm, not polluted like New York's smoggy air. She watched winged Olympians and large birds soaring together in the clear blue sky. Butterflies the size of cars fluttered around, playing a kind of tag with some young children. Down in the square, centaurs and giants walked and talked together as casually as people in her own world would. Everywhere she looked, Emily saw amazing things. But watching the world below only added to the feeling that things would never be normal again.

"Dad, where are you?" she said miserably. Emily no longer grieved over the death of her mother. Somehow in this strange and wondrous world, she always felt her mother's presence nearby, as though all she needed to do was reach out to touch her. It was her father who occupied all her waking moments. His rescue now seemed impossible. How could she help him if she couldn't even help herself? She was a dangerous monster—unable even to cry without possibly hurting or killing someone.

Lost in misery, Emily was unaware of time passing until she heard a gentle knock at her door.

"Emily?" a deep voice called. "May we enter?"

Emily was surprised to see Jupiter come into her room. Although she, Joel, and Paelen lived in his massive marble palace, she only ever saw him at mealtimes. But even then, those banquets were so big and noisy; she never got to speak with him. He had never been to her quarters, and the one time she did manage to speak privately with him was when she'd begged him to let her return to New York to rescue her father. That request had been denied.

"Jupiter." Emily bowed her head with respect.

"Emily, I was most disturbed to learn what happened at the theater yesterday. It seems your tears are very powerful. I hope you are all right."

"I'm fine, thank you," Emily said.

Behind Jupiter stood another man. He was equally large and had a commanding presence similar to that of the leader of Olympus. He was just as tall and had the same long white hair and full beard. But unlike the serious, somber face of Jupiter, this new man had a warm, smiling face filled with joy and mischief. The difference between the two could be found in their eyes: Jupiter's were dark and deep and seemed to hold the knowledge of the ages, while this man's eyes were so pale they were almost like pearls. In truth, to Emily he looked less like an Olympian and more like Santa Claus.

"I do not believe you have met my brother," Jupiter said casually. "This is Neptune." He turned to his brother. "And this is the Flame of Olympus. Although I have recently discovered she prefers to be called Emily."

"Emily," Neptune said as a huge smile appeared on his warm face. "My son told me what happened to you. How are you feeling?"

Emily's eyes grew wide as she remembered that Neptune was Pegasus's father. "I'm fine, thank you," she stuttered. She looked down at Neptune's strong, muscular legs beneath his tunic.

"Perhaps you expected a fish's tail?" Neptune started to chuckle.

Emily flushed and nodded. "I'm sorry, sir. I didn't mean to be rude and stare, but I'd always heard you lived in the sea."

Neptune's face wrinkled with booming laughter that seemed to fill the whole palace. "No doubt you thought I rode a chariot of shells drawn by a team of sea horses, carrying a trident in my hand as I stirred the seas into rage."

Emily's face turned redder and she nodded.

It was Jupiter's turn to chuckle. "Do not let him fool you, Emily. He does just that and more."

"But not when I am on land," Neptune finished, growing serious. As he stepped farther in the room, he turned back to the door. "Son, come in here."

Emily heard familiar and welcome clopping sounds coming from the corridor, and in moments Pegasus entered her bedroom. He was as blazing white as ever, and every feather lay smoothly on his wings. There was no evidence of the burns she had caused. Emily was grateful to find there was no trace of hesitation when he stepped up to her.

"Pegasus," she said softly as she stroked his soft muzzle. "Are you all right?"

"He is fine," Neptune said. "But he is very worried about you. After the incident at the amphitheater, he asked if I might be able to help. So I went to my most talented Sirens and asked them to weave their finest silk from the grasses that grow in the deepest part of the sea. It is my hope that this will help."

Emily watched Neptune produce a shimmering sea-green handkerchief from his tunic. It seemed to change color when it caught the light, and reminded her of iridescent fish scales. He handed it to her, and as she turned it in her hands, Emily saw an embroidered picture of her riding Pegasus in the center of the fine fabric.

"Pegasus gave the Sirens strands of hair from his tail for the embroidery," Neptune explained. "This is their best work."

"I just hope it works for the Flame's tears as well," Jupiter added. He stepped closer to Emily. "This was made with all the powers of the Sirens and the sea. Please keep it with you at all times. We believe it may be strong enough to collect and store your tears without causing any more damage to Olympus or yourself."

Emily looked at the beautiful, weightless handkerchief with the embroidered Pegasus. It was the most beautiful thing she'd ever seen in her life.

"All we need to do now is test it," Neptune said.

"Test it?" Emily said fearfully. "I'm not sure about that."

"Not today, child," Jupiter reassured as he put his arm lightly around her shoulders. "When you are feeling better. In the meantime, I want you to rest. That was a rather nasty surprise you had yesterday. When you are more recovered, ask Pegasus to take you to the new arena we are building for you. It will work as a much better training ground for your powers. Now that we have seen their extent, we need to ensure everyone's safety until you have better control of them."

Emily looked up at Jupiter and nodded. She thanked Neptune again for the beautiful gift and stood beside Pegasus as they left the room. When they had gone, Emily threw her arms around the stallion's thick neck.

"I'm so sorry I hurt you!" she cried. "It got away from me, and I couldn't stop it."

Pegasus nickered softly.

"Pegasus, what am I going to do? One more mistake like that and I could kill someone. I might do more damage to Olympus than the Nirads did."

Pegasus gently nudged her, to let her know he understood. He then invited her to stare into his eyes. As Emily locked into his gaze, a clear vision filled her mind. She was sitting on Pegasus's back, flying away from the palace—her fears and worries eased in that glorious moment.

"Can we?" she asked hopefully. Of all the wonderful things to do and see in Olympus, Emily's favorite was riding Pegasus and discovering new places she'd never been before.

Emily quickly changed and tied her new handkerchief to her braided belt. She climbed onto the stallion's back. When she was settled comfortably behind his large wings, Pegasus stepped up to one of the wide windows and confidently leaped through it.

Emily clung to the stallion's mane as they soared in the skies over Olympus. Riding Pegasus was better than all the roller-coaster rides she'd ever been on in her life! She felt safe with him, but at the same time, there was the wild exhilaration of flying high in the air with no safety harness. It was just her and Pegasus.

On the ground beneath them, people and creatures waved greetings to the Flame. In the sky around them, other winged citizens flew in formation beside them.

After some distance their escorts drifted away, and the two of them were flying alone. In no time her troubles were put aside and she savored the freedom she always felt when riding the magnificent winged stallion. As they gently glided in the thermal winds over the mountain range in Olympus, Emily could feel Pegasus's wings beating confidently.

Soon the stallion started to descend down the side of the mountain. Emily recognized the place they had gone on the very first day after she emerged from the temple. It was a private, secluded beach with shimmering silver sands beside a beautiful sparkling lake.

After he landed, Pegasus moved smoothly along the diamond-dust shore, his hooves splashing lightly in the water. Birds sang in the trees just back from the beach, and the air was rich with the smell of the lush green forest. Spending time with the stallion always made Emily feel better and cleared the cobwebs from her troubled mind.

She wasn't sure how long they'd been there when the peaceful tranquility was shattered by loud, urgent shouts from Paelen and Joel. She looked up in the sky and saw Joel clinging to Paelen's back as Mercury's winged sandals struggled to carry the combined weight of the two.

"Emily, are you all right?" Joel asked as he climbed

off Paelen's back. "Diana wouldn't let us see you. She said you needed to rest after you went nuclear and blew up the theater."

"I'm much better," Emily answered, grateful to see her friends. She reached forward and patted Pegasus's neck. "We both are."

"Good," Paelen said, "because we have a big problem. Nirads are back in Olympus."

"What?" Her feelings of peace ended with that one word: Nirads. The four-armed savage fighters who'd nearly killed her and Pegasus in New York and who had damaged her left leg.

"Where are they?" she demanded. "Is this another invasion?"

"I don't think so," Joel said. "We've heard there aren't that many."

"One Nirad is too many," Paelen added.

Emily looked at Pegasus and then her two friends. They had all thought the war with the Nirads was over. After the Flame was relit and the Olympians' powers restored, the warrior race had fled Olympus. No one imagined they would return. "So, what do we do? Get ready to fight?"

"No. Jupiter is raising the army again," Paelen said. "He, Neptune, and Hercules have gone out to where they were spotted to find out how many there are and how they are getting here. While they are gone, Mars and Vulcan are arming everyone with the same gold as your brace and Pegasus's bridle." He held up a golden dagger and pointed to the one on Joel's belt. "Apollo and Diana are organizing the remaining fighters. They've ordered us to find you and take you back to the palace. They don't want us to fight. We are to remain there with you until this is over."

Emily felt fear constricting her throat. The Nirads were back. She knew this time that she, as the living Flame of Olympus, was their target. If she were to somehow be killed or even severely wounded, the Flame at the Temple could be extinguished, and then there would be no hope for anyone's survival. She couldn't let that happen.

"We're not going back to the palace," she said, deciding. "It's too dangerous, and the Nirads are too big and strong. We'd be sitting ducks! I think we should go to New York. We were planning to anyway. When we get my dad free, I'm sure he can help." Emily looked at the stallion. "Pegs, what do you think we should do?"

Pegasus pawed the sand, whinnied loudly, and nodded his head.

Emily patted the stallion's neck. "It's settled, then. We go back to New York right now."

3

AS THEY PREPARED TO LEAVE, EMILY'S FEARS and doubts rose. She didn't want to stay at the palace and await the Nirads, but deep down she felt like she was abandoning the Olympians in their moment of need.

Joel settled on Pegasus's back, behind her. Emily looked over to Paelen. "You ready?"

Paelen nodded. "Let us go."

Pegasus started to trot along the silver sands, moved straight into a gallop, and leaped confidently into the air. Both Emily and Joel felt the thick, strong muscles in his shoulders and back flex as the stallion flapped his huge wings. As they climbed higher in the sky, Joel's arms wrapped tighter around Emily's waist, and she wove her fingers through the stallion's thick mane for a stronger grip.

"We're ready, Pegs!" Emily called.

The last time they had flown like this, they were fleeing the Nirads at Governors Island. This time they were fleeing Olympus for the same reason.

Pegasus flew faster and faster as they climbed higher in the sky. Emily looked back and saw Paelen using Mercury's sandals to fly behind them. Moments before they entered a thick white cloud, she thought she caught sight of something else following them at a distance. But before she had the chance to tell Joel, Pegasus prepared to enter the Solar Stream—the portal that Olympians used to travel from world to world. Pegasus moved impossibly fast to reach the speed that would open the door to the Solar Stream. Suddenly the stars around them turned into a brilliant blur, and they were gone.

Emily was certain she'd seen . . . something. She kept looking back, but within the powerful Solar Stream, with its blinding white light and the near-deafening whoosh of crackling energy, the most she could see was Paelen flying directly behind the stallion's tail.

"What is it?" Joel called.

Emily concentrated on him and had to shout to be heard over the tremendous power of the Solar Stream. "I thought I saw something following us!"

Joel quickly turned back. "I don't see anything!" he shouted.

"It's probably nothing!"

The journey through the Solar Stream seemed much longer than the last time. But then again, last time she had been traveling to her death. Eventually they burst out of the noisy brightness. The stars around them seemed to slow down to a stop, and they emerged into a brilliant, clear night sky. Emily sucked in her breath as her heart thrilled at the lights of New York City rising straight ahead.

The sense of joy and relief was a surprise to her. Emily never realized just how much she'd missed her old home.

"I thought I'd never see the city again," Joel said, as awestruck as she was.

"Joel, look," Emily called excitedly. She pointed to a tower rising majestically in the sky. "They fixed the

Empire State Building after Jupiter's lightning bolt blew the top off!"

"And it's got its Halloween colors on," Joel added as they both looked at the orange lights shining brightly at the top. The Empire State Building was unique. The colors were always changed at its top to reflect the season or special events. "It was May when we left. Now it's October? We've been gone almost six months?"

Joel's words filled Emily with dread. It felt like they'd only been in Olympus for a short time. But the Empire State Building's Halloween colors and the cold temperature of the air around them proved it true. In the past six months, what had the CRU done to her father?

Before long, they were approaching Governors Island. Emily looked down and felt sick as she remembered what had happened there. Joel's arms squeezed her tighter, and she knew he felt the same.

Pegasus began to descend, and Emily's fears increased. "No, Pegs, not here. We can't go back to Governors. The CRU are here!"

But her pleas were ignored. Pegasus was going to

land at the far end of Governors Island, a side of the small island Emily hadn't seen before. The Central Research Unit had their facility under the beautiful homes on the part of the island closest to Manhattan. There was no mistaking the military look to this area, with its several tall barracks, presumably where the soldiers stationed here lived.

They touched down in an open space between two barracks. The cold autumn wind was blowing off the water and caused Emily to shiver uncontrollably in her light Olympian dress. But apart from that, Governors Island was eerily quiet.

"Pegasus wants you to stay on his back," Paelen whispered, holding up his hand. "He has brought us back here to see if any Nirad warriors remain."

"How will we know?" Joel asked in alarm. "Stay here and wait for them or the CRU to come after us?" Joel leaned past Emily to speak to the stallion directly. "Pegasus, please, this is their base. We shouldn't be here. We've got to go."

"Joel, calm yourself," Paelen said. "I have an idea. These sandals always know where to find things I ask them for. Let me try now." He looked down at his winged sandals. "Search the island for Nirads. Are there any more here?"

Emily and Joel watched in the moonlight as the sandals obeyed Paelen's command and their tiny wings started to flutter. They lifted Paelen in the air, stopping when he was about ten feet high. They turned once, then came back down to the ground.

"The sandals have never failed me before," Paelen explained. "I do not believe they have done so now. There are no Nirads here."

"Then what happened to them?" Emily asked. "There were lots here right before we left. Bullets couldn't stop them, so what did?"

Pegasus started to neigh.

"I do not know," Paelen said. "Neither does Pegasus. He cannot smell any soldiers on this island. He believes the government has abandoned it."

"This was a huge facility. Why would they do that?" Joel asked.

Emily shrugged. "Maybe it was too difficult to explain the Nirads' presence in New York? When our picture was in the newspaper, they said we were a hoax. But maybe enough people saw Nirads and the damage they did and started to ask a lot of questions. So the CRU had to move."

"Could be," Joel agreed. "But where did they move to?"

"Perhaps to where they are holding Emily's father," Paelen suggested. "The sandals were taking me there before. I am certain they will do so again."

"Then let's go," Emily said as another shiver coursed down her spine. "There is nothing here but bad memories for all of us."

Once again Emily couldn't shake the strong feeling that they were being watched. She searched the darkened area but couldn't see anything out of the ordinary. She leaned forward and whispered in Pegasus's ear. "Pegs, I have a strange feeling. Is there someone else here?"

Pegasus lifted his head and started to sniff the air.

"What is it?" Joel softly asked.

"We are not alone," Paelen whispered as he, too, started to look around. Pegasus pounded the ground angrily and snorted. Without warning, he bolted forward. He galloped across the open area, toward one of the dark barracks. Shrieking in fury, the stallion rounded the building and charged a figure lurking in the shadows. Emily and Joel were nearly thrown off Pegasus's back as he reared and kicked out at the mysterious figure.

"Pegasus, no!" a frightened voice cried. "Please, it is me, Cupid. Please stop!"

"Cupid!" Emily gasped. Pegasus went back down on all fours and snorted furiously. He shoved Cupid brutally in the back of his folded wings to drive him out of the shadows.

"What are you doing here?" Joel demanded as he slid off Pegasus and charged forward.

Paelen poked an accusing finger at Cupid. "You have been following us! Why?"

Cupid stood before the group. "The Nirads are in Olympus."

"So you decided to follow us?" Joel challenged.

"Emily is the Flame, perhaps the most powerful of all Olympians. I thought the Nirads might come after her. So I came to help protect her."

"Liar!" Paelen accused as he shoved Cupid. "You are a coward. You came because you thought Emily would use her powers to protect you from the Nirads.

But you were wrong. Go back to Olympus, Cupid. We do not want you here."

"I will not go!" Cupid shouted back. "And you cannot force me, thief!"

"Just watch me," Paelen cried as he lunged at Cupid. Soon the two Olympians were rolling around on the ground and throwing powerful punches at each other. "Stop it!" Emily shouted.

"We don't have time for this!" Joel moved to break up the fight, but Pegasus stepped forward and blocked him.

"No, Joel. Don't," Emily warned. "They're much stronger than you. You'll get hurt. Pegs, do something. Please, stop them!"

Pegasus lunged forward and caught Cupid's wing in his sharp teeth. The Olympian howled in pain as Pegasus dragged him away. Joel caught Paelen, holding him back.

"Ouch! Let go," Cupid cried. "Pegasus, let me go!"

"Stop it, both of you!" Emily ordered as she slid off the stallion's back. She shivered and wrapped her arms around herself to keep warm. She stepped between the two fighters. "Just stop it."

Paelen tried to push past Joel to challenge Cupid again. "Go back to Olympus!"

"No!" Cupid shouted. "I will not!"

Joel caught hold of Paelen's shoulders and blocked his view of Cupid. "Calm down, Paelen," he said as his own teeth started to chatter. "This isn't getting us anywhere. We're wasting precious time."

"But he should not be here," Paelen cried. "He will get us all killed."

"I will not," Cupid said. "I can help." He turned to Pegasus. "I want to help the Flame."

Emily split her attention between Paelen and Cupid. The last thing she needed was another Olympian here to worry about; especially another one with wings.

"Cupid, please," she finally said through chattering teeth. "Go back to Olympus. We are only going to be here for a short time, then we're going right back."

Cupid turned his full attention on Emily. "You are here to free your father. I want to help."

Emily shook her head. "It's too dangerous. Hiding Pegasus's wings and keeping him from being seen is going to be tough enough. I can't see how we'll manage with you as well."

"I have done it before—I can do it again," Cupid challenged defiantly. "I used to come to this world regularly before Jupiter put a stop to all visits. I will not leave you here, Flame. If you refuse to allow me to travel with you, I will follow you anyway. You have many powers, but you do not have the power to send me home."

"Maybe she cannot," Paelen agreed. "But she can burn you to a cinder. That will stop you from following us."

"Paelen, enough," Emily warned. "I told you, I'm not using my powers again. They're too dangerous."

Pegasus started to whinny. Whatever the stallion was saying, Emily could see it was putting fear in both Paelen's and Cupid's eyes.

Paelen lowered his head guiltily. "I am sorry, Emily," he said softly as he hoisted her up onto the stallion's back. "I have been a fool. I should have seen that you and Joel are shivering and in need of protection from this cold night air. Perhaps we should go back to one of the homes and take shelter there for the night."

"No way!" both Emily and Joel said in unison.

"I don't care how cold I am," Emily continued. "I won't stay here. Maybe we can get closer to where they are holding my dad and find somewhere there."

Joel nodded quickly in agreement. "If it's not too far, let's do it."

BACK IN THE SKY, EMILY WAS NUMB FROM
the cold. She could feel Joel shivering behind
her. Paelen's sandals led the group north over the
Manhattan skyline. Emily looked to her left and saw
Cupid flying closely beside them. His wings were
smaller than Pegasus's, but not by much. She shook
her head in frustration as she watched him fly. How
were they supposed to keep those wings hidden?

As it was, she feared they weren't flying high
enough. What if someone saw them? Would they
call the CRU? Would the hunt start all over again?
Her simple plan of rescuing her father was suddenly
becoming very complicated. She realized she hadn't
considered how she was actually going to free her

father once they discovered where he was being held. That had been a mistake.

It wasn't long before they were moving away from the bright lights of the city. The sandals kept them going in a steady northern direction. Emily looked down and realized that they were passing over Yonkers and, finally, into the less populated areas on the way up to the Catskills.

"I know this area," Joel said from behind her. "My parents used to take me and my brother here when we were kids."

"Really? Me too!' Emily looked back at him in surprise. "There was a great rest stop we always went to—"

"The Red Apple Rest?" Joel asked.

"Yes!" Emily said excitedly. "It's where my mom and dad met."

"We always went there too," Joel said. "Wouldn't it be funny if we were there at the same time?"

"It sure would," Emily agreed through chattering teeth. She was chilled to the bone. If they didn't get out of the night air soon, she was certain she and Joel would catch pneumonia. Paelen, Cupid, and Pegasus didn't seem to notice the cold at all.

"There it is!" Excited, Joel pointed down to his right. "Look, it's the Red Apple."

Emily leaned over and saw that the restaurant was boarded up and abandoned. "It's closed," she said sadly. "I wonder what happened."

Both Emily and Joel were too absorbed by the closed restaurant to notice that Paelen's sandals were directing them downward. But when Pegasus started to neigh, they looked forward.

"We are going down," Paelen called.

"We must be near your father!" Joel added excitedly.

"Here?" Emily said. "But there's nothing around here but mountains, forest, and the Red Apple."

"And a great place to hide the CRU," Joel said.

Emily saw bright flashing lights in the distance. But they were descending in the opposite direction and farther over a dark forest. As they came down to the level of the treetops, Pegasus whinnied and sharply veered away.

"What is it, Pegs?" Emily called nervously. She looked down and still couldn't see anything hidden in the dark trees beneath them. "Have they seen us?"

Cupid glided closer to the stallion's side. "He

doesn't want to approach, as you and Joel are too chilled to confront them. He says we must find you warmer clothes first."

Emily was conflicted. If they were close to finally finding her father, she hated to leave the area. But she was freezing. Pegasus was right. She and Joel needed to warm up soon or they'd both be in big trouble.

"I've got an idea!" Joel called from behind her. "Pegasus, get us to those flashing lights. I know exactly where we are."

Pegasus neighed once and changed direction in the sky again. He took the lead as Paelen and Cupid flew at his side.

Emily turned back to Joel. "Where are we going?"

"Down there," Joel pointed at the bright lights. "Pegasus, you'll have to land before we get there. We don't want to be seen yet."

As they approached the flashing lights, loud pounding music and screams filled the air. Emily saw the flashing lights were from amusement rides. The screaming was from people on the rides.

"Land right there!" Joel called, and pointed toward

an opening in the forest near the fence surrounding the amusements.

Once on the ground, Joel slid stiffly off the stallion's back. He called Paelen and Cupid closer. "This is perfect. A few years ago, my dad took me up there for Halloween. It's the Haunted Forest Festival. There's a big haunted house and all kinds of things to see and do."

"Joel, we don't have time to go to the festival," Emily said irritably. She was cold and worried about hypothermia. "We need clothing, and then we've got to find my dad!"

"I know," Joel shot back. "But look at us. We can't go anywhere dressed like this. And look at them." Joel pointed at Cupid and Pegasus. "Look at those wings. We've got to find a way to hide them."

"So?" Emily challenged.

"Emily, it's the Haunted Forest! Don't you get it?" Joel continued. "They have performers dressed in scary costumes. We could walk right in there and everyone would think we were part of the show. I bet we could get into the actors' trailers and find some clothing."

"Oh," Emily said, finally understanding. "I get it. But wait, we don't look scary. We still don't fit in. We're dressed like Olympians, not vampires, ghouls, or ghosts."

"I do not understand," Paelen interrupted. "In this place, people are dressed as the dead? Why would they do that?"

"To scare the people who come to visit," Joel explained.

"And these people wish to be scared?"

Joel nodded.

"I still do not understand," Paelen said.

"Neither do I," Cupid added.

"And me," Emily agreed. "I always hated the haunted house."

"Maybe," Joel said. "But right now, with all of us looking like this, it is the only place for us."

They started to walk toward the festival. In the chilly night air rose the sweet aroma of cotton candy, caramel apples, and all the other amusement-park delights.

"They have food here?" Paelen asked eagerly.

"Oh, yeah," Joel said.

Pegasus also lifted his head and sniffed in the strong fragrance of festival food.

Before long, they crept up to a chain-link fence. On the other side they saw bright flashing lights from the countless game booths as visitors tried their luck at winning large prizes. Further in, they spotted all the carnival rides. There was a tall Ferris wheel filled with excited people, while the Octopus spun its riders around in the air to the beat of music. Across from the Octopus was the Merry-go-round, its horses rising and falling in steady rhythm as they chased each other around in the never-ending race. Not far from the fence they saw the biggest, brightest ride of all—the Monster Roller-coaster. Moments later, the coaster's car whooshed down the steep tracks past them, its occupants screaming in both terror and delight. Joel was right. Emily spotted countless performers dressed in costume.

"This is madness," Paelen grew quiet as his wide eyes tried to take in all the sights of the carnival. "I have never seen a sight like this before. I must see more—"

"Paelen, wait," Joel said. "I've got another idea." He

bent down and scooped up a handful of wet mud and decaying leaves. He rubbed the mess on his face, arms, and tunic until he was covered. Joel grinned at Emily. "There, now I fit right in. I'm an Olympian zombie."

Emily laughed at the leaves and twigs sticking up in Joel's hair. "Good idea. Help me down off Pegs. I'm going to be a zombie too." She turned to Cupid. "And you. You're going to be a winged zombie."

Cupid shook his head and looked mortified. "You are not suggesting I rub that filth on myself."

Emily bent down and filled both hands with freezing, wet mud. She stepped up to Cupid. "Not at all." Before he could protest, Emily threw the mud at him. "I'll do it for you. There, now you're a zombie too."

She turned to Paelen. "What about you?"

Paelen quickly held up his hands. "I will do it, thank you. I do not understand why, but I will."

Finally everyone turned to Pegasus. In the dark cover of the forest, the stallion was glowing brilliant white. "Sorry, Pegs," Emily said softly as she stepped up to his head. "But you're glowing. We've got to make you look like an ordinary horse again. Will you let us cover you in mud?"

Pegasus gently nudged her.

"All right, everyone," she said. "Let's cover Pegasus."

A short time later they were all covered in mud and dead leaves, except for Pegasus's and Cupid's feathers. Joel demonstrated how zombies were supposed to move with a slow, lumbering walk. Emily laughed as she watched Paelen and Cupid trying to mimic him.

"And remember," Joel warned Pegasus and Cupid, "no matter what you see or what happens, try not to move your wings. They're supposed to be part of your costume, that's all."

Getting over the tall fence was a problem for Pegasus, who needed more space to launch into the air. They kept watch and waited for the area to clear before flying over the top.

Finally they were all within the grounds of the Haunted Forest Festival. Despite their disguises, nerves bunched up in Emily's stomach. She was seated on Pegasus, and even with her gold leg brace hidden under his folded wing, she still felt exposed and vulnerable.

As they walked through the early evening crowd, people seemed curious and stared at them but kept their distance. On one occasion, Emily caught two girls looking at Cupid and smiling radiantly at him. "Cute guy," she heard them say, giggling, as they walked past.

They traveled deeper into the festival. The air was filled with screaming as costumed performers crept up on people unawares and did their best to frighten them. Not far ahead, they saw the main attraction—the Haunted House. Emily saw a performer dressed as the Grim Reaper carrying his scythe. He stalked the entrance, inviting people in and doing his best to terrify those waiting to enter.

"People do this for fun?" Paelen asked as he watched the Grim Reaper driving girls into screaming terror.

"I wonder how they would react if they saw a Nirad?" Cupid added. "That would soon teach these humans the real meaning of fear."

Joel sighed. "You don't get it. People come here to be frightened because it's safe fear. No one gets hurt. It's meant to be fun."

"I still do not understand your world," Paelen said.

"You don't have to," Joel finished. "Let's just grab

what we need and get out of here before Emily and I freeze to death."

Joel led the way through the thickening crowds. Emily watched Paelen's and Cupid's faces as they stared in curious wonder at the costumed people around them.

"Over there," Joel said. "There're all the trailers. C'mon."

They approached a quieter area filled with a long line of performers' trailers. They walked past a large sign that read PRIVATE AREA. DO NOT ENTER.

"You and Pegasus keep watch," Joel said to Emily. "We'll go grab some clothes." He turned to Paelen. "I know you gave up stealing. But for now, you're a thief again."

"If I must," Paelen said in mock regret. He looked at Emily and flashed his crooked grin. "But I will not enjoy myself."

Emily shook her head and laughed. "Just go!"

Emily waited with Pegasus. "I sure hope they hurry," she said, wrapping her arms tightly around herself.

As the minutes ticked by, she heard the sound of

voices. People were heading their way. Emily looked back at the trailers and couldn't see Joel or the others. She slid off the stallion's back. "Easy, Pegs, let me handle this."

Four men in heavy makeup approached. Two were dressed as vampires; the other two were a zombie and a Frankenstein monster. "You there," called the zombie. "Can't you read? This area is off-limits to the public. What are you doing here with that horse? The costume competition is on the other side of the festival."

"I know," Emily said. "I'm sorry, but my horse was getting spooked by all the crowds, so I brought him here to calm down."

"It was stupid of you to bring him here at all," a vampire shot back. "This is no place for animals. That's why they don't allow pets."

The Frankenstein monster came forward. "What are you supposed to be, anyway?"

"Olympian zombies," Emily answered as she watched the performers start to circle them.

They all laughed. "Olympian zombies?"

"I've never seen a horse zombie before, let alone one with wings," said a vampire.

"He's supposed to be a Zombie Pegasus," Emily explained.

They came closer and started to inspect Pegasus. "Great wings," Frankenstein said, reaching out and patting the stallion's folded wing. "How long did they take you to make?"

Emily's heart nearly stopped as Frankenstein closely studied Pegasus's wing. The stallion never took his wary eyes off him and seemed to be getting agitated by the man's closeness. "Please don't touch him. He doesn't like strangers," she warned.

"That's another reason why you shouldn't have brought him," challenged the zombie.

"You're right—I shouldn't have," Emily agreed. "If you give us a few more minutes alone, we'll go."

"How about you go now?" suggested a vampire. "Or should I call security?"

The sound of running footsteps came from behind one of the trailers. Emily turned and was grateful to see Joel, Paelen, and Cupid emerging from the shadows.

"Are you all right, Em?" Joel ran up to her. Paelen was right behind him, carrying a bundle, followed by Cupid.

"What were you kids doing back there?" the zombie demanded. Then he saw the bundle in Paelen's arm. "And what have you got in your hands?"

"Who, me?" Paelen said innocently.

"Hey, isn't that Jamie's coat?" the vampire said to his friends.

"I think it is," agreed Frankenstein as they all approached Joel. "Have you kids been stealing from the trailers?"

"Not stealing," Paelen said. "Borrowing with intent to keep."

The zombie moved toward Paelen. "You've got yourself a smart mouth, kid. Give me that stuff and get out of here."

"Or you will do what?" Cupid challenged as he took a step.

"Or we'll take it from you."

"I should like to see you try, human."

The situation quickly deteriorated. Emily saw the wings on Cupid's back flutter slightly. He was getting ready to fight. Quickly she moved forward and stood between the two groups. "C'mon, guys, let's just go."

Cupid shook his head. "Flame, stay back. I will not have these humans speak to us like this."

"Okay, that's it!" the zombie said. He turned to one of the vampires. "Jimmy, go get security. We'll keep them here."

But Pegasus blocked Jimmy's path. When he moved to the left, Pegasus did the same. To the right, Pegasus moved again. Each move Jimmy made was stopped by the stallion.

"Hey, call off your horse," Jimmy said as he tried to get around Pegasus.

"Please," Emily pleaded. "We don't want any trouble. But we're freezing and need those clothes. Please just let us take them and go."

"No, Flame," Cupid said, "you must not beg. It is beneath you." He turned to the performers and opened his wings threateningly. "Now we are going to leave here and you will not stop us."

The costumed men took a nervous step back as they stared up at the large set of open wings. "What's going on here? How'd you do that?"

"Cupid, stop it! Close your wings," Emily cried. She looked at the stallion, "Pegs, tell him to stop."

Pegasus snorted, shook his head, and pawed the ground before he reared on his hind legs and spread his own wings wide. After an angry whinny, he lunged forward.

When the actors saw Pegasus and realized his wings were as real as Cupid's, they tried to run. But Paelen and Cupid stopped them. The fight was quick but brutal. Within seconds the four men were unconscious on the ground.

"Why did you do that?" Emily demanded furiously. "You might have killed them with your strength!"

Paelen pointed angrily at Cupid. "We had to because of him!" He charged Cupid and shoved him violently back. "Joel told you not to show your wings. We are trying to blend in here, not expose ourselves. Because of you, we had to hurt these innocent men!"

Once again Pegasus whinnied loudly.

Paelen turned to Emily and Joel. He took a deep breath to calm himself. "Pegasus says we must bind the men and hide them. Then we must leave before they are missed." He bent down and went through the bundle of clothes. "Here," he said as he held a full-length coat up to Emily. "Please put this on and get warm."

Emily and Joel dressed in the coats while Paelen and Cupid used the men's belts to bind their hands behind their backs. They carried them over to one of the trailers and deposited them inside.

Back on the midway of the festival, the evening was in full swing. There were even more costumed performers charging through the heavy crowds to scare the visitors. Countless people stared and pointed at Pegasus walking among them. They commented on his wings, but all seemed to accept him as part of the show.

They walked past a man dressed as a clown at a dunk tank. He was seated on a plank over a glass tank of water, hurling insults at visitors. It was his job to goad them into throwing balls at the target that would cast him down into the water.

When he saw their group, his eyes settled immediately on Paelen. "Well, folks, what have we got here?" he called through a loud microphone. "Ain't he simply adorable! What a pretty little boy walking with his pet pony. Does your mother know you're out tonight, sweet thing?"

Paelen looked at the clown but said nothing.

"What's the matter, toga boy? Don't you wanna

come over here and play? What about your friends? Hey, freaks, this is Halloween, not a toga party! Get it right."

"Are you going to accept his rude comments?" Cupid challenged.

"Yes, he is," Emily said. "We've caused enough trouble here already." She looked at Paelen. "He's only teasing you so you'll go over there and pay some money to throw a ball at the target to knock him in the water. That's how he makes his salary."

Paelen frowned at the clown above the water-filled glass tank. "He wants me to throw a ball at him?"

"Not at him," Joel said, pointing at the bull's-eye. "That target beside the tank. If you hit it, it drops him in the cold water."

Paelen walked closer to the dunk tank.

"Paelen, no," Emily cried. "Don't do anything. Please come back."

But Paelen was already standing before the line of balls to throw at the target. The clown's assistant was tossing one in the air and telling Paelen the price for three balls.

"What's the matter, toga boy? Are you chicken?"

The clown started to cluck like a chicken. "Maybe your little winged pony can help you."

"Let's go," Emily said as she caught Paelen's arm. "Please."

When they started to walk away, the clown whistled. "I guess we know who wears the pants in your relationship, huh? You gonna let a dumb girl with a bum leg tell you what to do, toga boy? Or maybe you're frightened she'll take off that brace and beat you with it!"

Paelen stopped. "He may insult me," he said softly, "but never you. That man should be taught some manners." With lightning speed, Paelen snatched up a ball and used all his Olympian strength to throw it at the target. The ball exploded on impact with the bull's-eye and shattered the target's arm. As a bell rang, the plank holding the clown split, and he was cast into the freezing water.

Paelen rubbed his hands together and smiled at Emily. "He will not insult you again."

Part of Emily wanted to scold Paelen for losing his temper. But she realized he'd done it for her, so she stayed quiet. She shook her head, "C'mon, hero, let's get going."

Before long, they were walking past stalls of food.

"I'm starving," Joel commented as he looked enviously at all the food.

"Me too," Cupid agreed. He crossed to a stall selling caramel apples and cotton candy and held out his hand. "Give me one."

"Not you now. . . ." Emily moaned as she chased after him. "Cupid, wait, you can't go around demanding things. We do things differently here. If you want something, you have to buy it."

"But I am hungry."

"Yes, so is everyone else, but we don't have any money." Emily looked apologetically at the vendor. "I'm sorry. My friend is new here and doesn't understand. We can't pay for that."

The vendor shrugged and took back the caramel apple. "With that outfit, why doesn't he enter the costume competition?" He pointed at a large, colorful tent with people pouring inside. "The prize is two hundred bucks. It's just about to get started."

"Really?" Emily looked at Cupid. "Did you hear that? Two hundred dollars!"

Excited, they returned to the group, and Emily

explained about the competition. "I know we've got to get out of here, but we need money. If Cupid won, we could buy a lot of food and more clothing."

"What would I have to do?" Cupid asked.

"Nothing," Joel said. "Just walk around the way I showed you. We could enter you as a zombie angel."

"But I am no angel."

"It's pretending, Cupid," Emily said tiredly. "You would pretend to be a zombie angel, that's all."

Cupid looked around. "Just as these people are pretending to be dead creatures to scare the others?"

"Exactly!" Joel agreed. "It's simple. Just walk in there, and with those wings, you're guaranteed to win."

"He can't do it," Paelen said skeptically. "He is a coward, too frightened to try."

"I am not!" Cupid challenged.

"Prove it," Paelen said. "Enter the competition. If you win, I will apologize."

Cupid turned to Emily. "I will do it. I will prove to you that I am not a coward or selfish. I will win the money for all of us."

Emily kept close to Pegasus as they made their way through the dense crowds and toward the tent hosting the competition. Outside the entrance, costumed contestants gathered together.

"Anyone else?" called a man with a microphone. "This is your last chance. Best costume wins two hundred dollars cash! Sign up here and enter!"

Emily stepped up to the registration table. "We'd like to enter, please."

The woman looked up at Emily, then over to Cupid. She eyed him up and down in his short, mud-covered tunic and smiled. "And what is your name, handsome?"

"Cupid," Cupid answered softly, leaning closer and smiling back at her.

"Hmmm, the god of love," sighed the woman.

"No," Emily said quickly, "not Cupid. This is Zombie Angel."

The woman repeated the name dreamily and slowly handed over a card with a number on it. "Stand over there, Angel, and wait to be called forward. Good luck."

Cupid reached forward and caught the woman's hand. He gave it a soft kiss. "Thank you."

Emily's own heart fluttered as Cupid turned on

his charm. "Um, come on, Angel," she stammered. "It's over here."

Emily stood in line with Cupid while Joel and Paelen remained with Pegasus, well away from the tent. One by one they watched the contestants being called forward. There were chain-saw killers, mummies, grotesque aliens, ghouls, and countless murder victims covered in fake blood, all climbing up on the stage to show off their costumes. When Cupid's number was finally announced, he caught Emily by the hand. "Come, Flame, I want you with me for this. Remove your coat."

"Cupid, no," Emily quickly said. "I don't want anyone to see my gold brace."

"If you wish to win this, you will do as I say."

Emily looked helplessly over to Pegasus but allowed Cupid to pull off her long coat and draw her into the crowded tent.

"Here now, number thirty-one, Zombie Angel!" the announcer called.

Cupid held on to Emily's hand as he walked zombielike up to the stage. He drew her up the steps with him.

Dressed only in her silk tunic and gold leg brace, Emily looked over the cheering crowds that greeted Cupid as he stepped onstage. It was as though she were invisible. Everyone's eyes were on the winged Olympian covered in drying mud.

"It is I," Cupid announced theatrically, waving his hand in the air and bowing dramatically, "Zombie Angel!" He smiled radiantly at the crowd, and Emily could feel them reacting to his charm. "And here now, the one who holds a zombie's heart, the Flame of Olympus!"

Cupid went down on one knee and knelt before Emily. He bowed his head and slowly opened his beautiful wings and extended them fully. The crowd roared with excitement. Girls screamed and jumped up and down, chanting "Angel, Angel, Angel" as they reached across the stage to try to touch him.

"No!" Emily cried. "Don't show your wings!"

Her eyes were wild with fear as she looked into the audience. But they were all fooled. They loved Cupid without realizing it wasn't a costume. Cheers and roars filled the tent for several minutes, until the announcer came onstage. He held up his hands, trying to calm the frantic crowd.

"Close your wings," Emily quietly ordered as she continued to nervously scan the audience.

Cupid rose and wrapped his arm and one wing around Emily. "I believe we have won," he whispered softly into her ear.

"All right," the announcer roared. "All right, calm down, everyone! I can see by your reaction we have our winner!"

Once again the cheers reached fever pitch as the announcer pulled an envelope from his pocket. "Tonight's first prize for best costumes goes to Zombie Angel and his Flame of Olympus!"

The announcer handed the envelope to Cupid. As he struggled to gain control of the screaming crowds, he pushed the microphone into Emily's face. "What's your name, sweetheart?"

"Um, Emily," she answered nervously. Her heart pounded fiercely, and she was certain the announcer was about to discover the truth about Cupid.

"And you?" he asked, moving the microphone over to the Olympian.

"I am Cupid."

Once again the girls in the tent roared with excitement in response to Cupid. Emily had never seen anything like it before. She looked across the worshipping and adoring masses in the tent, but then Emily noticed one particular pair of eyes that weren't cheering or screaming at Cupid. They were staring only at her.

"No, it can't be!" she uttered. "What's he doing here?"

"What is it?" Cupid asked.

Emily pointed at the man as he spoke urgently to some young, costumed men around him. She watched him shout into his cell phone. When he hung up, he and his men started to shove their way through the hysterical crowds. His eyes were locked onto Emily, and there was no mistaking the recognition.

"The CRU!"

5

AS THE CROWD SURGED AND TRIED TO GET
closer to Cupid, Emily's eyes searched madly for
Agent O. There was no mistaking him—Emily would
remember his cruel eyes anywhere. He was one of the
agents who had tortured her at the Governors Island
facility and who was going to let Pegasus die when he
was hurt.

"We must go," Cupid cried.

He passed Emily her coat and took her by the hand.
But as they descended the stage steps, the crowd of
girls swarmed around him. Emily was pushed and
shoved until her hand was torn free of Cupid.

"Cupid!" she cried.

"Flame!" he called back. But it was from the rear

of the tent. The mass of girls had forced him against the canvas of the tent. Emily struggled to reach him, but the crowd was too dense. As she turned to head out, she walked straight into a nightmare.

"Emily Jacobs, what a questionable surprise to see you back here," said Agent O as he and two men dressed as aliens blocked her path. His hand closed on her arm with a viselike grip. "Or should I call you Flame of Olympus?"

"No, you can't be here," she cried as she tried to pull away. "I saw Pegasus kill you!"

Agent O shook his head. "He killed Agent J, but he left me with this," he opened his shirt to reveal a deep, angry hoof-shaped scar. "Because of you and that thing, I was transferred upstate to this boring hick town. My only escape from the monotony has been coming to this Haunted Forest with some friends. But now that I've found you, I'll get my promotion and get out of this place. You are my ticket back to New York City."

"Let me go!" Emily demanded as she struggled to pull away.

"Let you go?" Agent O repeated. "Never! You

owe me, Emily. I had a life back in the city before you stole it from me. Now I'm going to steal something from you—your freedom!" He started to haul her away.

Emily looked back toward Cupid.

"Don't worry about your winged friend back there. My men will take care of him soon enough."

As he dragged her toward the exit, Emily spotted the four costumed performers that Paelen and Cupid had attacked. They entered the tent with a group of police and security guards. "There she is," called Frankenstein as he pointed at her. "She was with the others!"

Emily was losing control. The CRU, the police—it was all happening too fast. Her inner Flame started to rumble and come to life as she began to tremble.

"Let go of me," she warned Agent O. "You don't understand. I've changed. Please, I might hurt you!"

"Shut up!" Agent O ordered, forcing her through the crowd.

As the performers, festival security, and police rushed forward, Agent O and his men pulled out their ID badges. "Back off! This is my prisoner."

"No, stop it, Em!" Emily cried to herself, fighting back the flames. "Don't do it. Hold it back!"

But her emotions and the powers wouldn't be stopped. The tingling in the pit of her stomach rose. It flowed along her arms and, finally, down to her hands. "Everyone, get away from me!" she screamed. "The Flame is coming, and I can't stop it!"

"I said shut up!" Agent O shouted furiously as he wrenched her forward. "I don't want to hear it."

Emily's powers let go.

Uncontrolled flames shot out of her fingertips and hit Agent O in the legs. He fell to the ground, rolling and screaming in pain as his trousers caught fire.

Emily pointed her hands away from the people around her and aimed the powerful flames down so that they burned deep holes in the grass and earth.

Agent O continued screaming and writhing in pain as his men tried to put out the fire on his legs. Those closest to Emily cried out in terror and ran for the exit. But the rest of the audience, those who couldn't see its origins, cheered at the unexpected fire show.

"Stop it!" Emily roared at herself. She was growing

close to panic as the flames intensified. No matter how hard she tried, she could not pull them back.

Suddenly a screaming whinny came from the tent entrance. Emily looked up and saw Pegasus rearing and spreading his massive wings. Police gathered around the stallion, trying to catch him, while the crowds roared and cheered in hysterical delight. Pegasus whinnied again and charged forward into the tent.

"Pegasus," Emily cried gratefully. Seeing the stallion coming for her calmed her somewhat and slowed the flames so she was able to regain control. Finally Emily stopped them completely.

She looked down at Agent O. "I'm so sorry! Please don't come after us. I don't have any control of my powers."

"You freak!" he howled as he clutched his burned legs. "I'm going to lock you so far underground you'll forget what daylight looks like!"

But when Agent O saw Pegasus arrive at Emily's side, his voice broke and he was paralyzed with fear. "Keep him away from me!" he squealed at his men, pointing a shaking finger at Pegasus. "Keep him back!"

As the crowd surged forward to get a better look and actually touch the stallion, Emily caught hold of Pegasus's wing and climbed up onto his back. When he began trotting toward the exit, she heard Agent O's cutting words.

"You can't escape me, Emily," he howled. "No matter where you go, I'll never stop looking for you. I'll find you and make you pay for this. . . ."

She turned back and saw the hatred blazing in his wild, frightened eyes.

From the back of the tent, girls were still chanting, "Zombie Angel, Zombie Angel!"

"Enough!" Cupid shouted, and leaped high into the air. His tunic was shredded, and it barely covered his muscular form. He was bleeding from deep scratches on his chest, arms, and face.

With wings unfurled, Cupid flew unsteadily over the heads of the cheering crowd and out of the tent. Pegasus followed closely behind. Once outside, the stallion galloped at full speed along the crowded festival midway before launching himself into the air.

Emily looked back down and saw hundreds of

flashes from camera phones as the people waved and called to them while they flew up into the night sky. Just outside the fence, in the parking area, she watched several black cars and military trucks arrive and the soldiers pour out.

"Em, are you all right?" Joel was clinging to Paelen's back as the tiny winged sandals carried them up to the stallion. "The performers broke free and called security. We had to fight the police to get away. Then we saw them going into the tent!"

"Joel," Emily cried, "Agent O and some of his men were down there!"

"What?" Joel and Paelen cried together. "Where? In the tent? Did they see you?"

"Yes," she replied. Emily pointed back to the military trucks and soldiers gathering at the festival. "They caught me, but I lost control of my powers and set Agent O on fire."

Joel punched the air in celebration. "Yes! Serves him right!"

"It was awful!" Emily cried. "He threatened me! Said he'd never stop looking for us. What are we going to do?"

"They are empty threats, Emily," Paelen called. "But we do need to find somewhere to stop and gather our thoughts."

"Let's go back to the Red Apple," Joel suggested. "It's abandoned. We could hide there and plan our next move."

Several minutes later they were landing in the dark parking lot of the abandoned rest stop. There were large, heavy boards on all the windows, and the building was completely locked up. Very little traffic was on the road, and there were no neighbors to worry about. They were alone.

"This should be perfect," Joel said, scanning the area. "No one has been here for ages."

Emily was still trembling as she slid off Pegasus and approached the rear door. "But how do we get in? We don't want anyone to know we're here."

"Leave that to me," Paelen offered. He stepped back to use his unique Olympian power. Paelen had the ability to stretch out and manipulate his body to fit into any space, even the tiniest of areas. It was very painful and noisy as his bones elongated and cracked while his body thinned. But it had saved his life on more than one occasion. He ordered the winged sandals to take him up to the roof, and they watched him squeeze into a painfully narrow kitchen exhaust chimney.

"I'll never get used to seeing him do that," Joel commented as he shivered and shook his head uncomfortably.

Moments later they heard stirring from behind the door and the sound of the locks being turned. Finally the door opened, and Paelen bowed graciously and grinned. "Come in. Welcome to my home. It is not perfect, but I like it."

Pegasus led the way in, followed by Emily, Joel, and then Cupid. They were in the gutted kitchen of the restaurant.

"I don't suppose there are any lights," Joel asked. "I can't see a thing."

"Me either," Emily agreed.

Pegasus gently nudged her. He nickered softly. "Hold on to Pegasus's wings. He will lead you," Paelen said. He closed and locked the kitchen door as Pegasus led Emily and Joel into the main seating area of the closed rest stop. It was pitch-black and cold.

"Em, do you think you could do something about the temperature in here?" Joel asked. "I'm freezing."

"Like what?"

"Like start a fire so we can see and maybe finally get warm."

"I-I don't think I should," Emily said nervously. "I set fire to Agent O's legs and nearly burned the tent down. You know I don't have any control."

Pegasus was still at her side, and he neighed softly. "You were frightened back in the tent," Paelen translated. "This is different. Pegasus says you can control it if you are calm."

Emily strained her eyes, but she couldn't see a thing. Finally she accepted that they needed light. But more than that, they needed heat. "All right," she hesitantly agreed. "But we need somewhere safe for me to do it, otherwise I could burn this whole place down."

"Come, Cupid," Paelen said as he started to move. "Help me find something for Emily to start a fire in."

Emily and Joel stood together in the dark and

listened to Paelen and Cupid go through the restaurant. They heard smashing wood coming from the kitchen and then something heavy being dragged into their area, followed by the sounds of old tables and countertops being broken up.

"All right, Emily," Paelen said as he took her by the hand and led her carefully forward. "Just a few steps and you are at the pile of wood. It is waist high. If you start with a very small flame, it should catch easily."

Emily felt the reassuring presence of Pegasus directly behind her. She tried to imagine herself back on Olympus and the lessons that Vesta had given her. She held out her hands and envisioned a small flame flowing from her fingertips down into the pile of wood.

The tingling in her stomach started and flowed up into her arms. Suddenly light and flames sprang from her fingers and shot into the pile.

"Easy," Joel warned. "That's it. Just keep it nice and small."

When the pile was burning brightly, Emily pulled back on the flames. This time her powers obeyed and the flame stopped. She saw that the pile had been built on top of an old steel stove and there was no risk of the fire spreading.

"Well done!" Paelen said as he patted her on the back. "I knew you could do it."

Emily grinned as she looked at the controlled fire. This was the very first time her powers had actually done what she asked of them. The flames drove away the darkness and were giving off much-welcome heat. She held her hands over the fire and was starting to feel warm for the first time since they left Olympus. Joel was beside her, also enjoying the heat.

Emily started to relax and looked over to Cupid. He had been silent since they landed and was standing away from the group. She left the fire and approached him. She saw the deep scratches all over his body.

Cupid was looking at the tatters of his tunic and shaking his head. "I do not understand," he said in a quiet voice. "Women used to worship me. They were shy and needed coaxing. But tonight those girls were mad. They were ripping at me. They pulled out my hair and my feathers and tore my tunic. It was as though they were all trying to steal a piece of me."

"Welcome to the new world," Emily said quietly. "Cupid, we told you this isn't the same place you used to visit. We've changed. You were like a rock star up there. Those girls wanted you."

"They wanted to kill me."

Emily shook her head. "No, not kill you. Just to touch you and perhaps have something to remember you by."

Cupid opened his wings and showed Emily the heavy damage done by the hysterical girls. She could see large holes where flight feathers used to be. "I can barely fly," he commented. "It will take ages for all these to grow back."

"Maybe not," Emily said. She reached out and stroked his colorful wings, enjoying the softness of the feathers. Wherever she touched, missing shafts sprouted and started to grow. Before long, the shafts split open and new feathers emerged.

From his wings, Emily moved to his back. She lightly traced her fingers along the deep gouges and watched them start to heal. As she worked, she looked in fascination at where Cupid's powerful wings joined his back. They seemed to be part of his shoulder blades but were able to move independently of his arms. Heavy muscles surrounded the area and gave him strength in flight. She wondered how he was able to sleep with the large, bulky wings or if he could even lie on his back. But she was too shy to ask and figured he must only sleep on his side.

Finally Emily moved to his front and healed the deep scratches on his face and chest. When she finished, she felt her own face flush. In the flickering firelight, Cupid was more painfully beautiful than she could ever imagine.

Cupid inspected his newly healed wings. He stroked the new feathers in wonder. "I had heard that you could heal Olympians," he said in awe, "but I did not believe it. Thank you, Flame."

"How many times must I tell you, her name is Emily," Paelen protested loudly as he charged over. He looked angrily at Emily. "You should have left him as he was. It might have given him some humility!"

"But he was hurt," Emily said.

"He brought it on himself," Paelen challenged. He poked furiously at Cupid. "I know what you did in the tent. You showed too much of yourself and put Emily in danger. Do you realize what might have happened if there had been more CRU people there? She would be in their facility right now being tortured!"

Cupid dropped his head in shame. "I am sorry, Emily. I was not thinking."

"No, you were not," Paelen continued. "Now the CRU knows we are here."

"All right," Joel said quickly. "That's enough. We don't need any fights in here. We've got enough problems already. What was Agent O doing there, anyway? Did you see Agent J?"

Emily shook her head. "He told me Agent J was dead. You should have seen him—he was so angry. He blamed Pegasus and me for ruining his life and said he was transferred up here because of us. But now that we're back, when he catches us, he's going to be promoted and move back to New York."

"It seems too convenient for me," Joel argued. "That he should be there the very same night we arrive."

"Perhaps they have been waiting for us," Paelen

offered. "Perhaps they have been using Emily's father as bait in a trap, knowing that she would eventually come for him. Perhaps there are agents posted everywhere around here."

"Then what do we do?" Emily asked. She started to pace the area. "We are *so* close. We can't just leave him here."

"We fight," Paelen said simply. "We are much stronger than these humans. Emily, you have your own powers. No one can stand against you."

Emily shook her head. "No way! I don't have any control. You didn't see what I did to Agent O. I might have killed him."

"I wish you had," Joel said darkly, "after what they did to us on the island."

"What did they do to you?" Emily asked. "Why don't you ever talk about it?"

"I just can't," Joel said angrily. He turned away and dropped his head. "I still see them in my nightmares. I hear myself screaming and begging them to stop. I remember the pain—"

Emily wrapped her arms around Joel and held him tight. She could feel him trembling. She had suffered at Governors Island, but she knew that both Joel and Paelen had been through much worse. They had both been tortured for information. "I'm so sorry, Joel."

Joel looked down into Emily's face. "Em, face the facts. Whether you want to or not, you are going to have to use your powers to free your father."

"I know," she answered in a hushed whisper. "But I'm so scared. What if it gets out of control again? What if I hurt you or even kill my dad? I couldn't live with myself if that happened."

Pegasus came closer and rested his head on her shoulder. Paelen and Cupid also moved forward. "We will not let it happen," Paelen said. "Emily, we will all be right with you. You are not alone. We will work together. And together we will free your father."

EMILY HAD A RESTLESS NIGHT. HER SLEEP was disturbed by terrible, haunted nightmares. There were the terrors of losing control of her powers and setting the whole world on fire. In one dream, she watched her father and Joel bursting into flame as she stood back, unable to stop the fire. In another, she was locked away in an underground laboratory as Agent O and his doctors poked, prodded, and experimented on her, trying to find the source of her powers.

Several times she awoke, gasping for air and filled with terror that she would never learn to control the fire beast that had been awakened within. That eventually it would consume everyone she cared for, leaving her alone in her misery.

The next morning Emily awoke beside Pegasus. The stallion was lying on the floor next to her, with his wing draped over her to keep her warm. She had slept but not rested. She felt tired and on the verge of tears.

"Morning, Pegasus." She patted the stallion's wing.

Pegasus reached forward and licked her cheek. She could see concern in his eyes.

"I'm fine, really," she said. "I just had a bad night."

"You sure did," Joel agreed. He handed her a plastic cup filled with orange juice. "You were crying and moaning. Those were some pretty bad nightmares. Do you want to talk about them?"

Emily shook her head. "Not really."

"Then drink your juice. That should wake you up."

Emily sat up and looked around in confusion. The fire on the stove was stoked and burning brightly. There were bags of shopping on the floor. But the biggest shock was seeing Paelen and Cupid sharing a box of glazed donuts and dressed like normal teenagers. Paelen was in jeans and a plaid lumberjack shirt, while Cupid was wearing an oversize college sweatshirt. The lower parts of his wings were tucked into his loose-fitting jeans, while the upper parts were covered by his top. From the front he looked like an ordinary seventeen-year-old. But when he turned, Emily saw the large, thick lump on his back. He looked a bit like a hunchback. But unless you knew the truth, no one would ever suspect the lump was actually wings.

She stood up and walked over to the shopping bags. "What's been going on?"

"You weren't the only one having a bad night," Joel answered, "so Paelen and I left before dawn to go check out the CRU facility. On the way back, we found a twenty-four-hour superstore on the other side of town and used the prize money to do some shopping. We got you some clothes as well."

Paelen handed her a shopping bag. "I hope the sizes are correct." He looked down at his own outfit and grinned. "So, what do you think? Do I look like a human?"

Emily was almost too stunned to speak. She smiled gently at Paelen's eagerness to blend in. "Paelen, you look wonderful." Her eyes trailed over to Cupid again. "You both do."

Cupid fidgeted uncomfortably. "I understand why I must wear this disguise, but it is not comfortable for me. I cannot sit down properly without hurting my wings."

"If you do not like it, you could always fly back to Olympus," Paelen offered. "No one asked you to come here."

Cupid shook his head. "I said I wanted to help and I will."

"No, what you wanted was to get away from the Nirads," Paelen accused. "You followed us here to get away from them in Olympus, not because you wanted to help us free Emily's father."

"All right," Emily said, stopping the fight before it got started. "That's enough." She looked at Joel. "Why did you go to the CRU facility without me?"

"Please don't be angry. It was still dark when we left," he explained. "We couldn't risk going in daylight, especially now that the CRU knows you and Pegasus are back. They don't know about Paelen and me. We figured they'd be expecting you both to show up, not us."

Emily sighed, realizing he was right. "What did you see there?"

"Not a lot," Joel answered. "It's deep in the forest, surrounded by dense trees. It's probably like Governors Island. Most of the facility is underground. There's only one small building aboveground. The rest is a large parking area and guardhouse. There's a single road going in and a tall electric fence surrounding the whole property. We saw cameras everywhere. Some were pointing down, but most were patrolling the sky. So it looks like they are expecting us to fly in."

Paelen took over speaking. "I asked the sandals to take me to your father, but they could not find a hidden way in. I believe the CRU may have discovered what I can do. They have sealed all the small entrances. There is only one entrance, and it is heavily guarded."

"With soldiers carrying big guns," Joel added. He dropped his voice. "Em, I'm so sorry. I don't think we can get to your dad. Not without help."

"But Jupiter won't help us," Emily said desperately. "Especially now that the Nirads are back. He doesn't care about my dad or the CRU. It's got to be us who free him."

"How?" Joel asked. "Em, they've got guns! None of us are bulletproof, even if you are the Flame of Olympus."

"We've got to think," Emily said softly as she started to pace. "We can't go charging in there. They'll stop us before we get anywhere. What we need is a plan."

They ate breakfast as they bounced different ideas around. It was finally Pegasus who offered the best possible solution by suggesting that they capture a couple of CRU agents and force them to describe the facility and help in the rescue.

"How?" Emily asked. "We can't just go to the facility and grab a couple of agents. We'll get captured!"

"What else is there?" Paelen asked.

Joel grinned. "I know. We go back to the festival. I bet there are still CRU agents poring over the place, looking for traces of us. What if we go see, and if they're still there, we'll grab a couple of their guys? We bring them back here and make them tell us where they're keeping your dad. Then we take their ID badges and clothing and drive right into the facility like we belong there."

Emily shook her head. "One problem: We can't drive."

"Joel can," Paelen offered. "He was driving this morning when we stole a car and bought all this food."

Emily frowned at Joel. "You did what this morning?"

"We stole a car," Joel said guiltily. "But we had to. The sun was coming up, and we couldn't risk being seen flying. Besides, we had all this food to carry."

"How could you know what to do?"

"Em," Joel said finally, "before we met, I was living in an awful foster home. I used to get very angry and frustrated. So I'd go out at night and steal a car and go driving around the city for a few hours until I wasn't angry anymore. That's how I got my criminal record."

"So, you're a car thief?" Emily said in shock.

"Not really," Joel said. "I wouldn't steal them to sell or strip for parts. I'd just drive them for a while and then return them when I was done."

Emily was almost too stunned to speak. "Joel, are you telling me that right now, right here, outside of where we are hiding from the CRU, you've got a stolen car?"

Joel nodded. "Think for a moment. We don't have a lot of time before Jupiter and the others come looking for us. We need to get your father out of there. We can't wait until night to go out. How else are we going to get around in daylight? We certainly can't fly. We need a car. Besides, we got it from a used car lot, so it's not like we're hurting anyone."

Emily looked from face to face and realized Joel was right. There was no other way for them to travel around the area. But with a car, how were they supposed to travel with Pegasus? They needed a horse caravan. When she voiced her concerns, Pegasus reached over and gave her a gentle nudge.

Paelen said, "Pegasus can't go out in daylight. It will be too dangerous for all of us if he is seen. He has asked you to stay here with him while Joel, Cupid, and I take the car and capture the CRU men."

"I can't stay here while you guys risk your lives," Emily said. "Besides, I can help."

Paelen rested his hands on her shoulders. "Emily, Pegasus will go wherever you go. If you insist on coming with us, he will not stay here. He will follow you."

Emily looked over into the stallion's big brown

eyes. Pegasus *would* follow if she tried to go without him, and to do that, he would endanger himself. She stroked his soft muzzle. "All right, Pegs," she said softly, "we'll both stay."

"And I shall stay with you," Cupid volunteered.

"Oh no, you will not," Paelen said angrily. "I do not trust you. You claim you are not a coward and followed us here to help. But you only want to stay with Emily so she can protect you from the Nirads."

"You are wrong," Cupid protested. "I will protect her should anyone come here. Besides, even dressed as I am, I do not look human. I will be a burden."

"Pegasus is here for Emily," Joel said. "And you won't be a burden. Cupid, we need your help. I may be bigger than you are, but you're much stronger than I am. If you really want to help, this is how you can do it."

"Pegasus and I are safe here," Emily added. "Joel and Paelen need you more than I."

Emily saw fear rising in Cupid's eyes. He had heard about the CRU and what they did to Pegasus, Diana, and Paelen. She realized Paelen was right: Deep down, Cupid was frightened.

"But there may be more screaming girls."

"They'll be long gone," Joel said. "We'll just go back to the festival, grab a couple of CRU agents, and come right back here. You'll see—it will be easy."

AFTER BREAKFAST, PAELEN, JOEL, AND CUPID left Emily and Pegasus at the Red Apple.

Joel drove their stolen car out of the parking lot. Paelen sat in the front seat beside him while Cupid was stretched out in the backseat complaining constantly about having to lie on his wings and all the damage he was doing to the feathers. His fidgeting was starting to drive Paelen crazy.

"If you do not be quiet," Paelen warned as he turned to the back, "I will pluck out all your feathers myself. Then you will not have anything to complain about!"

"I do not see why you are so angry," Cupid said. "You are not the one with your wings stuffed down your trousers. You are still wearing Mercury's sandals and can fly anytime you wish, whereas I am burdened with this uncomfortable clothing."

"And I'm burdened with the two of you," Joel shot back. "Geez, you're like two spoiled children! Shut up so I can concentrate on driving and not getting us caught in this stolen car. Cupid, lie on your stomach and keep quiet."

"Of all the indignities . . . ," Cupid complained as he turned over.

"How far is it to the festival by ground?" Paelen asked, looking forward again. They were entering a town with a main street and buildings and houses on either side. It was still early in the morning, and people were out and rushing to get to work.

"A few miles," Joel said. "When my dad brought me up here, we stayed in a hotel. We'd eat at the Red Apple and then go to the festival. So it's all in this area called Tuxedo."

Paelen fell silent and stared out the front window. He was astounded at how different this world was from Olympus. Here the people traveled around in cars and always seemed to be in a hurry.

Above them the sky was gray and heavy as the first snow flurries of the season started to fall. "What is this?" Paelen asked in wonder as he opened the window and felt snow landing on his hand. "What is falling from the sky?"

Joel looked at him. "Haven't you ever seen snow before?"

Paelen shook his head. "It does not do this in Olympus. Until I came to your world, I had never left there before."

"Child!" Cupid yelled from the backseat. "I have been here many times and seen snow all over this world."

"I am not a child," Paelen argued.

"You are much younger than me," Cupid responded. "Younger than most Olympians. That makes you a child."

"How old are you?" Joel asked.

Paelen shrugged. "I do not know. You have lived in Olympus. Have you ever seen us measure time?"

"I never noticed," Joel admitted. "But I guess not."

"We do not," Cupid continued. "There is no need. We do not race around like you humans, trying to fill every moment of your short lives with one kind of action or another. We live, love, and enjoy ourselves."

"Until the Nirads attacked," Joel added. "I saw a lot of running around then."

Paelen heard Cupid's breath catch and knew he was terrified of even the mention of Nirads. "That is the exception," Cupid said. "Though I am certain there is not a human in this world who would not flee the Nirads."

"They'd be crazy not to," Joel agreed. "Now keep your eyes open for police, soldiers, or the CRU. We're not far from the festival."

Paelen's eyes scanned the area, searching for anything that might look out of place.

"There are a lot of extra police out," Joel muttered as they all watched two police cruisers drive past their car. "This could be a problem."

They continued out of the town and entered a wooded area. The road followed along the Haunted Forest's property. They saw the tall chain-link fence and some of the rides behind it. Finally the Haunted House came into view. In daylight there weren't a lot of festival workers about. But what they did see were soldiers and a lot of men in dark suits.

"The CRU," Joel said nervously. "Pegasus was right. They're searching for anything to tell them why we were here last night. We just might be able to capture a couple of their men."

"Do you think they will be expecting us to come back?" Paelen asked.

Cupid hauled himself up from the backseat and peered out the front window. "It could be a trap."

Joel shrugged. "It could be. I think I'll drive past the parking lot a few times to see what it's like there. Just keep your eyes open."

As expected, the parking lot was filled with black CRU cars and multiple military trucks. Several soldiers stood behind one of the trucks, taking a break. "Well, we can't drive in. I think we should abandon the car away from here and walk," Joel said.

"But how will we transport the men we are going to capture?" Paelen asked.

"We'll have to steal a CRU car," Joel suggested. "We're going to need it to go to the facility anyway. So we'll get both at the same time."

"That does not sound like much of a plan," Cupid complained.

"You got any better ideas?" Joel challenged.

Cupid fell silent and lay back down on the seat. Joel drove the car past the festival and turned in along a dirt road, heading higher into the mountains. He parked, and they abandoned the car. As they hiked through the woods, back toward the festival, Cupid continued to complain. Finally he stopped and freed the lower part of his wings from his jeans.

"Cupid," Paelen said tiredly. "You cannot show those."

"I am not going to," Cupid said. "I am going to leave my top on. But I could not walk another step with the feathers scratching against my legs. This will be fine. No one will notice."

Joel raised his eyebrows and looked at Paelen. "Is he kidding?"

Paelen finally gave up. There was just no reasoning with Cupid. "Fine, do as you wish. But if you get into trouble, do not expect us to help you."

They approached the chain-link fence and followed it until they reached the large parking area.

They ducked down behind some trees and studied the flow of men in and out of the parking lot. Not far ahead, they saw an open truck that contained scientific-looking equipment. Men were wearing white outfits that looked like space suits. They were carrying sealed containers with the word QUARANTINE printed on the sides.

"Do they think we're infectious?" Joel asked. "What could they have in there that they think is so dangerous?"

"I do not know," Paelen answered. "Did we leave anything behind last night?"

"Feathers," Cupid suggested. "The girls tore out a lot of my feathers. Perhaps they think they are dangerous."

"Maybe," Joel agreed. "Emily also set fire to the ground. Maybe they think that's contaminated as well. Whatever it is, there're a lot of men here. We're going to have to be extra careful."

Joel led the way forward as they kept low and crept into the parking lot. They crossed over to where most of the black cars were parked. When they ducked behind a large bush, Joel peered over the top. "I think these are the CRU cars," he said. "Those green trucks over there are for the soldiers. We should wait here until a couple of agents come along. Then we can make our move."

Light flurries soon turned into a full snowstorm with large, heavy flakes falling and collecting on the ground. Before long, a film of snow covered the vehicles. After what seemed an eternity, they heard the sound of muffled voices drawing near.

Paelen stole a peek and saw three CRU agents walking toward the black cars. Their heads were down against the weather, and they were talking softly. When one of them looked up, Paelen sucked in his breath. "Joel, look, it is Agent T! Do you remember him from Governors Island?"

Joel peered at the agent walking with the two others. "He was almost as bad as Agent J. He was part of the team that interrogated me. I remember his smile when they gave me those terrible drugs."

"The plan was to take two agents," Cupid said nervously. "Perhaps we should wait for others."

Fury rose on Joel's face. "No, I've got a score to settle. I want him! Let's just grab all three."

"I agree," Paelen said. "I should like to 'speak' with Agent T myself. Besides, we do not know how long it will be before more agents come, and I do not wish to leave Emily alone for very long. This may be our only opportunity."

The other two men were walking closer while Agent T stopped before another car and pulled out his keys. Paelen said, "I have an idea. Cupid, take off your top and go out there to get their attention. See if you can get them to follow you back here."

"Me?" Cupid said fearfully. "Why must I do it?"

"Because Agent T will recognize Joel and me and raise the alarm. Also, your wings will act as a diversion," Paelen explained. "Display them. Then, when the men are distracted, Joel and I can make our move."

"This is a bad idea," Cupid complained as he removed his sweatshirt and walked from their hiding spot and toward the men. Paelen and Joel crept out from behind the bush, then moved into position beside a black car.

"I am sorry," Cupid said softly as he approached, "but I am lost. Would you please tell me where I am?"

"You're gonna be more lost if you don't get out of here, kid," one of the agents said. "This is government business. Get moving."

Paelen watched Agent T step away from his car to investigate. "Look, it is working," he whispered. "Get ready."

"Please," Cupid said to the men. "There is no need to be rude. I was simply flying around and lost my way in the storm. If you could tell me where Olympus is, I will gladly go."

"Olympus?" Agent T said suspiciously. "Did you say 'Olympus'?"

It was only then that one of the other agents noticed Cupid's wings. "Oh my . . ." But he never finished the comment. Cupid struck out with a mighty punch.

Paelen and Joel dashed forward and knocked Agent T and the other agent to the ground. Joel unleashed his pent-up rage at Agent T for everything that had been done to him at Governors Island. Before long, Agent T and the others were unconscious.

Joel panted heavily as he looked up and peered around. With the heavy snow now falling, no one saw or heard anything. "Hand me his keys," he said to Cupid. "Let's get them in the car and get out of here!"

BACK AT THE RED APPLE, EMILY PACED THE
confines of the dining area, feeling like a caged animal. It seemed ages since the others left. There were
so many ways that things could go wrong. She was
afraid the police might have noticed the stolen car
and stopped them along the way. What if they'd been
arrested? Were they in a prison cell? Or perhaps the
CRU had captured them at the Haunted Forest and
taken them to the facility.

"They've been gone too long," she said as she crossed
over to the stallion and stroked his soft muzzle. "Something's wrong. We should be with them."

As more time passed, her panic increased until
Emily was ready to jump out of her skin. Finally they

heard the door opening in the back kitchen area.

"They're back!" Emily ran toward the kitchen, expecting to find Paelen, Joel, and Cupid. Instead she came face-to-face with a stranger holding a flashlight in one shaking hand and a gun in the other. Emily screamed. In that same instant the startled man's finger twitched on the trigger and fired.

The bullet hit Emily square in the chest. She flew backward and fell to the floor. It felt as if she'd been hit by a baseball bat. Her chest was on fire, and the blood was rushing in her ears. She heard Pegasus's furious whinnies as he charged the man, and then the man's frightened cries as he faced the enraged stallion.

Emily knew she'd been shot. But even as she wondered what would happen to her father without her, she felt the metal of the bullet heating up. It was melting in her body as the large wound burned itself closed. In the darkness of the unlit kitchen area she could see a bright glow rising from her chest. Her hands reached up to check and found her clothing wet from her blood. But as she poked her finger in the bullet hole, she could find no trace of the wound.

Beneath her fingertip she felt smooth, unblemished skin.

She sat up slowly. Emily looked over at the man and saw him cowering in the corner. He was still clutching his flashlight, but the gun was gone. Pegasus was standing before him, his wings open and nostrils flared in fury.

"Easy, Pegs, I'm all right," Emily said as she climbed unsteadily to her feet. She was slightly dizzy and felt strange, but other than that, she was in no pain. "I'm just a little shaken up."

Emily went to the open back door and shut it. "Who are you?" she demanded of the terrified man. "What are you doing here?"

"I-I own this place," he stuttered in fear. His flashlight was shining on her blood-soaked top, and his terrified eyes watched her as though he were seeing a ghost. "I saw smoke comin' out of it and thought vandals had broken in again. Please don't kill me!"

"Kill you?" Emily challenged. "You're the one who had a gun. You shot me!"

"I-I'm sorry," he said. "It was an accident. You came at me so fast, you startled me and my finger slipped."

Pegasus pawed the ground furiously and whinnied. He stalked forward, closer to the terrified man.

"What is that thing?" he cried in terror.

"Pegasus is not a 'thing'!" Emily said irritably. "He's a he."

"Pegasus?" the man repeated. "That the flyin' horse from them Greek myths?"

"And he's not a horse, either!" Emily replied as she stepped up to the stallion and patted his quivering neck. "It's all right, Pegs. I'm sure this was an accident. He didn't mean to hurt me." She looked at the man. "Did you? You'd better tell Pegasus the truth. He knows when people are lying."

"I swear," the man said. "It really was an accident."

Emily felt overwhelmingly tired and needed to sit down. "Come out of there and into the seating area, where I can see you better. What's your name?"

"Earl," the frightened man said as he walked cautiously around Pegasus, never taking his wary eyes off him.

"Sit down over there," she said tiredly. "Don't make any sudden movements or try to leave."

Earl sat down by the fire, still looking at Emily as

though she were an apparition. "What are you?" he timidly asked.

"You really don't want to know," Emily said. "But I can tell you this. We're here for a very good reason and need to stay hidden for a while. So please don't try to escape. I don't want to hurt you, but if you try anything, I will."

Emily felt sick threatening the man, but she couldn't have him escaping and calling the police. To illustrate her point, she stood before the fire. She called up the flames, and they shot from her fingertips into the burning wood. "I can do this faster than you can run. So just settle down and relax. When we're done, you can leave here completely unharmed."

Earl's eyes grew wide with terror as the flames moved from the raging fire back to Emily.

"Do we understand each other?" she demanded.

The man nodded. Emily patted Pegasus on the side. "Would you keep an eye on him for a while? I'm not feeling very well. I think I need to sit down for a bit."

As Emily settled down, Pegasus stood protectively beside her but never took his angry eyes off Earl.

He was still snorting and pawing the ground furiously. Emily was sure if Earl tried to move, Pegasus wouldn't hesitate to attack him. She took a deep breath and tried to relax. She was more tired than she'd ever been in her life and couldn't keep her eyes open a moment longer. Before long, she fell into a deep, healing sleep.

9

"EMILY!"

Emily awoke to Joel shaking her arms. "Em, please wake up!"

"I'm awake," she said groggily. "Please stop yelling!" Joel's frightened face hovered above her. Paelen was beside him. Pegasus was behind them, staring at her.

"Are you all right?" Paelen asked. "Pegasus told us what happened."

"It was an accident," Emily muttered, now fully awake. "We startled each other in the kitchen, and the gun went off."

"But you're hurt," Joel said as he inspected her sweatshirt. "Look at all this blood. We've got to get you to a hospital."

Emily shook her head. "No, it's all right. I don't understand how, but the bullet melted and the wound closed by itself. I'm fine."

"How?" Joel argued. "Em, you were shot!"

"She is the Flame of Olympus," Cupid explained. He was standing before their unconscious CRU prisoners. "She can heal herself as easily as she heals others."

"Yes, but a bullet in the chest should have killed her," Joel challenged.

"If she were human, it would have," Cupid continued. He approached Emily, knelt down, and stroked her cheek lightly. "Emily, the human in you died in the Flames back in Olympus. Your other life ended that day. Now you are as we are. You can no longer be killed."

Emily rose to her feet. "No way. I'll admit that something weird happened to me in the temple. But I'm still me. I'm still human."

Pegasus approached her and neighed softly as Cupid gently shook his head. "No, you are not. I know this has been a difficult transition for you, but believe me, you are not human. You are the Flame of Olympus. The human Emily died that day in the temple."

"No, that's impossible!" Emily argued. She turned desperately to Pegasus. "I still feel the same. I feel the cold and I get hungry. I can be hurt. I'm human and I'm alive."

The stallion moved closer and gently pressed his head to her. He neighed softly.

"Of course you are alive," Paelen reassured her. "You were reborn in the flames. And you feel pain as we all do. But you feel the cold only because you believe you should. Your body is Olympian, but in your mind, you still think of yourself as human. This is why you can't control your powers. You do not believe you can control them."

"But I still feel the same," Emily insisted. "What am I supposed to tell my dad? That I'm some kind of freak just like Agent O said I was?" She tried to wrestle with the truth. Tears rose to her eyes.

"Emily, don't cry!" Joel warned fearfully. "Your tears—remember what happened at the amphitheater! You could blow us all up."

Emily panicked, fearing what could happen here

if her tears fell. She reached into her jeans and pulled out the beautiful handkerchief Neptune had given her. She brought it up to her eyes and gently patted her tears.

"I can't even cry right." She sniffed and looked at the handkerchief. Her tears were beading on the surface like water on wax paper. But as she watched, a secret pocket seemed to open, and the tears slid in. Soon the surface looked as though they'd never been there at all. She looked at Pegasus. "What do I do with this now?"

The stallion nickered softly.

"He says that your tears are collected in the Siren's weave," Paelen explained. "They are not gone, nor have they been neutralized. If you ever need them, you can call them back to you. He says you must keep that with you at all times."

"What would she need her tears for?" Joel asked. "They're like nuclear weapons. They should be destroyed."

"They cannot be destroyed," Paelen said.

A sudden moan from one of the CRU prisoners reminded Emily why they were there. "I'm sorry," she said, shaking her head and sniffing a final time. "I've been thinking only about myself." She walked over to the three unconscious men lying on the floor. Agent T was starting to stir. "Shouldn't we tie them up or something? And I thought we were only going to get two CRU agents?"

"We didn't have much choice," Joel said. "The whole area was crawling with them. We were lucky we got these guys."

"There is no need for us to bind them," Paelen added. "We are stronger and faster than they are. It would be a fatal mistake if they tried to escape."

As she looked at the men, Earl approached them. "Don't kill me for talkin', but are you kids crazy? Bringin' them CRU agents here when everybody knows you're just the kinda things they're lookin' for."

"You know about the CRU?" Emily asked.

Earl nodded. "I know 'em and don't like 'em. A few years back a whole mess of them government folk moved into the area. Soon there was all kinds of crazy talk about aliens and other creatures. . . ." His eyes trailed over to Cupid, who'd taken off his sweatshirt for comfort, exposing his wings. They moved over to

Pegasus. "I also know that anyone who strays onto their property ain't never seen or heard from again."

"That's the CRU all right," Joel said. "What do you know about their facility?"

Earl shrugged. "Nothin', and I want to keep it that way. They hired a bunch of locals to build their underground bunkers. Some say the place is like a huge hidden fortress. My best friend's brother was an electrician who worked there. He talked about them deliverin' all kinds of freaky things. A few months back we were all out at a bar. He was drunk as a skunk and spoutin' stories of them bringin' in these big, four-armed gray aliens. It wasn't long after that he up and disappeared. A bunch of us tried to find him, but some agents came round and said it was best for everyone to just shut up. Not long after that, this place was condemned and my business shut down. I know it was them doin' it to warn us off."

"Nirads?" Cupid asked fearfully. "You are talking about Nirads?"

Joel snapped his fingers. "I bet those are the same ones from Governors Island. But how could they capture them? Bullets couldn't stop them." He looked at

Paelen. "Tranquilizers couldn't stop you, Diana, or Pegasus; I doubt they'd have worked on Nirads."

"Are you saying them things was real?" Earl asked fearfully. "That he wasn't tellin' tales?"

Emily nodded. "Yes, they're very real, but they're not aliens," she said softly. "They were trying to kill Pegasus."

"And you," Paelen said to her.

"They damaged my leg," Emily explained. "Now the CRU are holding my father at the same facility where they're keeping the Nirads."

"The CRU has your daddy?" Earl said. "Is that why you're all are here?"

Emily nodded.

"Where are you from?" he asked.

"The less you know, the safer it is for you," Joel warned.

"I don't hardly think so," Earl said. "The moment they find out I've been talkin' to you, I'm a goner."

"He's right," Emily said. "The CRU will kill him if they find out he's been here with us."

"I believe they already know," Paelen said as he pointed at Agent T, who was sitting up. He climbed to his feet and looked around. When his eyes settled on Pegasus, he inhaled. "It's true. You're back."

Emily looked at the man, with his black suit, perfectly groomed dark hair, and fiery blue eyes. He was tall, lean, and cruel. She instantly felt her fury rising. She remembered everything about him from Governors Island. "Yes, we're back," she responded. "We're here for my father, and you're going to help us get him out of there!"

"No, you've got that all wrong, young lady," Agent T said coolly. "You are going to surrender to *me*, and we'll all go back to the facility."

Joel stepped forward. "Do you remember me, Agent T? Because I sure remember you! The only thing keeping you alive right now is the information you've got. So look around you. In case you hadn't noticed, you're outnumbered. We've taken your weapons and phones. I'm sure you remember how strong Olympians are. Do you really want to make them angry?" Joel pointed at Paelen, Cupid, and Pegasus. "Emily and I have changed as well. Show him what you can do, Em."

Emily didn't hesitate. Talking to the arrogant agent

brought all her terrible memories of Governors Island back to the surface. She looked at the fire, held up her hands, and released the flames. They were wild and barely contained as they flashed and burned the wood in the fire to cinders.

When she looked back at Agent T, she saw a trace of fear rise in his eyes, but his shroud of arrogance quickly returned. "From what Agent O tells us, you can't control it."

"I can control it enough," Emily warned. "So you are going to tell me where my father is before I lose my temper."

"No, I'm not," Agent T responded. "We've all been trained to withstand torture. There's nothing you can do to us that will make us speak. So do whatever you like. It won't work. "

"That's right," the second agent agreed as he and the third agent rose to their feet and stood defiantly beside Agent T. "Surrender now, or this will turn very ugly for all of you."

No one expected this standoff. The CRU agents were unafraid as they faced the powerful Olympians.

"What are we going to do?" Joel muttered softly.

"Well, we can't reason with them," Emily answered. "Look at them. They don't care what we do to them." She started to pace the area. They had come so far. But it seemed everything was against them. There didn't seem to be any way to free her father.

"I know what will work." Paelen pointed at Cupid. "He can make them talk."

Cupid's eyes went wide, and he stepped back. "Oh no. I know what you are suggesting, but I will not do it."

"Do what?" Emily asked.

Paelen continued. "He can make the agents speak without the use of force. All he needs to do is use his powers."

"What powers?" Joel asked.

"The powers of love," Paelen said. "No one can resist Cupid when he turns it on." He pointed at the agents. "Not even them."

"Whatever you kids are planning, forget it," Agent T said. "Just surrender now, and no one needs to get hurt—" He looked at his men and picked up a large plank of wood from the burning pile. "Now!"

Before anyone could react, Agent T struck Joel in

the back of the head with a brutal blow. When he fell to the floor, unconscious, the agent turned on Paelen.

The restaurant erupted into fighting. Pegasus, Cupid, and Paelen had strength on their side, but the agents were better trained in combat and blocked most punches thrown at them. Despite being out-numbered, they held their own against the powerful Olympians.

Emily crouched beside Joel and watched the fight from the sidelines. Earl received a powerful spinning kick from Agent T that knocked him out while the two other agents pounced on Paelen.

She could feel her powers rising and aching to be freed. It was taking all her strength and concentration just to hold them back. She couldn't risk unleashing them and hitting those she cared for. She would only use her powers as a last resort.

Pegasus reared and kicked out at one of the agents on Paelen. But the man was quick and ducked beneath the lethal hoof. With a sudden roll, he sprang away from the stallion and was back at Paelen. As the fight intensified, Cupid was struck by Agent T's plank of wood. The force of the blow sent him hurtling across the restaurant. He landed on his wings and cried out in pain.

"Cupid!" Emily cried.

Cupid rose to his feet, his face blazing with fury. His wings flew open, and he howled in rage. Raising his hands in the air, he pointed at the agents and charged forward.

"Stop!" he ordered. "I command you to stop!"

As if they'd been suddenly frozen, the agents stopped fighting and stood perfectly still. The plank of wood in Agent T's raised hands fell noisily to the floor. They all stood unmoving, staring at Cupid, eyes wide, mouths hanging open, and arms limp at their sides. There was no mistaking that they were completely under Cupid's control.

"Go on, Cupid, finish it," Paelen coaxed as he rose from the floor and dusted himself off. "You must use your power to make them speak."

Cupid shook his head. "No, I will not. Mother always said charm is the best weapon. I believe she is correct."

The screaming girls! And her own feelings of attraction to him. It suddenly all made sense to

Emily. She had felt Cupid turn on his charm before but never realized it was an actual power he could control. She thought it was just his good looks. "So, you could actually charm them into talking?"

Cupid nodded reluctantly.

As Joel stirred and started to come around, Emily helped him to his feet. She turned back to Cupid. "Please, you must do it! If you don't, they won't talk. We need that information about my father and how they are controlling the Nirads. I'm begging you, Cupid, please help us."

Cupid shook his head. "You do not understand, Flame. Once I do this, they will love me forever. There is no going back, no reversing it."

"We don't have a choice," Emily pressed. "It's the only way we can save my dad."

Cupid hesitated. Finally he sighed and hugged Emily. He wrapped his wings around her tightly and whispered in her ear, "I will do this only for you, Emily, no one else. Not because you are the Flame and can command me, but because I choose to do it for you."

Emily's face flushed, and she felt her heart pounding as Cupid held her. "Thank you."

"That is enough," Paelen said gruffly as he forced them apart. "Save your charm for the agents, Cupid."

Everyone stood well away from the winged Olympian as he faced the mesmerized CRU agents. Cupid said nothing. But the wings on his back fluttered lightly with annoyance.

Earl had regained consciousness. Although he had a headache, he was unharmed. Standing between Emily and Joel, he tapped her lightly on the shoulder. "That there fella, is he the real Cupid? You know, the one with the bow who shoots love arrows and stuff at folks?"

Emily nodded. "But I'm not too sure about the bow. I've never seen him with one."

Earl whistled softly. "I always seen pictures of him as a chubby little angel baby with wings, not a teenager."

Joel looked at Earl. "It's amazing when you're in Olympus and see just how much we got wrong."

All eyes focused on Cupid as he stood before the agents. His head was down, and his wings drooped as his arms hung straight down. His body language showed just how much he didn't want to do this. Finally he lifted his head and faced the agents.

Emily watched the agent's faces as Cupid unleashed his powers. At first they were staring blankly. But that was soon replaced by an expression of awe, which turned into undisguised love.

"It's working," Joel said softly. "Look at them. They'll do anything for him."

"Cupid may be a coward and a troublemaker, but he does have his uses," Paelen said. He nudged Joel with his elbow. "Can you imagine what we could accomplish with a power like that?"

Joel chuckled and winced at the pounding in his head. "I can think of a few things."

Cupid closed his wings and turned back to the group. "You may ask your questions now," he said softly. "They will answer you."

Emily was the first to come forward. She stood beside Cupid and faced Agent T. "Where is my father?"

Agent T looked at Cupid and grinned foolishly.

"Answer her," he commanded.

Without further hesitation, the agent spoke. "He

is at the facility in the forest. We are keeping him on sublevel ten."

Over the next hour, the agents willingly answered every question posed to them. They gave the exact location and condition of Emily's father. They explained everything they knew about the Nirads being held at the facility. They told the group how they could enter the underground facility without being exposed. When the questions ended, Cupid ordered the men to sit down and remain silent. They obeyed the winged Olympian like eager puppies anxious to please their scolding master.

"Twenty-one Nirads," Paelen said. "I would never have thought it possible so many could be in this world."

"I still don't understand what happened?" Emily said. "Why would the Nirads surrender and become docile? Twenty-one could easily destroy the facility and go anywhere they pleased."

Paelen shrugged. "Perhaps when they failed to kill you and we left, they had nothing left to fight for, so they just surrendered."

Joel shook his head. "I don't think so. You saw

them. They were savage and uncontrolled. I don't believe they could surrender; it would mean they were thinking about it. The Nirads we saw showed no signs of intelligent thought, just animal instincts and reactions."

"Well, whatever it is," Emily said, "I hope they stay that way. I just want to go get my dad out of there and return to Olympus."

EMILY HELPED CUPID PULL ON ONE OF THE
agent's black suit jackets over his wings, then helped
him into a heavy wool coat.

"I do not know why I must dress as one of them,"
he complained as he fidgeted with the tie at his neck.

"How many times must we explain it?" Paelen
said tiredly as he dressed in one of the other agent's
suits. "You have wings. We must hide them. You do
not hear me complaining. I have had to take off my
sandals and wear these uncomfortable shoes."

Joel was doing up the shirt buttons and pulling on
the jacket of the last suit. "Will you two stop complaining? You're making my headache worse!" He
went over to Cupid and spoke to him as though he

were speaking to a troublesome child. "We've got to look like CRU agents. They dress in white shirts, black suits, and black coats, so we dress in white shirts, black suits, and black coats. It's as simple as that."

"But what about him?" Cupid said. He pointed to Agent T.

Agent T was wearing Joel's jeans and a checkered top, and his adoring eyes never left Cupid.

"We're taking him with us, since he has a valid ID badge. And he's going to wear the long black winter coat. I don't think he'll be a problem."

As Cupid protested further, Pegasus whinnied loudly and pounded the floor angrily with his golden hoof. Both Emily and Joel looked to Paelen to translate, but he said nothing. However, the look on Cupid's face was enough to say that Pegasus had lost patience with him.

"All right," Joel said to Emily, "you know the plan. We're just going to get in there. Agent T will take us to where they're holding your dad. Then we'll get right out again. I'd love to take my time and destroy the place, but I won't. With luck, we should be back here in a couple of hours."

"I really wish we were going with you," Emily said as she stroked Pegasus's strong neck.

"So do I," Joel agreed. "We could use that fire trick of yours. But I'm sure they're waiting for you and Pegasus. Just be ready to go the moment we get back."

Emily reached up and hugged his neck. "Thank you for doing this, Joel. It means everything to me."

Joel blushed. "Emily, you and your dad are the only family I've got. I don't want him trapped in there any more than you do. Just keep the door locked and say a prayer for us."

"I will," Emily promised as she watched Joel stroking the stallion's soft muzzle.

"Take good care of her, Pegasus," he said.

Cupid stepped up to the two agents remaining with Emily. They looked eagerly at him, grateful for his attention. "You two will stay here. You will do whatever Emily tells you to do, and you will protect her with your lives. If you fail her, you fail me, and I will be most displeased. Do you understand me?"

Both agents nodded and grinned foolishly at Cupid. Cupid's charm had worked too well. Emily almost felt sorry for them. The poor agents seemed to only want to serve him now. But what was to become of them once this was over?

"Be careful," Emily said for the hundredth time. "Please don't do anything foolish to endanger yourselves."

Paelen grinned his crooked grin and kissed her lightly on the cheek. "We will be careful," he said. "But you must take care also. Do not answer this door unless you hear it is us. We cannot have you hurt again."

"I won't," Emily promised.

Cupid, with his shaggy blond hair, looked painfully handsome in his long black coat. Once again her heart fluttered. "Stay safe, Cupid," she said softly.

"I will," he promised. He bent down and gave her the softest kiss on the lips. "You too. Wait for me, Flame. I will return shortly."

Emily could barely breathe when Cupid moved away.

"C'mon, lover boy," Joel said as he tugged Cupid's coat, "that's enough. Let's go."

Emily closed and bolted the door behind them. "We should be going with them, Pegs. It's not fair for them to risk their lives for my father while we sit here babysitting a couple of CRU agents."

Pegasus nickered softly. He put his head on her shoulder and pulled her closer.

They both heard movement in the kitchen and saw Earl standing there. "Are you all right?" he asked.

Emily nodded. "I'm just really scared for them. I wish I could have gone too."

"I'm sure everything will work out fine," he said. "Those boys care a lot about you and'll do the best they can."

"Thanks, Earl," she said softly. She crossed to the door and unbolted the lock. "It's not fair to keep you here any longer. You can go. But please promise me you won't tell anyone what you saw here."

"Well, now, you know I wouldn't say a word," he said as he shuffled his feet. "But if it's all the same to you, I think I'll stay a bit to keep you company."

Emily frowned. "Why would you want to do that when you could be free?"

"To tell you the truth, I want to see those boys beat the CRU and bring your father back here to you. So why don't we sit down a spell and wait for the good news."

THEIR CRU PRISONER DROVE THE BLACK CAR
out of the Red Apple parking lot, through Tuxedo,
New York, and toward the secret government agency's hidden forest facility. The snow that had started
earlier that morning continued to fall. By late afternoon there were several inches covering the ground.
The driving was treacherous and painfully slow.

Paelen sat up front in the passenger seat, while
Cupid and Joel took the backseat. As they drove
along the private road leading to the guardhouse,
Paelen looked back at Joel. He saw deep worry
lines etched on his friend's face. Cupid's face also
revealed fear, reflecting his own concerns for this
rescue. They were actually planning to go deep

inside a CRU facility. The chances of something going wrong were astronomical.

"We're approaching the gate," Agent T announced.

"Very good," Cupid said. "I want you to say whatever you must to ensure we get in there."

"Anything for you," Agent T said as he turned back and gave Cupid a silly grin.

"And stop smiling at me," Cupid spat. "Remember how you used to be."

The agent's grin disappeared, and he nodded. But he winked at Cupid before facing forward again.

Paelen laughed. He winked and kissed the air. "Anything for you," he teased Cupid.

Cupid leaned forward and grabbed a handful of Paelen's dark hair. He yanked his head back. "If you ever tell anyone what I have done in this world, I swear I will set the Hydra on you!"

"That's enough, you two," Joel warned. "Cupid, let him go. Let's just get this done, and you can finish your fight later."

"What fight?" Paelen said innocently.

They were drawing up to a guardhouse. A heavy chain-link gate blocked the way in. There were cameras everywhere, some pointing at them and others scanning the sky. This would be the first major obstacle.

The car pulled up to a tiny window at the guardhouse. A large, angry-looking man with an even larger weapon draped around his shoulder stood inside. When he saw Agent T at the wheel, he nodded in recognition. But then his eyes found the other passengers.

He opened the door and walked toward the car as his finger rested on the trigger of his weapon. "Identification," he demanded.

They were prepared for this. Paelen and Joel both showed the identification badges from the other agents. They silently prayed he wouldn't study the photos too closely, as they were not even close to what Paelen and Joel looked like.

But as the guard noticed the difference and became suspicious, he straightened and raised his weapon. Cupid reluctantly turned on his power. They watched the same reaction as before rising on the guard's face. At first suspicion, then awe, and, ultimately, adoration.

"It will please me if you let us in," Cupid said tightly through gritted teeth.

"Of course," the large guard said sweetly. "Anything

for you." He returned to his guardhouse and pressed the button that opened the large gate. Just as the car moved forward through the snow, they saw the guard blowing kisses at Cupid.

"How precious!" Paelen howled with laughter.

Despite his attempts to hold it in, Joel started to chuckle as well.

"I am warning you, Paelen," Cupid muttered furiously, "if you say one word about this back in Olympus—just one—I will have your head. . . ."

The rest of the journey passed in silence. Everyone seemed to understand the danger they were about to face, and the laughter stopped. Agent T drove the car to the parking lot at the side of the single building.

"This is it," Joel said tightly as he climbed out of the car and stood facing the small, squat redbrick building.

Paelen looked around and noticed how quiet and calm the area was. The heavy blanket of snow seemed to still even the birds. "Is it always this quiet?" he asked the agent.

"It's the snow," Agent T said. "No one likes coming out in it. They'll all be inside."

"And you know what you must do?" Cupid asked.

"Yes, if it pleases you, I will take you all in there to Steve Jacobs."

Cupid walked beside the agent, and Paelen and Joel followed closely behind. Joel stayed particularly close to Cupid's back to help hide the large lump made by his wings.

At the front entrance of the building, Agent T pulled out his ID card and passed it through the scanner. The door whooshed opened, and they all walked in. Just inside the door was a sign-in desk. A guard was sitting and reading a newspaper. He put it down when they approached. "Some storm, eh, Agent T?"

The agent nodded. "It's getting worse out there. He turned to Cupid. "This is Agent C."

Paelen felt his heart stop as their prisoner smiled at Cupid. "He's here to visit Jacobs."

"That wasn't on the schedule." The guard said as he frowned. He reached forward and checked a clipboard. "I have no visits listed here."

"I know. Change of plans," Agent T said. "The head is thinking of moving him. Especially now that the winged horse and the girl are back in the area.

These agents here are to assess the logistics of the move and to see if Jacobs is fit to travel."

"I'm sorry, Agent T, but if it's not on the list, I'd better check." The guard reached for the telephone.

Paelen gave Cupid a shove. "Do it," he quietly ordered.

Cupid looked at him furiously but reached out and grasped the guard's hand. "It is all right. You do not need to check. We will just visit the prisoner for a moment. Then we shall leave. Please, return to your reading. Do this for me."

The guard's face turned brilliant red. He cleared his throat and shuffled awkwardly on his feet. "Of . . . of course, anything for you." He fiddled around his desk and quickly drew up clip-on passes. "If anyone asks, just show them these." He grinned as he handed them the Cupid. "Is there anything else I can do for you today?"

"No, thank you," Paelen said.

The guard gave him only a passing glance as his adoring eyes rested on Cupid. "Please have a wonderful day."

As their agent-prisoner led the way to the elevators,

Cupid dropped his head. "This is by far the worst day of my life. My mother would be furious if she knew what I was doing." He shivered visibly and looked at Paelen. "I shall never forgive you for this."

Paelen was about to say something when Joel stepped forward. "Cupid, Venus would understand. She would be proud if she knew how much you were helping Emily." The elevator arrived, and they piled in. The agent pressed the button.

"How deep does it go?" Joel asked.

"There are twelve sublevels," Agent T said.

"And what levels did you say the Nirads are being held on?" Cupid nervously asked.

"On the bottom three."

Paelen frowned. "Wait—you told us that Emily's father is on sublevel ten. That means there are Nirads on the same level?"

"Yes. But they are dormant. They spend all their time sleeping. I assure you, they will not trouble you." He looked at Cupid again and grinned sheepishly.

A heavy silence filled the elevator as they descended. Paelen felt as if they were entering the maze of the Minotaur. One wrong turn and they would come face-to-face with the beast. Only this time, it wasn't the furious Minotaur they would encounter. It would be a hoard of deadly Nirads. Dormant or not, a Nirad was a Nirad, and he wanted to stay as far away from them as possible.

They arrived on sublevel ten, and Agent T led them forward through a maze of corridors. Halfway down a long, twisting corridor, they approached a heavy metal door. It had a sliding plaque mounted on the front that read STEVE JACOBS. The door was painted shiny white and had a coded lock. It looked identical to the doors from the facility at Governors Island. The agent entered the code on the security lock and pushed open the door.

Paelen entered first and felt a shiver pass along his spine. The room was so similar to the one he'd been held in. It even smelled the same. In the center of the room was a bed with a big lump. A blanket was pulled high over the occupant's head.

"Steve?" Joel called.

The lump stirred as a muffled voice called, "Go away."

"Steve, it's me, Joel!"

"And me, Paelen," Paelen added. "Emily is safe."

"Emily?" the lump said. Emily's father pushed down the covers and quickly rolled over. His eyes went wide at the sight of Joel and Paelen.

"Is it really you?" He leaped from the bed and gave Joel a brutal bear hug, then did the same to Paelen. His eyes darted around the room. "Where is she? Where's Emily?"

"Not here," Paelen said. "We thought it best if she stayed away. She is with Pegasus. They are waiting for you."

Tears rose in Steve's eyes, and his shoulders started to shake. "Is she all right? The Nirads hurt her. What happened? The CRU wouldn't let me see her or tell me how she was."

"She is fine. Calm yourself," Paelen said. "Vulcan built a brace for her leg. She walks perfectly."

"I really began to think I'd dreamed it all," Steve said shakily to Joel. "But it was real, wasn't it? Pegasus was here. He had a broken wing, and you kids dyed him black and brown."

"Yes it was," Joel said. "It wasn't a dream."

"Wait," Emily's father said, alarm rising in his

eyes. "The war? Olympus was destroyed. What happened?"

"We do not have time to explain," Paelen said. "We must get you out of here." He noticed that Steve was wearing a hospital gown. "Do you have any clothes here? It is very cold out."

"No, they won't give me anything but this. They won't even let me shave or cut my hair." He pointed to his thick, bushy beard and long brown hair. "I guess they're afraid I'd try to kill myself—" Steve's eyes suddenly landed on their agent prisoner. "Agent T!" His fury rose, and he launched himself at the agent. Knocking him to the floor, he started to pound him. "You did this to me! You refused to tell me about my own daughter!"

"Steve, no!" Joel cried as he struggled to break the men apart. "Please, we don't have time. He's working for us now. Stop, we've got to go. Emily needs you."

The mention of Emily's name held his fist in the air. "He's working for you?"

"Yes, Cupid charmed him. Now he is ours."

"Cupid?" Steve said.

"I am Cupid," the winged Olympian said, coming

forward. "It is an honor to meet the father of the Flame."

Steve shook his head in confusion as he regarded Cupid in his poorly fitting black suit and lumpy long coat. He looked at Joel. "What flame? What's he talking about?"

Joel grasped Steve by the arm. "We have a lot to tell you." He turned to Cupid. "Take off your long coat. Steve is going to need it." Then he looked back to Emily's father. "Do you remember how Pegasus was here to find the Daughter of Vesta? Well, that was actually Emily. She's the Flame of Olympus."

"My Emily?" he said in disbelief. "But . . . but . . . Diana, she said the Daughter of Vesta had to sacrifice herself to save Olympus. She had to die."

"Emily did sacrifice herself," Paelen said gently. "You should be very proud of her. Emily saved our world, and she saved yours. She was reborn in the flames. But she has never stopped thinking about you or wanting to free you from the CRU. So we slipped away from Olympus to get you."

"But she's alive, right?" Steve asked. "Emily is alive?"

"Very alive," Joel said. "And she's waiting for you. So please put on Cupid's coat—we need to get moving."

Steve quickly put on the long black coat. But as the group moved toward the door, the loud, furious sounds of sirens suddenly filled the air.

"They've found us," Joel cried.

Both Paelen and Cupid started to sniff the air. Cupid's expression turned to terror. "No, it is not the CRU."

"What is it?" Steve asked.

Paelen groaned. He shook his head. "Not again! This cannot happen to me twice!"

"What is it? What's happening?" Joel demanded.

Everyone heard the deep, guttural roars coming from the hall and the sound of shattering doors. Automatic gunfire mixed with the screaming of men.

"Nirads," Paelen said darkly. "They are awake."

PAELEN AND JOEL LED THE WAY OUT OF
Steve's quarters. The halls quickly filled with armed
soldiers preparing to fight the Nirads. They moved
down the corridor, toward the bank of elevators.

"I can't believe this," Joel said. "It's just like last
time."

"The Nirads will kill us all," Cupid cried as his
wild eyes darted around in terror. The wings on his
back were fluttering, and he was shaking like a leaf.

"I will protect you," Agent T said eagerly. He drew
his weapon. "They will not harm you."

"No, they won't!" Joel agreed. He reached into his
suit pocket and pulled out his golden dagger. "Did
you bring yours with you?" he asked Paelen.

Paelen nodded, and held up his dagger. "If we must fight, we will."

Having Agent T with them meant the other agents did not try to stop them or block their way. But as they stood waiting for the next elevator, they heard deep growls and roars.

Everyone watched as doors along the long corridor exploded and two Nirads charged out of their rooms. They turned toward the group and lumbered forward.

Soldiers in the hall opened fire, but the bullets bounced off the Nirads' gray marble skin and ricocheted around the area, knocking out lights and hitting other soldiers. "Their weapons will not work against them." Paelen shook his head. "When will these foolish people learn?"

"We're trapped here!" Cupid cried as he frantically searched for a way out. The elevators were still several levels away. "They will tear us apart! We are all going to die!"

"Cupid, calm down!" Joel said as he pointed. "Look, there're the stairs. Let's move!"

The group entered the stairwell. From above they

heard the sounds of fighting. "We're surrounded," Steve cried as the two Nirads from sublevel ten entered below.

The Nirads were gaining on them as they dashed for the next level. They weren't going to make it. Paelen and Joel stopped running. They turned and raised their gold daggers. "Keep moving," Joel ordered Steve. "Get back to Emily. She's at the Red Apple!"

Paelen's mind flashed with the terrible memories of what the Nirads had done to him on Governors Island. Of the pain he felt when they tried to rip him apart and the sounds of his own bones breaking. His hand started to shake.

"You okay?" Joel asked quickly.

"No," Paelen admitted.

"Me neither."

Further comment was cut short as two creatures rounded the bend and faced them. The Nirads' bead-black eyes settled on Joel and Emily's father. They bared their sharp, pointed teeth and snarled with vicious rage as their clawed hands opened and closed into fists. With renewed energy, they charged forward.

Joel held up his dagger. But he'd never fought with a knife before, let alone a dagger against a Nirad. As he flashed the golden blade in the air, it nicked one of the Nirad's four arms, causing a spray of black blood. Howling in pain, the creature swung a brutal fist and knocked the golden blade out of Joel's hand, sending it flying away. The creature roared and lunged at him.

Paelen tried to reach Joel to help, but the second Nirad was moving. It swatted him aside as though he were shooing away a troublesome fly. Paelen was knocked off his feet and sent tumbling back down the stairs.

When he hit the bottom, he looked up, and his eyes went wide in horror. The one Nirad had Joel in a brutal grip and was hoisting him in the air. Without a backward glance, the creature roared triumphantly and carried him up the stairs. Despite Joel's size, he was helpless against the terrifying strength of the four arms wrapped around him.

"Paelen!" Joel cried as he was carried away from the group and up and around the bend in the stairs. "Paelen, help me plea—" Suddenly the voice was cut off.

"Joel!" Paelen shouted. He feared his best friend had just been killed by the Nirad. "Joel!"

Above him, the other Nirad was still fighting to get hold of Steve. As Paelen reached for his gold dagger, he heard Cupid order Agent T to shoot.

"No!" Paelen cried as he dashed up the stairs. He knew human weapons were useless against the Nirads. In these tight quarters, firing the weapon at the Nirad was a disastrous idea.

The agent's weapon went off. The bullet struck the creature, ricocheted off its marblelike skin, and hit Steve in the chest. The Nirad caught hold of Emily's father just as he crumpled to the floor. Paelen shouted and sprang forward. He drove his gold dagger deep into the creature's back.

The Nirad released Steve and howled in pain and fury as it tried to dislodge the dagger. But it was too late. The Olympian gold's deadly poison was already doing its job. The fearsome creature staggered on the steps as its strength ebbed. In a final, agonized cry, it swooned and tumbled noisily down the stairs.

Paelen jumped aside as the huge creature somersaulted past him. He didn't pause to check on the

Nirad. "Cupid, help Steve," he ordered as he chased after Joel.

Paelen was close to panic as he climbed floor after floor, searching for his friend. "Joel!" he howled, "where are you?" But his calls went unanswered.

Paelen finally reached the ground level. He burst through the stairwell doors and into the lobby. Destruction was everywhere. Just like on Olympus, the Nirads had left nothing standing. Bodies of CRU agents and soldiers littered the floor, and the sign-in desk was in pieces and scattered around the room. The main entrance doors had been ripped off their hinges and tossed aside.

Paelen ran outside. Large tracks were impressed in the snow. They were all headed in the same direction, deeper into the forest. In the distance, he saw the electric fence had been knocked down as the army of Nirads had torn through it.

Paelen studied the tracks. His eyes caught hold of a sight that nearly stopped his heart. Red stains in the snow. He didn't need to see more to know what it was. It was human blood. It was Joel's blood. Paelen's knees gave out, and he collapsed to the ground.

EMILY SAT WITH EARL AND THE TWO AGENTS, snacking on the last of the food supplies. The moment Cupid left, the two agents clung to Emily like bees to honey. They were anxious to please her so she would tell Cupid what a great job they were doing. But what they were really doing was driving her insane.

"Please just sit down and eat something," she said as they hovered near her. "Geez, now I know what the president goes through with the Secret Service. . . ."

Pegasus was standing beside her, enjoying the last of the glazed doughnuts Emily handed up to him. "I've got all the protection I need with Pegasus."

"What's it like on Mount Olympus?" Earl asked. "I ain't never been to Greece."

"Neither have I," Emily answered. "The real Olympus isn't in Greece. It's another world. You have to go through this highwaylike thing called the Solar Stream to get there. But it's really awesome. More beautiful than anything you could ever imagine and filled with amazing people and animals."

Earl sighed. "I'd sure like to see it someday."

"Maybe you will when all this is over."

"You could come with us," one of the agents suggested, a brilliant, almost crazed smile lighting his face, "when we go there with Cupid."

Emily and Earl looked at each other knowingly but said nothing. They lapsed into silence as they waited for news from the others.

Time seemed to stop. As each moment ticked by, Emily felt her fear growing. "How long has it been?" she finally asked.

Earl checked his watch. "'Bout an hour and a half; they should be back here any time."

Emily started to pace the area. "I just wish they'd hurry."

The two agents also stood and began pacing along with her.

"Would you two please sit down!" Emily shouted. "I'm fine. See? There's no one here to hurt me!"

The words were no sooner out of her mouth than a huge crashing sound came from the kitchen area. Pegasus whinnied loudly and charged forward into the darkness. Emily strained her eyes in the firelight but couldn't see anything.

The two agents burst into action. "Stand over there," they ordered, driving her away from the kitchen. "We'll check this out." One of them pointed at Earl. "Keep an eye on her."

Emily could hear Pegasus's shrill and furious whinnies. "Pegs!" she cried. She began to feel the Flame within her start to stir. "No!" she told herself. "Not again. Not now!"

From the kitchen came more sounds. Mixed in with Pegasus came grunting and squealing. "What the heck is that?" Earl cried as a large animal charged into the dining area, knocking aside the two agents.

After all her time in Olympus, Emily thought she had seen just about everything that world had to offer.

But now, standing before her was a massive, winged boar. It was covered in coarse brown hair, with sharp, pointed tusks curling out of its large, threatening snout. But stranger still were the wings. They were folded close to the stocky body and stuck out almost a meter past the boar's hind end. Its feathers were as brown and coarse as its hair. The raging animal charged forward but stopped just short of Emily.

Pegasus followed quickly behind. He bent his head down and hit the boar with enough force to send it rolling away from Emily.

The enraged animal righted itself and turned. It charged at Pegasus. The stallion stood his ground and lowered his head again. As the two heads met, the sound of their skulls knocking together was sickening.

"Pegasus!" Emily cried.

Earl was beside her and holding her back. "Don't!" he warned. "I don't know what that thing is, but if it's anythin' like the wild boars we got around here, it ain't no friend! We gotta get outta here!"

"I'm not leaving Pegasus," Emily said, pulling away.

Pegasus reared on his hind legs and kicked out at

the ferocious boar. Although the animal was big, it was lightning fast and darted away from the stallion's lethal hooves.

"Stop it!" Emily roared. She could feel flutters in her stomach turning into heavy tingling as the power of the Flame increased with her fear. Soon it would rise and flow along her arms, and there would be nothing she could do to control it. "Please, stop fighting. The Flame is coming!"

The fight was terrible. The boar charged forward and darted under the stallion's kicking legs. When it reached Pegasus's vulnerable underside, it threw its head up, and the sharp tusks tore into the flesh of the stallion's underbelly.

Pegasus shrieked in pain as both his hooves came crashing down on the boar's back. It squealed and darted away but then turned and faced Pegasus again. In the dim light, Emily could see blood pouring from the stallion's wounds. But Pegasus wouldn't stop. He reared again and charged the winged boar.

Suddenly, from all around the boarded-up rest stop came a sound Emily knew all too well. Her eyes flew wildly around the dining area. Thick, filthy fingers with sharp claws were tearing away the boards on the windows. As they fell away, daylight showed the horrors yet to come. An army of Nirads were outside the Red Apple and were tearing their way in.

"Nirads!" she cried, running closer to the fighting stallion. "Pegasus, stop, we've got to get out of here! Nirads are here!"

"Them the four-armed aliens attackin' Olympus?" Earl asked as his terrified eyes darted around the room. "The ones that hurt your leg?"

Emily nodded. The sounds of breaking windows, tearing wood, and roaring Nirads in the confines of the tight area were deafening. "They're here to kill us." Emily had to shout to hear herself. "Get the agents and go! Leave before it's too late!"

"I ain't leavin' you," Earl called. "You're comin' with me."

Emily's powers were rising. In moments fire would burst forth from her fingertips. "I can't. The Flame is coming and I have no control!" She shoved Earl away as the tingling rose from her stomach and moved along her arms. "Go now before it's too late!" she howled.

Just as the first Nirads touched down on the floor of the Red Apple, Emily's powers let loose. Despite her terror, she forced herself to concentrate. The flames shot wildly out of her fingertips, but as a Nirad charged toward her, she pulled back and tightened the Flame into a thin red beam.

She pointed her hands at the Nirad. The red beam struck the ferocious nightmare and burned right through the creature, cutting it in half. The air was filled with howls of pain as it fell to the floor and died.

But there was no time to celebrate. More and more Nirads were pouring into the restaurant. Emily ran forward and fired at a second Nirad and then a third. But in her panic, her aim was off, and she only managed to wound the rampaging creatures.

With the red beam still firing from her fingers, Emily's wild eyes found and shot at more Nirads. But as they went down, more and more seemed to replace them. She had no idea how many there were, except that it was countless more than they had ever fought before. Even with her powers, they were badly outnumbered.

"Pegasus!" she cried. The stallion and boar were still fighting. As she stole a glance back, she saw several Nirads joining the fight and moving in on Pegasus. Earl and the two CRU agents were taking on a single Nirad. She ran toward them.

The Nirad quickly dispatched one agent and then the second one. It turned on Earl.

"Earl, no—"

The Nirad caught hold of him and raised him in the air. Emily was there in a flash. She pointed her hands at the Nirad as it squeezed Earl in a crushing embrace. Her red beam struck the vicious creature's leg and cut it off. It roared in pain and threw Earl across the restaurant.

Emily couldn't see where Earl had landed. She didn't know if he was dead or alive. But she didn't have time to find out. She turned her hands toward the Nirads attacking Pegasus. But fear of striking the stallion kept her aim off.

As Emily struggled to control the red beam so that it would hit only the Nirads, she was charged from behind. A Nirad caught her around the waist and hoisted her easily off the ground.

Her arms flew around wildly as she lost control of the Flame. It shot in all directions throughout the restaurant. The beam burned its way through the walls, the ceiling, the floor, and any Nirads in the way. Everything the powerful red beam touched was sliced like a knife through soft butter. Soon the walls of the Red Apple blazed furiously.

"No!" she cried. As terror threatened to overwhelm her, Emily finally regained some control and pointed her hands down at the Nirad. Fire burned the creature's legs. It roared in agony and released her; they fell to the floor together.

Emily scrambled away. But the relief was short lived. Before she could raise her hands again, she was tackled and driven down to the floor. Pain exploded in her head as more arms wrapped around her.

As the brutal arms squeezed tighter, Emily continued to fight. But it was in vain. Her powers stopped, and she had no strength against the Nirads. She looked up, searching for Pegasus.

The stallion had been knocked to the ground, and his pain-filled cries split the air as the Nirads swarmed over him. "Pegasus!" she howled.

The Nirad holding Emily lifted her off the ground. But as more creatures moved forward, everyone heard the loud creaking and moaning coming from the building itself.

Emily looked up and saw the latticework of cuts and scars in the ceiling from her powerful red beam. The entire roof was a roaring flame. Then the weight of the snow above and the fire below proved too much for the weakened timbers. Before anyone had time to react, the beams broke and the entire burning ceiling came crashing down.

EMILY REGAINED CONSCIOUSNESS AND
opened her eyes. A scream escaped her lips before she
could hold it back. She was being carried in the arms
of a Nirad. The creature looked down at her as he
clamped his third hand across her mouth.

He shook his head. The message was clear. Don't
scream.

Emily struggled. Yet despite the Nirads' unbeliev-
able strength, his grip on her was surprisingly light
and causing no pain.

When the Nirad was certain she wouldn't scream
again, he removed his hand from her mouth. Emily
nearly gagged at the taste of filth on her lips. She
looked around and was terrified to discover she was

no longer at the Red Apple. She was surrounded by the huge, lumbering creatures as they trudged through the deep snow of the forest.

It was only then that Emily noticed all the cuts, burns, and large tears to her clothing. She was covered in blood and smelled of smoke. But she wasn't in any pain. Her jeans were badly damaged, and most of the gold leg brace was exposed. The Nirad was being careful not to touch any part of the brace. As if it somehow knew that touching it would be dangerous.

Her hands were covered in dried blood, dirt, and ashes. But the skin was smooth and unblemished. She could also move them without any trace of pain. She suddenly realized that despite the torn shreds of her clothes, she wasn't feeling the cold of being outside in a heavy snowstorm. Cupid was right. She really was an Olympian after all.

Only then did she remember what happened. How the entire roof of the Red Apple had burned and then collapsed on them.

What about the others? Emily suddenly remembered Pegasus. The last thing she recalled seeing was the

Nirads swarming all over him. "Pegasus?" she cried as panic set in and she struggled to escape the arms that held her. "Pegs, where are you?"

From far behind the group, Emily heard the stallion whinny. Her heart filled with relief that he was still alive. "Are you all right?"

The Nirad holding her gave her a light squeeze and grunted. It shook its head again. Emily focused on its eyes. They were different from those of the other Nirads she'd seen. This Nirad appeared to possess intelligence and understanding. When it looked at her, instead of the normal glazed expression and desire to kill, it really seemed to see her. The color of the creature's skin was also different from that of the Nirads she had previously encountered. Those had a gray, marbled skin.

This Nirad had the same marbled skin tone, but the color was dark orange. Emily looked around and saw an array of different-colored Nirads—orange, gray, even lilac. Leading the group deeper into the forest was the winged boar. Bleeding hoof scars were imprinted on its back and wings from the fight with Pegasus. One of the boar's wings was held at an odd angle and dragged along the surface of the snow, broken.

"Please put me down," Emily said softly to the Nirad.

The creature looked at her but remained silent.

"Can you understand me?"

At the front of the group the winged boar stopped. It turned and trotted back to Emily. It stopped before the Nirad holding her, and Emily felt the creature react. It lifted her higher, away from the sharp tusks of the vicious animal, and gripped her more securely.

The boar squealed and fluttered its good wing threateningly at her.

Pegasus responded immediately and whinnied angrily from behind. The boar looked back, squealed again, and then returned to the front of the procession.

High in the Nirad's arms, Emily stole a glance over its thick shoulder. There were a lot more gray Nirads surrounding Pegasus. They growled, drooled, and poked him with sticks to keep moving.

Emily inhaled sharply at the sight of her beloved stallion. Pegasus was covered in deep scratches, burns, and filthy debris from the roof collapse. But worst of all were his once-beautiful wings. The fire had burned most of his feathers off, leaving only singed, downy feathers behind.

"Pegs," she whimpered. "I'm sorry."

The Nirad holding her lowered her until she could no longer see Pegasus. It looked down into her face, and for a moment Emily saw profound sadness resting there as it gave her a gentle squeeze.

"Were you ordered to capture us?" she asked in a hushed whisper.

The creature nodded slightly.

"You can understand me!"

The creature looked up toward the boar leading the group before looking back down at her. Once again it gave a slight nod.

Emily's mind was in turmoil. Ever since she'd encountered the first Nirad in New York she had thought of them as mindless creatures set on only one thing: destruction. But if this Nirad could understand her, could the others? Was there more to them than she first thought?

As she was carried deeper into the forest, she continued to study the Nirads around her. She started to notice other significant differences. It was more than just the color of their marbled skin. She observed that the gray Nirads were stockier. They drooled, shuffled, and seemed to follow the others rather than lead. The lilac Nirads appeared to be in control of the gray ones. She watched as they occasionally barked growling instructions at them.

Emily then looked back at the face of the orange Nirad carrying her and noticed a big difference. It stood taller and straighter. Although it had the same muscular build, long dark hair, four arms, and claws as the others, these orange Nirads had a presence that suggested intelligence and perhaps even empathy.

Emily stole a look forward at the winged boar before asking the Nirad carrying her, "Can you speak my language?"

The creature shook its head, then opened its mouth to reveal a row of terrifyingly sharp, pointed teeth. It had a very tiny tongue and made a soft sound, but nothing she could understand. She realized that without a proper tongue, it could never speak her language.

When she opened her mouth to ask another question, the Nirad brought its third hand down across it again. It motioned to let her know the winged boar was slowing down to listen.

Emily nodded. The creature removed its hand, and they walked on through the forest in silence. After a time, Emily saw the ground beneath them rising and realized they had reached the base of a mountain.

But instead of climbing up, they were walking to the left. Up ahead, Emily saw a dark area that could have been a cave entrance blocked by huge boulders.

The winged boar squealed, and the group stopped. The Nirad carrying Emily stood well back as the gray Nirads moved forward. Grunting and growling, they started to shift the huge snow-covered boulders away.

Emily could see Pegasus again. Several orange Nirads surrounded him, but they left him untouched. His head was down, and his eyes were closed with exhaustion. His beautiful silky mane was matted with blood. Emily desperately wished she could touch him to heal him. But she knew the Nirad would never allow it.

She was certain it was holding her at an angle so that she could see Pegasus. The way it looked at her told her so. But it would do no more than that.

"It'll be all right, Pegs," she called to the stallion, heedless of the winged boar standing just a couple of yards away. "We'll get out of this somehow."

The boar turned and squealed at her again.

"What are you going to do?" Emily angrily replied. "Kill me? Go on, then, try it. But if you dare to touch Pegasus one more time, I swear I'll unleash my powers and kill us all! Do you understand me?"

The winged boar looked at Emily and tilted its head to the side curiously. It moved closer. Once again the Nirad lifted Emily higher, out of reach. But the winged boar was having none of it. It squealed angrily at the Nirad until Emily was lowered to the boar's level.

Emily was now face-to-face with the large animal. She looked into its deep brown eyes and saw great intelligence there; it immediately reminded her of Pegasus. The boar's sharp tusks were a few inches away from her face. But Emily felt no fear for herself. All she cared about was keeping Pegasus safe.

"I don't know who you are or why you are doing this," she said, "but I mean it. If you hurt Pegasus again, I will turn my powers against you. Even if it kills me—I don't care. Leave him alone."

The boar moved even closer to Emily, until the end of its whiskered snout touched her cheek. At the moment of contact, the boar squealed in shock and jumped back. It looked down at its broken wing and moved it slightly. Then it looked over to Pegasus and grunted. Finally, it moved forward and pressed its snout against one of Emily's hands.

Against her wishes, Emily's powers healed the boar. The hoof marks on the animal's back faded and disappeared while the wing set and moved into its normal position on the boar's back.

"You're an Olympian!" she said in shock.

The boar stared at Emily for several heartbeats, until it eventually drew away. It walked over to Pegasus and squealed.

Pegasus raised his head proudly and faced the boar. He whinnied several times and pounded the snowy ground with his sharp golden hoof. She wished more than ever that she could understand him. Something very serious was happening here, and she needed to know what.

After a long exchange the winged boar looked back at Emily. It turned and walked through the deep snow to where the Nirads were uncovering the cave entrance. When it was opened, the boar entered.

Everyone started to move. They streamed one by one into the dark cave. Soon the Nirad carrying Emily stepped forward. As she looked back toward Pegasus, she struggled to see past all the Nirads surrounding him. He was being led in behind her. Emily couldn't see a thing as her eyes adjusted to the pitch-dark of the cave. She could hear the occasional grunt as the Nirads piled into the tight area. A moment later something brushed against her leg—a Nirad arm—and as it grazed along her exposed gold leg brace it howled in agony and fell to the ground, clutching its wounded arm and bellowing in pain. It rose to its feet and charged toward Emily, desperate to kill. Before Emily could react, the orange Nirad holding her struck out at the attacker with one of its strong arms. She heard the fist make brutal contact with the face of the attacking Nirad. It fell backward, roaring as it went.

As it gained its feet for a second attack, more orange Nirads surrounded Emily in protection. By the time her eyes adjusted fully to the darkness, she realized it had been one of the gray Nirads attacking her.

The shrill sound of the winged boar filled the air, and all the Nirads stopped. The animal charged through the creatures and approached Emily. It looked up at her Nirad and squealed.

The Nirad grunted and growled in response. It knelt down to show the boar Emily's exposed leg brace. It sniffed the gold, turned to Pegasus, and squealed loudly.

Emily strained to see around her Nirad to look at the stallion, but her view was blocked. She heard Pegasus pounding the stone floor of the cave, but he said nothing.

The winged boar concentrated on Emily again and grunted. It snatched a cover from the nearest Nirad and draped the filthy rag over the exposed gold. A second rag was then torn from another Nirad, and the boar ensured that all the gold of the leg brace was covered.

The boar charged through the gathered creatures and approached the back wall of the tight cave. It opened its wings and made several loud and short sounds.

Suddenly the rear wall burst to life as if there had been a silent explosion. Blinding white light poured into the dark cave, followed by ferocious winds and the sounds of crackling electricity. Emily inhaled sharply and realized this was a portal to the Solar Stream. It was how the Nirads had traveled to her world. As the winged boar entered the blinding light and disappeared, the Nirads followed closely behind.

Fear coursed through her as her Nirad approached the portal.

"No, don't," she begged as she struggled in its arms. "Please, I belong here. This is my world. I don't want to leave!" She struggled against the Nirad's strong arms, but they would not give. It held her close and grunted softly but moved forward. Moments later Emily was carried through the bright portal and she disappeared.

PAELEN WEPT AS HE KNELT IN THE SNOW.
How could the rescue plan have gone so wrong? He
cursed himself for not bringing Emily and Pegasus.
She could have used her powers. Joel wouldn't have
had to die.

His tears fell unchecked down his face as he
grieved over the loss of his best friend. Until Emily
and Joel had entered his life, Paelen had been alone,
scavenging and stealing his way through a life apart
from the other Olympians. Always on the outside,
never part of anyone or anything. But Joel and Emily
had changed all that. They brought joy and adven-
ture into his life. More than that, they had become
his family.

Now Joel was gone and Emily's father was hurt. What words could he ever tell her to make up for that? He had failed them all.

"Paelen," Cupid called. He was standing at the entrance of the building, clutching Emily's father. Agent T was beside him. "Go start the car," Cupid ordered as he carried Steve closer. "Paelen, this human is badly wounded. We must get him help."

Paelen rose to his feet and looked at Emily's father. His eyes were closed and his face pale, but he was breathing. He felt for the pulse in Steve's neck. It was still beating strongly. But for how long? Inhaling deeply, he drew himself away from the Nirad tracks and reluctantly followed Cupid and Agent T.

Paelen sat in the backseat of the car, cradling Emily's father and keeping pressure on his bullet wound. The stain on the front of his hospital gown was slowly spreading. He was losing a lot of blood.

Cupid was in the passenger seat up front with Agent T. "Get us back to the Red Apple," the winged Olympian ordered quietly. "And hurry."

While Agent T drove them away from the CRU facility, Paelen shook his head. "Why Joel and Steve?"

he wondered aloud. "The Nirads were only after Joel and Steve."

Cupid looked back. "No, they were after all of us."

Paelen shook his head. "You are wrong. That creature could have killed me. But it was as though he barely even saw me. He knocked me away as though I meant nothing and was focused only on Steve. Why?"

Cupid faced forward. "And why did the Nirad take Joel away?" he mused. "He could have simply killed him and left him behind. But he took Joel's body with him."

Paelen shuddered. Cupid had given voice to his worst fear. That Joel was really dead. "What are we going to tell Emily?"

"That Joel died bravely defending her father," Cupid said. The winged Olympian leaned forward and looked out the window at the sky above them. "The snow is getting heavier. We must collect Emily and Pegasus and leave this world soon."

They traveled in silence as they made their way along the slushy roads, back through Tuxedo and toward the rest stop. Everyone noticed a large number of fire trucks and police cruisers out on the roads. Paelen also saw several military trucks driving past.

"They must be searching for the Nirads," Agent T suggested.

Cupid shook his head. "How can they? The Nirads went in the other direction. These men look like they are heading to—"

Cupid stopped and looked back at Paelen, and they said together, "The Red Apple!" He looked over at Agent T. "Move faster."

The car sped toward their hiding spot. When they drove along the road in front of the rest stop, they saw flashing lights from fire trucks, police cruisers, and military vehicles crowded into the parking area. The building itself was all but collapsed. Part of the roof was still burning as the firemen struggled to put out the flames. Everywhere they looked, they saw destruction. Nothing of the rest stop remained intact.

"Emily!" Paelen cried.

As Agent T started to turn the car into the crowded parking lot, Cupid ordered him not to. "Continue down the road."

"Cupid, what are you doing?" Paelen asked.

"We must not let them see us. Emily and Pegasus are already lost. Why should we surrender ourselves so easily?"

Paelen's fear turned to fury. "Emily is not lost!" he shouted. "We must go back and find them!"

"Paelen, calm down," Cupid ordered. "We will. But we must not be seen. This is the time for stealth. For once in your life, trust me. I am older than you, and I know what I am doing."

Paelen was too frightened to know what to do. Steve was wounded, Joel dead, and now this. It was beyond anything he'd ever experienced.

The car continued past the Red Apple and farther down the road. Cupid instructed Agent T to pull into the empty parking area of a closed gas station. Paelen gently lowered Steve's head onto the backseat as he climbed carefully from the car.

"All right," Cupid said. "We have two choices. I can fly back to Olympus to get help—"

"No!" Paelen cut in as he brutally shoved Cupid. "You are not leaving for Olympus, you little coward! Emily and Pegasus are in that wreckage. They need us to get them out before the CRU does."

The wings under Cupid's suit jacket fluttered as he righted himself and stepped closer to Paelen. Looming above him, his eyes blazed with fury. "I am not a coward!" he shouted. "Are you so incapable of believing that I can care for Emily and Pegasus? That I would abandon them in their time of need? I do care, Paelen. And I am not going to leave them to the mercy of the CRU. I was going to say that I could fly back to Olympus for help or that we could both go over there to find Emily ourselves. I was going to suggest we stay and do this ourselves."

Paelen was shocked into silence by Cupid's outburst. In all the years he'd known him, he'd never seen him this angry. "I am sorry, Cupid. I have been unfair. You are not a coward. You have done everything we have asked you to, even though it hurt you to do so." Paelen looked over to Agent T and saw his besotted eyes following Cupid. "We could not have made it this far without you. But losing Joel and now seeing the Red Apple and knowing Emily and Pegasus are in there, I am not thinking clearly."

Cupid calmed. "I know I have not always proved myself to you and the others. And yes, perhaps I came here as much to get away from the Nirads as to help Emily. But believe me, Paelen, I do want to help. Now, let us ensure Steve is safe, and then we can walk back to the Red Apple and see about Emily and Pegasus."

They checked on Steve in the backseat. He was still unconscious, but his bleeding had stopped and he was breathing well. After they made him as comfortable as possible, they started back toward the Red Apple.

The snow was now falling heavily. The thick flakes settled on their hair and shoulders and limited their vision to only a few yards in front of them. Keeping in the dense trees that grew behind the large rest stop, they approached the area.

One of the first things they noticed was Agent O supervising the search. He was walking with two crutches, and his legs were covered in thick bandages. Yet despite his wounds and obvious pain, he was well enough to bark orders at the others working in the area, demanding they not stop until they found Emily.

"They have not found her yet," Paelen said gratefully. "There is still hope."

His eyes scanned the whole area. The destruction was all but complete. "What happened here?" he asked in a hushed whisper. "Could it have been Emily's tears again?"

They watched in silent shock as several men emerged from the wreckage. They were struggling to carry a heavy stretcher. A sheet completely covered the body. But as the men moved to put the stretcher on a truck, an arm fell out from under the cover. It was the color of gray marble.

"Nirads!" Cupid said. "While we were gone, Nirads attacked our hiding place!"

"How is this possible?" Paelen asked. "The Nirad tracks at the CRU facility showed they were moving deeper into the woods. How could they get here before us?"

Cupid shrugged. "They could not. But if it was not the same Nirads as at the facility—"

"Then there are more here in this world," Paelen finished.

As they concentrated on the wreckage, Paelen, Cupid, and Agent T crept closer, trying to see any signs of Emily or Pegasus. There were CRU agents and military personnel poring all over the area and searching through the wreckage. But there were no traces of their missing friends.

A short while later another stretcher was carried out of the smoldering debris. Paelen and Cupid could tell by the size that it was another Nirad body. But it was different. The lump under the sheet ended at the waist. Moments later, a third stretcher emerged, with an equally strange shape. The men carrying it slipped in the snow and fell. When they hit the ground, the body fell off the stretcher, revealing only a heavy set of legs and lower torso.

Paelen pointed. "Look at the cut edge. It has been burned."

"Emily can kill Nirads," Cupid mused. "It is no wonder they came after her. If they knew she and Pegasus could kill them, they would have to get them first, before completing their attack on Olympus."

"Or here," Paelen added. As he scanned the debris, Paelen shook his head. "We have seen Nirads pulled out of there, but where are the others?"

"Maybe he can tell us?" Agent T offered helpfully as he pointed at yet another stretcher being pulled from the debris. Unlike the others, the occupant was not fully covered by a sheet. He was wrapped in a blanket. His face was badly burned, but he was alive and moaning loudly.

"Earl!" Paelen said. "We must get to him. He can tell us what happened here."

They watched Earl being loaded into an ambulance. Cupid turned to Agent T. "Where will they take him?"

Agent T smiled radiantly, grateful to contribute. "They can't take him back to the facility, not with what the Nirads did to it. If it were me, I would secure a hospital and take him there."

Paelen realized if the CRU managed to take Earl away, they would never learn what happened to Emily or Pegasus. He looked at Cupid. "We must stop them."

"How?" Cupid asked. "This whole area is covered with agents. We will be captured before we get anywhere near him."

"If it pleases you, I can do it," Agent T offered. "They know me and will not suspect that I'm doing it for you. I could capture the ambulance, and we could get away from here."

Paelen looked at Cupid. "We have no choice. If he wants to do it, let him try."

Cupid said to their prisoner, "Yes, it would please me very much if you could do this. Go secure the vehicle. When you have it, take it to where we left the car. Paelen and I will join you there."

Agent T's face beamed as he stood, anxious to carry out Cupid's wishes. "I will do anything for you, Cupid."

Cupid cringed as the agent showed his undying devotion. From their hiding place they watched Agent T's demeanor change. He straightened his back and walked with the arrogance they were used to seeing. His voice was loud and commanding as he approached the group of agents standing beside the ambulance containing Earl.

They could hear him demanding a full report. Both Paelen and Cupid breathed a sigh of relief when they heard the others report that there were no traces of the girl or horse in the wreckage. Just the Nirad bodies, two dead CRU agents, and the one surviving man.

Agent T ordered them back to work in the debris. Alone with the ambulance, he secured the rear doors and stormed up front to the driver's side and climbed in. Moments later the ambulance burst to life. Agent T put it in gear and began driving away from the area.

"We must go," Cupid said as he rose and caught Paelen by the sleeve. "We do not want Agent T waiting there for us long. He may try to come back to look for me."

The ambulance was waiting for them beside the black car when they left the cover of the trees. Agent T was standing at the rear doors, bouncing with excitement.

"I told you I could do it!" He sounded like a hopeful child looking for praise. "Did I do well?"

"Yes," Cupid said. "You did very well."

They opened the ambulance doors and were immediately struck by the smell of smoke rising from Earl. His face was raw with burns, and he was moaning softly.

"Earl," Paelen said gently as he climbed in and approached the side of the stretcher. "It is us, Paelen and Cupid. Can you hear me?"

Earl's eyes fluttered open, and he turned his face to Paelen. "Thank God, it's you," he said weakly.

"What happened?"

"Monsters came. Them big four-armed things. They attacked us."

"Are Emily and Pegasus still in the rubble?" Cupid asked.

Earl shook his head slightly and moaned at the movement. "No," he choked. "I saw 'em take 'em away right after the ceilin' came down."

Paelen cursed. Then he hesitantly asked, "Was Emily alive?"

Earl took an unsteady breath. He shook his head. "No. Not at first. When the burnin' roof came down, she was buried in the worst of it. This big orange Nirad dug her out. It started to howl like crazy when it pulled her free, like it was grievin' or somethin'. I tell ya, Emily was nothin' but a little rag doll in its big arms—all burned up and broken. There was no mistakin', she was dead. But then she started to glow—you know, just like when I shot her. Right there in the Nirad's arms. After a few minutes she moved. Then the others found Pegasus and got him movin'. They left me for dead."

Paelen looked at Cupid. "An orange Nirad? We've

only seen gray ones." He looked at Earl. "This orange Nirad, was it their leader?"

Earl coughed and winced in pain. "Ain't certain. When they first got here, there was this big wild boar with wings—"

"A boar with wings? Are you certain?" Paelen asked.

When Earl nodded, Cupid cursed. "It is Chrysaor! What is he doing here?"

"It cannot be," Paelen said. "He would not betray us. Not to the Nirads." He concentrated on Earl. "Were the boar's wings as brown as the rest of him? Did they hang over his rump?"

Earl nodded. "That's him all right. Whatever he is, Pegasus didn't like him one bit. They started fightin' with all the fury they got. I couldn't see much, 'cuz this big Nirad caught hold of me. He darn near broke all my bones and squeezed the life outta me. Emily tried to help, but she lost control of the flames. Then the roof came down." Earl started to cough. When the fit ended, he asked, "You know that boar?"

"Chrysaor is Pegasus's twin brother," Paelen muttered, deep in thought.

Earl's burned eyelids shot open. "Pegasus has a twin that's a boar?"

Paelen nodded. "They have been fighting most of their lives. Now it appears that Chrysaor has sided with the Nirads against Olympus."

"But what does he want with Emily?" Cupid asked.

Paelen shrugged. "I do not know for certain, but it frightens me. Emily is the source of all our powers. Whoever possesses her could control Olympus."

Earl started to cough again.

"You need help," Paelen said. "So does Steve."

Agent T finally spoke. "If you don't want to be captured, you can't take either of them to the hospital. Once they realize Earl is gone, they will search the hospitals first."

"What can we do?" Paelen asked.

"Leave me," Earl said weakly. "Just go after Emily and Pegasus."

"You will die if we leave you," Cupid said. "Normally, as you are human, I would not care. But Emily does. So leaving you and her father is not an option."

They moved Steve into the ambulance, beside

Earl. Agent T proved invaluable with his first-aid skills. Using the ambulance supplies, he was able to treat the men. Earl remained conscious long enough to offer a safe place for them to hide. He and some buddies had a hunting cabin up on the mountain.

Agent T disabled the tracker device in the ambulance, ensuring that they wouldn't be followed, and drove up into the mountains. Just as Earl had promised, they found the small hunting cabin nestled deep in the trees. It was covered in undisturbed snow and offered them seclusion and protection from the CRU down in Tuxedo.

Once they had transferred Steve and Earl into the safety of the cabin, Cupid and Paelen built a roaring fire to warm the place. Earl was still on the stretcher, moaning softly.

"How is he?" Cupid asked.

Agent T grinned up at him before saying, "Not good. He needs a doctor. So does Jacobs over there on the sofa. Though the bullet went right through him, I don't know what damage it's done. He may be bleeding internally."

"If he needs a doctor, he shall have it," Paelen said

confidently. Then he frowned. "What is a doctor and where do we find one?"

Earl managed to tell them he knew of a doctor they could trust. He gave Agent T the telephone number before fading back into unconsciousness.

Paelen straightened and looked around the small cabin at the two wounded men. He'd never felt so helpless in all his life. He was in a strange, unfriendly world with no idea how anything worked. One of his best friends was dead, the other missing. CRU agents were hunting them once again, and everything was going wrong.

He looked at Cupid. The winged Olympian didn't show any of the fear or insecurities Paelen now felt. Cupid was calm and in control as he took notes from Agent T on how to contact the doctor. Despite everything he'd ever felt toward Cupid, Paelen had a new-found respect for him.

"So where do we find this thing called a tele-phone?" Cupid asked.

The CRU agent shrugged apologetically. "There aren't as many around as there used to be. Every-one has a cell phone these days. I'm so sorry, Cupid, but my phone was left at the Red Apple." The agent looked as though he were about to cry. Finally he said, "We might find one in town, though. The trouble is, by now the other agents will be on the lookout for me and the ambulance."

Cupid nodded. "You will not be going back into town. I will."

"Not alone," Paelen said. He looked out the cabin's window. "It will be getting dark soon. If you can carry me, we can fly back together. My winged sandals were also left behind at the Red Apple. I would like to see if we can get them back if they have not been discovered yet. Then we could use the telephone to get the doctor."

Cupid looked as though he were about to protest, but then closed his mouth. "I will carry you," he said softly. "Once it is dark we will leave."

While they waited for the sun to set, Paelen investigated the small hunting cabin. In the kitchen he found canned and dry food, but there was very little sugar or other food for the Olympians. Neither he nor Cupid had eaten since that morning, and he was feeling his strength starting to ebb.

In the bedroom there was a small closet with winter clothing that could help them blend in with the locals. Paelen carried a selection back into the main area. He started to check through the pockets of the CRU agent's suit he was wearing as well as the other clothing's pockets. He didn't find anything at all. He looked at Cupid and Agent T. "Do you have any money?"

Cupid found nothing. But Agent T was still wearing Joel's clothing from earlier that day and discovered almost fifty dollars left from the costume competition's winnings. He handed it eagerly to Cupid.

Paelen said, "I believe we should also buy some more food. There is plenty here for the humans to eat, but nothing for us. I do not know about you, but I am starving and getting weaker."

Cupid nodded. "Me also." He stepped over to the window. "It is dark out. We should change our clothes and go."

The snow had finally tapered off, and the clouds cleared as a cold, crisp starry night arrived. When they tried to leave, they discovered that asking Agent

T to stay behind proved more difficult than they expected. He followed them out into the snow and begged Cupid to take him with them. Tears welled in the agent's eyes when they refused.

Paelen felt his sympathy for Agent T rise. He was a wreck. Paelen now understood why Cupid had been so reluctant to use his powers on the men.

"We will not be long," Paelen reassured him gently. "And I know for certain it would please Cupid greatly if you were to stay with Steve and Earl and do your best to help them." Paelen looked over to Cupid. "It would make you happy, would it not?"

Cupid sighed and dropped his head. "Yes, it would make me very happy if you would do that for me."

That seemed to satisfy the teary agent. He sniffed and smiled sadly. "I will, just for you. You will be so proud of me. Just promise you'll come back safe."

"We will," Paelen promised.

After the agent went back inside, Cupid shook his head. "I have destroyed him. It would have been kinder to torture the agents rather than use my powers. There is nothing left of him."

"You did it for Emily," Paelen said. "She would not

have allowed us to hurt the men. I am sure when this is over we will find a way to restore him."

Cupid looked doubtful as he walked away from the cabin. The snow was knee-deep and heavy. They needed to find an area clear enough for Cupid to spread his wings and have a running start if he was to carry Paelen's weight as well.

Not far from the cabin they finally found the perfect spot. Cupid lifted Paelen into his arms and launched himself into the cold night sky.

EMILY WAS HELD TIGHT IN THE NIRAD'S arms as they traveled through the Solar Stream. On the two other occasions when she had ventured through it, she had been riding Pegasus. Perhaps it was the steady movement of the stallion's powerful wings or just being with him that had distracted her, but this time, with no Pegasus to reassure her, the brilliant light surrounding her and the booming sounds assaulting her ears left Emily feeling sick and dizzy. She looked up into the Nirad's face and could see that it was also not enjoying the experience. Its eyes were closed and its mouth was a tight, thin line. If the noise of the Solar Stream hadn't been so loud, she was certain she would have heard the creature whining.

They finally emerged in the back of another dark-ened cave. The Nirads filed out into the daylight, which was gray and miserable. As Emily recovered, she looked at the strange world around her and sucked in her breath. The sky was heavy with black storm clouds. Yet the air felt dry and arid. The ground beneath them was black and dusty, with every step stirring up dark gray dust clouds around their feet. There were no trees or any signs of plant life.

Not too far away she saw small animal-like crea-tures scurrying around on the dry ground. They were almost the size and shape of raccoons but didn't have fur. Instead they had dark gray and brown marbled skin. They showed no fear as the parade of huge Nirads, led by the angry boar, filed past them. In the sky above, large, leathery batlike creatures circled in the dull sky. Their wingspan was almost as wide as Pegasus's was. They were graceful and agile, and their wings cut silently through the still air. Occasionally they made strange calling sounds that seemed to carry for miles.

As she looked around, Emily continued to see no plant life at all. There were no trees, no grass, no weeds, and no flowers. Nothing appeared to grow in the black, dusty soil. They soon approached an area with roughly built stone structures.

The primitive stone houses had four solid side walls and a single stone slab for a roof. She almost expected to see a caveman emerging. Instead Emily was stunned to see what she realized was a female Nirad, exiting her home with a child held in her arms.

The Nirad woman was almost as big as the men were but with even longer claws and hair. She also had four thick, powerful arms, which she waved in the air threateningly at the sight of Emily and Pegasus.

Everywhere Emily looked, Nirads stopped to stare at the line of escorts around her. Most growled and shook their fists angrily at her when the group walked past, but some seemed to drop their heads and look away in sadness.

"So, this is your world," she said to her Nirad in awe.

He looked down at her and nodded.

"Do you have any children?"

The Nirad's eyes seemed to mist. Emily was certain she saw heavy sadness there as once again he slowly nodded.

"Are they in danger?"

He made several soft guttural sounds that Emily couldn't understand. His expression was pain-filled and earnest as he tried to explain.

"I'm sorry, I can't understand you," she said softly. "I wish I could speak your language. I don't even know if you have names. Do you?"

Her Nirad nodded and opened his mouth. He made a deep sound that he slowly repeated several times.

"Tange," Emily tried, hoping to get as close to the sound as possible. "Is your name Tange?"

The Nirad nodded.

Emily silently celebrated the breakthrough. She and the huge male Nirad called Tange were actually communicating!

"Do you know why I am here?" she asked.

Tange shook his head. But then he motioned toward the front of their group.

Emily strained to see around the line of Nirads blocking her view. Tange lifted her higher, and she saw their destination. It was a tall, white marble palace that looked completely out of place in the dark, mournful landscape. As she looked at the tall pillars and white marble steps leading up to the magnificent entrance, she instantly recognized the design. It was a replica of Jupiter's palace, reproduced in the Nirad world. Along the road leading to the palace stood a long line of statues that seemed to serve as an honor guard.

"That palace is from Olympus!" Emily breathed. "What's it doing here?" She looked back to Tange. "Is Jupiter here?"

Before Tange could answer, another large orange Nirad came up beside them and growled ferociously. His eyes settled on Emily, and he shook his head and barked a single harsh word to her. The message was clear. Stop talking.

Emily saw pure murderous hatred blazing in the Nirad's face. He wouldn't hesitate to kill her if he got the chance. She curled closer into Tange, wondering what she and Pegasus had done to cause such rage among the Nirads.

All along the journey to the white palace, Emily saw evidence of the Nirad hatred as crowds gathered to stare and growl at her. When some gray Nirads tried to approach, Tange and the orange Nirads drove them away with threatening growls and raised fists. The same happened when the crowds tried to throw stones and clubs at Pegasus. Only the orange Nirads prevented the stallion from being hit.

"Why do you all hate us?" Emily asked Tange softly.

Tange said nothing as he carried her steadily toward the palace. The closer they got, the more statues Emily saw lining the route. Some were back from the road, and a few had been knocked over and were lying in broken rubble. Scanning the area, she realized there had to be hundreds of these Nirad statues, if not thousands.

Whoever had carved them had put an expression of terror and pain on all their faces. Not one was smiling or standing in a normal position. They all seemed to be frozen midaction, trying to move or run, and not one of them looked happy. They all had that same horrible, pain-filled expression. Finally she had to look away. The sight of those horrible faces was making the journey worse.

Eventually they arrived at the steps of the white

palace. Emily watched the winged boar go up ahead of them. Two orange Nirads were standing guard beside the doors. At the boar's approach they hauled open the two heavy marble doors, and the group started to file in.

When Tange carried Emily up the steps, she strained to peer behind her. "Please let me see," she asked.

Tange looked down at her, then lifted her higher until she could see over his thick shoulder. The Nirad village sprawled out around the white palace. There were thousands of dark stone structures with even more statues in all directions. It was almost like a black-and-white film. There was no color, just varying shades of gray, black, and brown. The only brightness in the whole area came from the orange Nirads themselves. Even the strange batlike things in the sky were gray and black. Emily watched them circling and wondered if that was what pterodactyl dinosaurs had looked like.

Once again Emily noticed a lack of any plant life. She wondered what the Nirads ate. She remembered Tange's wide mouth and his sharp teeth and felt her first twinges of genuine terror. Were Nirads meat eaters? And if so, what or who was on their menu?

Before full panic set in, Emily was carried through the doors of the white palace. The entrance hall was huge. It was made of the same white marble as all the structures in Olympus. But, unlike Jupiter's palace, no art or anything beautiful adorned the walls. Just more horrific statues frozen in movement.

As they lumbered forward, Emily heard shrill screeching coming from one of the rooms off the entrance hall. The grating sound set her already strained nerves on edge. She didn't want to know who or what was making that awful sound.

As she was being led toward it, Emily struggled in Tange's arms. "No, please, Tange, no! I don't want to go in there!"

Pegasus started to whinny and scream behind her. She could hear his hooves clopping on the smooth marble floor as he strained against the orange Nirads who were directing him forward.

"Chrysaor, bring her in!" demanded a high, shrill voice. "We want to see the Flame of Olympus!"

Emily was carried forward. As Tange entered the

large hall, the Nirads parted in front of them and moved to either side of the room, giving her a clear view of the winged boar stepping up to the owners of the shrill voices.

Emily began to scream.

IT WAS A SHORT FLIGHT FROM THE CABIN TO the town. Streetlights were on, and the aroma of woodsmoke from countless fireplaces filled the air. When they soared silently over the wreckage of the Red Apple, Paelen was distressed to see that the entire area was covered by a large, secure tent with several heavily armed soldiers patrolling around it. No light was showing through the tent, so at least no one was inside.

Cupid glided closer and flew silently over the trees to the back of the wrecked rest stop. He found a clearing and lightly touched down. Paelen handed him his clothing, and he started to dress.

"I really hate this," Cupid complained as he pulled

up his trousers after tucking his wings inside. He reached for the red plaid flannel shirt. "You have no idea just how uncomfortable this is."

Paelen braced himself for another long series of complaints from the winged Olympian. "Well, it is better than letting them see you and raising the alarm. We must get in there without drawing their attention."

"I hardly believe whether they see my wings or not will make much difference. We are going to have to fight our way in regardless."

"You could always use—"

Cupid held up a warning finger. "Do not even suggest it. It is bad enough with Agent T. I will not use my powers on these men. It would be kinder if we simply killed them right now."

"We cannot do that!" Paelen said in hushed shock. "They have done nothing to us. We will do what we did at the carnival and knock them out. Emily would never forgive us if she knew we had killed innocent people."

"Who would tell her?" Cupid asked.

"I would."

"Then you are a fool," Cupid said. "For now, we will try it your way. But if they cause me any trouble, I will not hesitate to kill them."

Paelen was shocked at Cupid's ruthless streak. "I have an idea," he finally said. "I used to get into Jupiter's palace undetected all the time. I am certain I can do this. Then, once I am inside the tent, all I need to do is find the sandals."

Cupid looked doubtful, but he seemed satisfied to be told to stay behind and wait. "All right, I will give you a short time. But if there is trouble, I will fight."

This was the best he could hope for from Cupid. Using all the stealth of his thief's experience, Paelen crossed through the parking area and crept past two guards without being seen. He could feel more than see that two other guards would soon be approaching from the other side as they constantly patrolled the perimeter of the large enclosure.

After a short, silent sprint, Paelen reached the side of the tent. The main opening was around the other side. But a guard's station had been set up there, with two large, burly soldiers sitting at a table. Their weapons were drawn, and they looked ready for anything.

Paelen crouched down and tried to lift the edge of the tent. But he discovered it had been tacked down to the ground every few inches. Tearing it up would make too much noise. He groaned inwardly, knowing what he had to do.

Checking to see the position of the patrolling soldiers, Paelen used his power to manipulate his body. With each crack and pop of his bones, he feared discovery. Soon he was too thin to fit in his clothing. With a bit more stretching, he turned into the snakelike body he used to get into tight areas.

He lifted up the edge of the tent as far as it would go and slid easily inside. He returned to his normal shape and stood amid the debris that had once been the Red Apple.

Despite the complete lack of light, he was able to see clearly. He was in what had once been the kitchen area. He made his way back to where he, Joel, and Cupid had changed their clothes in preparation for their assault on the CRU facility. Paelen forced himself not to dwell on the memories of that disastrous rescue. He was here for his sandals, nothing more.

The acrid smell of recently extinguished fire stung

his nostrils as he quietly climbed over the charred debris. He cursed every time the destroyed timbers cracked under his weight but was grateful to discover that the area where they had changed look undisturbed. It had yet to be searched.

"Sandals, where are you?" he muttered softly, looking around.

There was a slight stirring in the burned debris. Paelen's sharp senses caught movement to his left. "Sandals?"

Once again there was movement. Paelen recalled what Mercury had told him when he'd given his sandals to Paelen. Mercury said the sandals didn't belong to him anymore, but to Paelen. Suddenly that comment made sense. Their initial devotion to the messenger of Olympus and now to him was because the sandals were alive. They were responding to his voice. Buried beneath the debris, they were trying to get back to him.

"Where are you, sandals?" he softly called.

Not far ahead a deep pile of rubble shifted. The sound of stirring and movement set Paelen's heart pounding. What if the soldiers outside heard it? He climbed over to the area as quickly and quietly as he could. His nerves were stretched to the limit. "Sandals, where are you?" he called softly again.

The movement was right in front of him. A large chunk of burned roof was covering the area. As Paelen caught hold of the edge, he hoisted it in the air. He peered beneath and, with a sigh of profound relief, saw his two sandals amid the ashes.

Quickly retrieving them, Paelen lowered the roof and made his way back to the side of the tent. He stretched his body and slid under the edge. His clothing was still waiting for him.

But so were the soldiers.

As he returned to his normal shape and rose, bright lights blazed to life and shone painfully in his eyes.

Two armed soldiers rushed at him. "Freeze or we'll open fire!"

Paelen barely had time to think before a soldier's rough hands caught hold of his arms and hauled him forward.

"Drop the shoes!" another voice ordered.

"They are sandals," Paelen corrected. "And if you want them, you shall have to take them from me."

As more soldiers came forward, they heard a bloodcurdling scream. Cupid dove down from the sky. His arms were filled with large stones, and he started hurling them at the unsuspecting soldiers.

After a first pass, Cupid swooped away, turned, and came at them for a second assault, throwing more stones at the men. They had been prepared for a ground attack but hadn't been warned about enraged winged teenagers coming from above.

As the soldiers scattered and tried to raise their weapons, Cupid landed and charged at them, fighting with all the Olympian strength he possessed. Paelen took the opportunity and wrenched his arms free of the man closest to him. He tackled him to the ground. With one punch, the soldier was unconscious.

Not thinking, just reacting, Paelen lifted another soldier in the air and threw him across the parking area and into the trees. The Olympians knew everything was at stake. They couldn't get caught. With Cupid fighting beside him, not one soldier had time to fire his weapon. Before long, they were all down on the ground.

"Grab your clothing and the sandals," Cupid ordered. "We must go before others arrive."

Paelen followed Cupid back into the trees. Pausing only long enough to dress, he was grateful to feel the winged sandals back on his feet, where they belonged.

"We must fly," Cupid called as he collected his own clothing. "We still need to make that phone call."

Cupid was first in the air. Paelen ordered the sandals to follow and was thrilled as their tiny wings lifted him easily into the sky.

Within minutes of their escape, they heard the sounds of sirens rising from below. Flashing lights of police cruisers, military trucks, and CRU vehicles illuminated the roads as they raced to the Red Apple. Both Olympians knew it had been a close call.

Paelen flew closer to Cupid. "They must have raised the alarm. We cannot go into the town to make the call. We should try the place where Joel and I bought food. They are always open. Perhaps we can find a telephone there."

Cupid agreed and let Paelen lead the way. He ordered his sandals to take him to the superstore.

They were both grateful to see it was on the far end of town, well away from the Red Apple and the gathering soldiers.

They landed a short distance away and walked back to the superstore. Paelen jumped when the sliding doors at the large entrance whooshed open at his approach. He still didn't understand how they knew he was there. Perhaps a small nymph controlled them?

"Come along," Cupid said irritably. "We do not have time to play. We must find the telephone and get back to the cabin."

"Who is playing?" Paelen asked as he nervously stepped through the mysterious doors, still convinced they would snap shut on him at any moment.

Inside, Paelen was once again struck by the sights, sounds, and smells of the brightly lit superstore. There was so much sugar there. But there were also a lot more people than when he and Joel had shopped. That made him nervous.

"Cupid, can you smell that?" Paelen asked softly as his stomach started to gurgle.

Cupid nodded. "We will make the call first, and

then we must eat. I have been too long without ambrosia, and I am feeling weak."

The two Olympians stood at the entrance, wondering what a telephone looked like and how they would find it.

Finally, Cupid approached an attractive young woman carrying several shopping bags and smiled radiantly at her. Paelen watched him working his magic. The winged Olympian didn't turn on his power—he didn't need to. His smile alone was enough to turn the woman's cheeks bright red.

"Can you help us, please," he said in his most charming voice. "We need to make a call, and I cannot find a telephone."

The woman's cheeks reddened further. She reached into her pocket and produced her cell phone. "You could always use mine if you like."

Cupid took the small device and looked at Paelen quizzically. When Paelen shrugged, he looked back at the woman. "Would you mind showing me how to use this?"

"Not at all," she said. "What's the number?"

Cupid handed her the piece of paper with the

doctor's telephone number. The woman dialed and held the phone to her ear.

After a moment she shook her head. "It's going straight to voice mail. Do you want to leave a message?"

"Does that mean you cannot reach the doctor?" Cupid asked.

"I'm sorry," she said. "Do you want me to leave a message? I could give them my number, and we could wait together for them to call?" There was no mistaking the offer in her soft voice. Paelen was once again struck by Cupid's power over women.

Cupid smiled. "No, thank you. Perhaps when I next visit and we have more time."

The disappointment on her face was obvious as she reluctantly put her cell back in her pocket and drifted away.

When she was gone, the smile dropped from Cupid's face. "No doctor. We shall have to manage on our own." Cupid sniffed the air again. "Come, Paelen, this place is filled with food, and I am starving. It is time we ate."

Paelen and Cupid went back to the entrance and

collected shopping baskets. Each step they took, Cupid fidgeted. "I really hate this. My feathers are poking into the back of my legs."

"It will not be long," Paelen promised. "We will just get what we need and go."

Following their noses, the two Olympians carried their shopping baskets deeper into the store. They walked down an aisle filled with chocolate, candy bars, and cookies.

As they filled their baskets, Paelen became aware of several children drifting away from their parents to follow Cupid. The winged Olympian looked back at the small but growing group and tried to shoo them away, but the children refused to go. Farther down the aisle, a boy of no more than four broke away from his mother and ran straight at Cupid. He hugged him around the legs and wouldn't release him.

Paelen laughed at the mortified expression on Cupid's face as he struggled to disentangle himself from the affectionate child. "Go back to your mother, little human," he cried. But the more he tried to push him away, the louder the child protested and refused to release him.

Paelen pulled the little boy off Cupid just as his mother arrived. The woman's face was red with embarrassment as she apologized for her son's odd behavior.

"Madam," Cupid scolded, "will you please keep hold of your child."

As she dragged her screaming son away, Cupid looked back at the group of other children pressing closer. "All of you, go back to your parents. I have nothing for you."

But they refused to leave. Paelen tore open a bag of miniature candy bars and handed them out to the children. "Go now, young ones, your parents will be looking for you. Go on. Cupid and I need to eat."

The children accepted the treats but still refused to leave. They followed at a distance, waving and calling to Cupid.

"There is only one thing I hate more than humans," Cupid complained as he tore open a bag of chocolate chip cookies and started to eat. "That is young humans."

"You do not," Paelen argued as he stuffed his

mouth full of chocolates. "If you did, you would have struck that little boy."

Cupid regarded him with a dark expression. "I did not wish to draw undue attention to us. That is all."

"Of course," Paelen said as he chuckled. "I believe you. No one else would, but I do."

The two continued to eat as they made their way down the long aisle of sweets. They were still being followed by the parade of children. Halfway down the next aisle, they were met by store security.

"You're gonna pay for all that," a guard confronted them angrily. "And for the candy you just gave to those kids back there."

Paelen's mouth was full of food, but he nodded his head. "We have money," he mumbled. "We intend to pay for everything."

"Then eat when you get home," the guard said sharply. "We don't allow grazing while you're shopping."

That comment caused the wings on Cupid's back to flutter with annoyance. He stood erect, and his pale eyes flashed. "Animal's graze," he corrected. "We are eating. There is a difference."

"Not to me, there isn't," answered the guard. "Now bring your baskets and follow me. It's time you checked out."

Paelen started to follow, but Cupid refused. "We are not finished here yet. We will leave when we are ready. Not a moment sooner. And neither you nor any other human can command us otherwise."

"Listen, kid," the guard said as he pressed closer. He poked Cupid in the shoulder with a bony finger. "You'll leave when I tell you to. And I'm telling you to go right now."

In a move too quick to follow, Cupid struck the guard with a punch that knocked him to the floor. The children screamed and ran forward. They jumped on the guard and pinned him down, ordering him to leave Cupid alone.

As the guard curled up in a tight ball, Cupid looked down on him and started shouting. "I have had it with you humans telling me what to do! I told you, we will leave here when we have finished and not a moment sooner!" He picked up his shopping basket and continued casually down the aisle as though nothing had just happened.

"We should go," Paelen said, looking at the group of children piling on the guard. Around them, other shoppers stared in shock. "People are beginning to stare at us."

"Let them," Cupid spat as he tore open a second bag of cookies. "I have not had a decent meal since we left Olympus. I am half-starved, my wings are driving me mad, and I am in no mood to deal with humans, big or small!"

Paelen looked around at the gathering crowds. Suddenly something Emily said rose to his mind. "Cupid, do you remember what Emily said? Agent O told her that since he moved up here, his only pleasure was attending the Haunted Forest Festival."

"So what?" Cupid said, spraying Paelen with cookie crumbs as he reached for more food.

"So that means he lives in this small town. It also means he would have to buy food. This is the only place to do that in the area. What if other CRU agents and their families shop here?"

Cupid stopped and looked back at the crowds gathering around the guard. Finally he shook his head. "They are far too busy with the destruction of their facility and the Red Apple to come here. I am sure we are perfectly safe."

Cupid had barely finished the comment when they spotted two men standing at the end of the aisle. They were dressed in jeans and winter coats, but they had weapons drawn and pointed right at Paelen and Cupid, despite the children hovering near Cupid. Their stance and facial expressions were immediately recognizable.

"Freeze!" the CRU agents called.

"Perhaps you were right," Cupid muttered.

"I wish I'd been wrong," Paelen said as he looked behind them and saw several armed soldiers moving into position at the other end of the aisle.

"Drop your baskets!" the lead agent ordered. "Do it now, nice and slow!"

"There are children here," Paelen warned. "Please put down your weapons and let them leave before they are hurt!"

"We give the orders here. Now, both of you, get down on the floor."

"You are making a grave mistake, human," Cupid warned. He slowly backed up toward the group of frightened children. As he moved, he pulled off his coat, tore open his shirt, and freed his wings. He opened them protectively around the children, gathering them close to him. "It would serve you well to let them leave here right now. I will not be as amiable if one of these children is hurt because of you. "

Paelen moved beside Cupid, further blocking the children from the soldiers' weapons. He could hear the shocked cries and muttered remarks of the adult shoppers around them. They all seemed to think Cupid was some kind of winged angel.

"No one is going anywhere, Cupid," called an all-too-familiar voice. Agent O moved to the front of the aisle. His legs were still bandaged from Emily's burns, and he remained on crutches. His eyes landed on Paelen. "Paelen, did you really believe we wouldn't be watching this place? We know all about your need for sugar. I'm surprised it took you so long to show up here. You are surrounded and won't get away from me this time. Now, where are Emily and Pegasus?"

"Well beyond your reach," Paelen spat as his anger grew. "You will not take us, Agent O. Not again."

Some of the children began to cry. They huddled

fearfully together behind the protection of Cupid's spread wings. "Let these young ones leave here before I lose my temper," Cupid warned. "They are not part of this and should not bear witness to what is to come."

"You care so much about human children?" Agent O challenged.

"Obviously, more than you do," Paelen shot back. "Tell me, would you really shoot at us with these children here? Are you so desperate to catch us that you would sacrifice them?"

Paelen saw hesitation on Agent O's face. There were gathering crowds of people watching. Agent O might be single-minded and obsessed, but he wasn't a fool. He motioned to the soldiers to lower their weapons.

"All right," Agent O said. "Let the children go first."

Paelen glanced back and saw the soldiers who blocked the end of the aisle following the order. He looked down at the children and pointed to the soldiers. "Go that way, children. Go find your parents."

The children hesitated and looked up to Cupid with tear-filled eyes. "It is all right, little ones, you are safe," he said kindly as he stroked a little girl's head. Cupid looked to the adults in the aisle. "Please take them to safety. Help them find their parents."

As the other shoppers approached to collect the children, Cupid shot a warning glance at Agent O. "You will let them all leave here unharmed. This fight is between us. They have nothing to do with it."

With a store full of witnesses, Agent O nodded reluctantly. He ordered the soldiers to direct the public out of the building. While the children left the aisle, Cupid whispered, "When they are gone, we must move. If we get separated, you know where to go."

"Good luck," Paelen said as the last child was escorted out of the aisle.

"Luck has nothing to do with it!" Cupid shouted as, in one swift move, he dropped his basket and ran toward the agents.

CUPID CHARGED DOWN THE AISLE. THE TIPS of his wings caught the edges of the shelves and knocked food onto the floor as he ran. The crowds behind the agents screamed when they saw the enraged Olympian storming straight at them.

Behind him, Paelen heard the soldiers preparing to fire. He turned and hurled his basket at the men.

"Sandals, take me up!"

Once airborne, Paelen ordered the sandals to take him forward. He skimmed the food on the top shelf and watched it rain down on the shocked soldiers.

Flying over the tops of the shelves and into the next aisle, Paelen found stacks and stacks of canned goods. He snatched up a handful and threw them at the soldiers. Gunfire rang out behind him, and Paelen felt a sharp stinging in his back. He turned to see two CRU agents firing their weapons at him. Their bullets did little damage. But they did hurt.

Screaming in rage, Paelen flew full speed at the agents working with Agent O and knocked them both into a tall display of baked beans, hurling cans everywhere. Paelen ordered the sandals to carry him higher in the air. His wild eyes searched for Cupid. He heard shooting to his right and saw Cupid going down. As the winged Olympian tried to rise, he was knocked over and pinned to the ground by countless soldiers.

Paelen reacted immediately. He collected several more cans of baked beans and ordered the sandals to take him to Cupid. Paelen threw the cans with the same deadly accuracy he'd used on the target at the clown dunk tank at the Haunted Forest Festival. Unable to defend themselves against the barrage, the soldiers released their prisoner and covered their heads. Cupid was on his feet in seconds and back in the fight.

Out of beans, Paelen reached for other bottles or cans to throw. Soon more soldiers ran along the aisle toward him with their weapons raised. Paelen screamed in fury and used his Olympian strength to shove the entire length of display shelves over, burying the men in all manner of items.

As he moved to get back to Cupid, Paelen heard gunfire and felt a sharp stinging in the side of his head. He turned and saw Agent O firing his weapon. The agent wasn't trying to capture him. He was trying to kill him!

The sudden pain brought back all the terrible memories of what Agents J and O had done to him at the Governors Island facility. Then he remembered they'd done the same to Joel. Those memories turned to rage.

"Sandals," he shouted, "take me to Agent O!"

The CRU agent heard Paelen's order. His eyes flew wide in fear as he struggled to run away. But the thick bandages on his legs wouldn't let him move very fast. Paelen was on him in an instant, unleashing all the pent-up anger he felt toward the evil government agent.

He was unaware of anything else. It was just him and Agent O. He couldn't see Cupid gaining control over the soldiers, nor did he see the other agents moving in to pull him off. All he knew was fury.

A loud shattering of glass finally caught his attention. Paelen lifted his head to see Cupid flying full speed through the glass of a large window at the front of the store. That sound brought him back. He looked down. Agent O was unconscious, and his men were trying to drag him off.

"This is for Joel!" Paelen shouted as he gave Agent O a final jaw-cracking punch. "Sandals," he shouted, "follow Cupid!"

The sandals reacted immediately. Despite all the men crushing him, Paelen was lifted in the air. With several soldiers dangling from his legs, he flew toward the broken window. Just as the last man released him, he passed through the opening and up into the night sky.

The urgent popping of gunfire followed as Paelen searched the air for Cupid. From above him arrived the heavy thumping sounds of military helicopters giving chase. Paelen looked back and saw the terrifying machines gaining on him. "Faster!" he cried to the sandals. "Fly faster!"

Ahead of him, two other helicopters cut through the night sky. They were moving away from him, so he knew they were chasing Cupid. He saw flashes as they fired their weapons.

Paelen had little time to worry about Cupid, because the other military helicopters were right behind him and getting closer. He turned back. "Let me see how high you can go. Sandals, take me up!"

With a sudden change of direction, the sandals shot Paelen straight up in the night sky. Beneath him, the helicopters tried to follow, but he was moving too quickly.

"Higher!" Paelen ordered. "Take me higher!"

The air became painfully thin. Paelen felt his breathing become more labored, but not so that he couldn't breathe. He looked down and saw the helicopters struggling to follow him. Eventually they gave up and flew away from the area.

"Yes!" he cried, punching the air in celebration. He looked down and followed the trail of the fleeing helicopters. They were joining the others chasing Cupid. But the first two weren't moving anymore. They were hovering in one position in the sky, over the trees. Paelen suddenly had a very bad feeling. The two helicopters that had chased him were also now hovering above one area. Their searchlights burst to life and started to scan the trees and snowy ground below. They were looking for Cupid.

"Sandals, be very careful, but get me to Cupid."

The sandals lowered Paelen down out of the sky. Well away from the probing helicopters' lights, he entered the trees. Hovering just above ground level, they carried him over the undisturbed snow, toward the area where searchlights sought Cupid.

Up ahead, he saw a large, dark shape in the snow. Even before he arrived, Paelen's heart pounded and his mouth went dry. It was Cupid. He had been shot out of the sky and crashed to the ground. Lying unmoving, in a broken heap. One wing was fanned out behind him, while the other was trapped beneath his unconscious form. The snow around his body was turning red from blood.

Above him the searchlights continued to pan the area. For the moment they couldn't see him or Cupid. But it was only a matter of time. Paelen felt Cupid's neck nervously. There was still a pulse, and he was breathing. As the ceaseless searchlights drew closer, Paelen hoisted Cupid up in his arms.

"Get me back to Olympus," he ordered the sandals. "Quickly!"

PAELEN CRADLED CUPID IN HIS ARMS AS
the sandals flew toward an opening in the trees and
climbed higher in the dark sky. But as they tried to
gain enough speed to enter the Solar Stream, the
combined weight of the two Olympians was too
much for them to bear.

After several failed attempts, Paelen was forced to
give up. He ordered the sandals to take them back
to the cabin. When he touched down on the porch,
Paelen carried Cupid forward and kicked open the
door. "Agent T!" he called. "Cupid has been hurt!"

"Cupid!" Agent T screeched as he ran forward. His
face was twisted in pain. "What happened to him?"

"There were these flying machines," Paelen

explained. "They had large weapons. They were chasing us. When they realized they couldn't catch us, they shot Cupid out of the sky. He hit the ground hard. I think he has broken a wing."

Agent T ran ahead and cleared the coffee table. "Put him here," he said shakily. "When is the doctor coming?"

"We could not reach him," Paelen explained as he carried Cupid to the table. "It is just us."

Paelen settled Cupid down, and together he and Agent T inspected his wounds. His back and wings were covered in blood. They found multiple deep and weeping bullet holes. Paelen had been right. Cupid's left wing was badly broken from the fall.

"Smaller weapons do not hurt us," Paelen mused as he lifted Cupid's unbroken wing to peer beneath it. "But look what those flying machines did to him. He has been torn to pieces."

"He needs a doctor!" Agent T insisted as he gathered together bandages and antiseptic for Cupid. "He is bleeding and is going to die without one. I can try to slow the blood loss, but I don't have the skills to help him."

"I cannot reach the doctor," Paelen insisted. "And a human doctor could not help him anyway. I tried to carry him back to Olympus, but my sandals could not bear the weight of the two of us—" Paelen paused. Finally his eyes went wide. "Wait a moment. Ambrosia! Cupid needs ambrosia. It is what keeps us healthy and strong in Olympus. It will help him heal." He looked back at Emily's father on the sofa and Earl on the stretcher. "Ambrosia will help everyone here heal."

"Then why are you just standing there?" Agent T shouted. He shoved Paelen toward the door. "Get out of here! Go! Fly back to Olympus and get some ambrosia. Save Cupid!"

EMILY COULDN'T STOP SCREAMING. THE
screams just kept on coming, even after Tange put a
hand over her mouth. Her eyes were wide with terror and locked on the two creatures sitting in a set of
thrones on a dais. She tried to look away but couldn't.
They were worse than anything she could have
dreamed and more horrible than any of the creatures
from the most terrifying movies she and her father
used to watch together.

They were women. But nothing like anything she'd
ever seen before. Their skin was covered in green and
gold snake scales. They had small golden wings that
constantly fluttered on their backs like humming-

birds. Their arms ended in hands of bronze, and their legs were long and bony and had lizardlike feet with long, sharp claws.

But most terrifying of all were their heads. Their green, scaly faces had no noses, just two breathing holes like a snake. They had no lips to speak of, but slits that opened when they let out their squeals. In place of hair, hundreds of green snakes grew out of the tops of their head, writhing around as their forked tongues spit and hissed.

As Tange carried her forward, Emily spotted more statues gathered around the dais. This time they weren't adult Nirads, but children. As she looked closer, her screams found renewed energy as a realization overtook her. The Nirad statues—they hadn't been carved. They were real Nirads that had somehow been turned to stone! These Nirads no longer had marblelike skin—they *were* marble. Their terrified faces revealed the final torturous moments of unbearable pain as their living tissue had turned to stone.

Behind her, Pegasus was going mad. He reared and whinnied furiously as they were led forward, until he broke free of the Nirads surrounding him and charged ahead.

The stallion stopped just before the thrones. He reared up high and opened his burned wings. His head was thrown back in fury as he faced the two snake-women. The winged boar, seated between the two thrones, rose on his haunches and squealed loudly at the stallion.

"Calm down, Chrysaor," one of the monstrous women said, stroking the furious boar's head.

"Listen to Euryale," said the other. "This is a time of celebration. We have the Flame of Olympus in our midst. We must not have her thinking ill of us, or that we do not welcome her visit." She turned to Pegasus. "So say what you will, Pegasus," she hissed through her thin, snakelike mouth, "it will change nothing. The time of retribution has finally arrived. Euryale and I will finally have justice. Jupiter and all Olympus will pay for the murder of your mother. Our beloved sister, Medusa, will be avenged!"

Emily had stopped screaming. But she trembled in terror as she looked at the two hideous women. Fear was making it hard to think clearly. But part of her almost remembered their names.

Medusa was a . . . a . . . Emily strained to recall what Joel had told her about Pegasus's mother. Gorgon! She finally remembered. His mother, Medusa, and her two sisters, Stheno and Euryale, were Gorgons. Pegasus was born when Jupiter's son, Perseus, cut off Medusa's head. Joel had also told her that the stallion supposedly sprang from the blood at Medusa's neck. But Emily never believed him. She suddenly remembered that one look at a Gorgon would turn you instantly to stone.

Emily looked at all the stone statues in the room and realized at least that part of the myth was true. But if one look at a Gorgon could turn someone to stone, why hadn't she been turned? Or Pegasus and all the living Nirads in the hall?

With Pegasus locked in a loud, furious fight with the two Gorgons, Emily took a longer look around the throne room. Her eyes fell on a large cage set up directly behind the repulsive snake-women's thrones. It was made entirely of gold, with fine, narrow braided bars that Emily knew even she could break out of. On the roof of the cage was a huge stack of more gold. The only part of the large cage that wasn't gold was the single black stone chair that sat in the very middle.

Seated in the chair was a female Nirad. She was the smallest Nirad that Emily had ever seen. She was certain if they stood together, they would have been the same size.

She looked very young, with fine, gentle features that were almost pretty. And although she still had four arms, she was a lovely shade of dark pink with darker pink marbling. Instead of wearing rags like all the other Nirads, she was wearing a gown of the palest pink, which made her skin even prettier.

Emily sensed there was something special about this young Nirad. But one thing was certain: Whoever she was, she was by far the saddest creature Emily had ever laid eyes on. Her shoulders were slumped, and her eyes were downcast as they lingered on all the stone children gathered around the thrones. When she finally raised her pale-gray eyes, Emily's heart nearly broke. The pain they held was unbearable.

Emily glanced away from the sad, pink Nirad and continued to investigate the throne room. To her right, she saw part of another large cage. Unlike the braided gold bars of the cage at the front of the room, this one had thick, solid black bars. As Emily strained to peer around Tange to get a better look at it, her eyes settled on the occupant lying on the floor of the cage. She gasped.

It was Joel.

If Joel was here, were the others, too? Emily desperately searched the room for signs of her father, Paelen, and Cupid. But all she could see was Joel. She tried to call to him, but Tange was still covering her mouth. Her hands flew up and tried to drag his away as she renewed her struggle in his arms. Yet the harder she fought, the firmer he held her.

Tange was shaking his head, trying his best to get her to stop.

But her squeals and struggle did not go unnoticed. As Pegasus stood before the Gorgons, he turned back to Emily. It was only then that the stallion also noticed Joel. He whinnied loudly and trotted over to the cage. Pegasus reared and tried to kick the large lock off the door. But even after several vicious blows, the lock remained undamaged.

"You will not break it, Pegasus," Stheno hissed. "That lock is secure. But do not fear, the human boy inside is unharmed. For now. . . ."

There was no mistaking the threat in the Gorgon's voice. Pegasus trotted back up to the dais and continued to protest loudly. But the louder the stallion became, the softer the snake-women spoke. Emily strained to hear what was being said, but she couldn't.

Joel's back was to her. She was relieved to see his sides moving with steady breathing. From what little she could see, he looked all right. Emily finally gazed back up into the face of Tange. She nodded her head, trying to tell him she wouldn't scream or fight anymore.

Tange removed his hand from her mouth. His eyes were locked on the stone children standing before the thrones. As her initial terror faded into a steady fear, another feeling started in the pit of Emily's stomach. She recalled the pained expression on Tange's face when she'd asked if he had any children. "Are those your children?" she asked him.

Tange didn't move for a long time, and she wondered if he'd even heard her. Finally he looked down at her and nodded.

Emily's eyes flashed back to the stone children. Her throat tightened when she saw the terror on their young faces. It looked like they had been running away from the throne when they were turned to marble. Suddenly a crucial piece of the strange puzzle fell into place.

"You invaded Olympus and came to New York because those Gorgons were threatening your children, right?"

Tange nodded.

"And if you didn't cooperate, they turned them to stone?"

Once again Tange gave a slight nod.

Emily looked away, too stunned to speak. She had become so accustomed to hating and dreading the Nirads that it was hard to imagine that these fearsome, powerful creatures were actually a conquered race of slaves. They deserved her pity and compassion, not fear and hatred! The Nirads were being forced to serve the cruel Gorgons or face the destruction of their children.

As she looked, she saw some of the child statues had been smashed and the pieces scattered around the room. It was bad enough that the Gorgons had turned them to stone. But to smash them as well was just too cruel.

Her eyes drifted back to the pink Nirad in the cage. "Is she important to you?"

Tange looked up toward the cage. She watched his eyes grow even sadder. He nodded his head slowly.

Before Emily could guess who the pink Nirad was, the conversation between Pegasus and the two Gorgons ended. The stallion turned away from the throne and tried to come back to her. But Chrysaor sprang forward and blocked his path.

Pegasus reared again and faced the boar. Chrysaor rose on his stubby legs and challenged the stallion. But before their fight resumed, the two Gorgons started to scream. The sound was loud and shrill and caused everyone in the throne room to cry out in pain and put their hands over their ears.

Emily had never experienced anything like it in her life. Even Tange reacted to the horrible sounds and covered his ears. His other arms gripped her tighter and quivered. When the sounds finally stopped, Emily removed her own hands from her ears and expected to find blood.

"Pegasus, enough!" screeched Euryale. She rose from the throne and stepped down from the dais, kicking aside a child statue as she went. The statue spun and fell over; one of its tiny arms broke. In the cage, the pink Nirad howled in pain.

"Silence!" Euryale warned. "Or I will destroy more." She turned and looked at the boar. "Chrysaor, we will have no more fighting between you two."

Emily tensed as the snake-woman drew near. She could feel Tange actually start to tremble. But was it fear or rage? Looking at Tange's face, she couldn't tell.

"So," said the Gorgon, "this child is the Flame of Olympus?"

The closer she got, the more Emily could hear the living snakes on her head hissing and spitting. She stood before Emily. "A human child? Vesta was a fool to hide the heart of the Flame in a human." She reached forward and stroked Emily's cheek with her cold bronze finger. "Humans are all so . . . delicate. What could she have been thinking?"

Emily felt sick at the touch. She couldn't look at the Gorgon. She kept her eyes locked on Pegasus. The stallion was pawing the marble floor and trying to get closer, but the boar squealed again.

"I told you to stop, Chrysaor," Euryale spat. "Leave your brother alone."

Emily's eyes flashed open as she looked at the winged boar. That was Pegasus's brother? She was far too stunned to be repulsed by the closeness of the snake-woman.

"What is this?" the Gorgon said as she studied Emily's face. "Did you not know that Pegasus had a twin brother? They were born when the murderous Perseus cut off our dear sister's head." She let out a horrible, harsh laugh. "See, Pegasus? See how ignorant the humans are? Is it any wonder that we used to feed on their flesh? Why you should choose to give your loyalty and time to this one is well beyond my comprehension."

Stheno flew down from the throne and approached her. Emily had to fight to hold back more screams. Her eyes were drawn to the squirming and hissing snakes covering the tops of their heads.

As she reached for Emily, Pegasus whinnied and charged forward, trying to put himself between the Gorgons and Emily.

"Hold your tongue, nephew," Stheno hissed as she smacked the stallion's muzzle. "You know we have killed for less. You will have her back. But not until she has done what we brought her here to do."

Emily grew cold. These horrible child killers expected her to do something for them? "I don't know why you brought us here. But whatever it is you want me to do, forget it. I won't do it!"

Both Gorgons laughed their terrible, screeching laugh. "Such fire!" Stheno said. "She truly is the Flame of Olympus."

Euryale drew closer to Emily and caught her by the chin in a painful and cold grip. "You are wrong, child. You will do exactly what we say exactly when we say it or you will know pain the likes of which you have never experienced before."

Emily tried to pull away, but Tange held her steady. "I don't know what you think I can do. You've got more powers than me. I'm nothing."

"True, child, you are nothing," Euryale agreed.

"But for reasons unknown, Vesta has imbued you with all the powers of Olympus. You alone have the power to do what no other being, alive or dead, past or present, could ever do."

"What's that?" Emily asked fearfully.

The Gorgons looked at each other. Then they turned together to Emily as both of their snakelike mouths spread in hideous smiles.

"Kill Jupiter."

DESPITE HIS LOUD PROTESTS, PEGASUS WAS
locked in a large cage. Emily was carried over to the
cage containing Joel. Tange lowered her to the floor
and started to close the door.

"Wait!" Stheno called. She held out her hand.
"Give me your golden brace."

Emily looked down at her leg. "But I can't walk
without it."

"Look around you, child. Where do you think you
will be walking? If you were to somehow escape that
cage and leave our palace, every Nirad in this world
would try to kill you. They know you are the cause
of all their misery."

"I didn't do anything!" Emily challenged. "It's you

who hurt these poor people. Look what you've done to their children. You're the monsters here, not me!"

The Gorgon stood erect and started to hiss. "Do not raise your voice to me. It is time you learned some manners!" She stormed over to the cage containing the pink Nirad. "Segan, call another child in here!" she ordered fiercely. "Do it now, or I will kill twenty!"

Emily watched the pink Nirad drop her head as her shoulders started to shake.

"Do it!" Stheno commanded.

The pink Nirad looked up and closed her eyes in concentration. Moments later a gray Nirad entered the throne room carrying a screaming and growling child. If it had been human, Emily would have guessed it to be no more than two or three years old. The child tried to bite the gray Nirad's arms and struck out with her clawed hands to scratch his face.

"Over here," Stheno ordered. "Put her in the cage with the humans."

The screaming child was carried over to their cage. Emily crawled closer to Joel as the hysterical Nirad was placed inside with them.

Across the room, Pegasus whinnied furiously, trying to break down the bars of his own cage.

"Silence, Pegasus!" Stheno cried. "The Flame of Olympus must be taught obedience!"

The Nirad child took one look at Emily and Joel and began to cry in terror. She stumbled back to the door and tried to get out. Her four arms rattled against the bars of the cage, and she began to howl mournfully.

"Now, Flame of Olympus, learn your lesson well!" cried the Gorgon.

Emily's eyes flew wide as Stheno's eyes turned from emerald green to a glowing gold. She looked down at the Nirad child. "You have caused this, Flame of Olympus. This child will die because of you!"

"No, don't!" Emily panicked. "Please, don't do it. You can have my brace. I'm begging you, please don't hurt her!"

"Too late, Flame," the Gorgon screeched. "Learn your lesson. You will obey us!"

The child's frightened wails turned to howls of pain as its skin darkened slowly and became solid. It tried to move, to get away from the deadly stare, but it couldn't. Each second, more and more of it was turned to stone.

"Stop!" Emily begged. "You're killing her!"

With a final agonized cry from the child, it was done. Emily was looking at a tiny marble statue. Up in the golden cage, the pink Nirad wailed in grief, and the other Nirads in the throne room dropped their heads.

"Segan, be silent," Euryale shouted at her, "or my sister will kill another!"

Emily's heart was racing as her rage toward the snake-women grew. The Flame was rising in the pit of her stomach, but she did not try to stop it. Emily rose to her knees. "I begged you to stop," she said furiously. "She was an innocent child. You had no right to kill her!"

She raised both her hands, and flames shot from her fingertips. But they did not hit the Gorgon as she intended. With her emotions running unchecked, the flames flew through the bars wildly and shot around the throne room uncontrolled. Tange growled in shock and pain as a stream of the flames glanced off his wide, muscular chest and tossed him backward as if he weighed nothing. At the front of the throne room, the pink Nirad was crying in fear as the living flames approached her cage. But before the deadly flames reached her, a gray Nirad jumped forward and sacrificed himself to save her. He howled in agony as his marble skin started to bubble and burn.

Emily panicked when she saw the pain and destruction her powers were causing. She pointed her hands down and tried to stop the flames before they did any more harm. But as the flames scorched the marble of the throne room's floor and caused the stone to smoke and actually melt, their intensity increased.

"Stop it, Em," she commanded herself. "Stop it!"

Suddenly, from the front dais, Euryale shouted, "Turn it off, Flame, or Pegasus will die!"

Emily's panicked eyes shot up to Euryale as she flew toward Pegasus. Her eyes were already glowing gold. "Do not be a fool, Flame. I will kill my nephew if I must. Turn it off now or he dies!"

"I'm trying!" Emily screeched as she fought to pull back the roaring flames. But her fear of the terrifying Gorgons was fanning the flames. They would not respond to Emily's commands. It was as though the flames had a mind and will of their own and would not be stopped.

"Must we kill again?" demanded Euryale. She turned from Pegasus and directed her deadly gaze at Chrysaor. The winged boar squealed and tried to dash away from his aunt. As his wings turned to stone he looked pleadingly at Emily.

When their eyes met, Emily saw pain and betrayal. For his final breathing moments he struggled to drag his stony body closer to her.

"Stop it!" Emily cried as her wild emotions fueled the flames further. She tried to pull them back, to gain some control, but her mind was too frightened and unfocused. "Please, you're killing him!"

"Then stop the flames!" Stheno commanded.

Emily concentrated harder than she ever had in her life. She could hear Pegasus whinnying loudly in the cage opposite her. Hearing the anguish in the stallion's voice gave Emily the power and determination she needed to finally pull back the flames. They weakened and tapered just as Chrysaor made it to the side of her cage. The boar's transformation was complete as the last of the flames died away. His dark eyes faded and turned to stone.

Stheno stepped closer to the cage and faced Emily with a cold, cruel expression. "You will control your temper, Flame, or I promise you, Pegasus and the human with you will suffer the same fate as Chrysaor."

Emily fell back to the floor, panting heavily. Her frightened eyes moved away from Chrysaor to look around the throne room at the havoc her unleashed, uncontrolled powers had wrought. Eventually guards arrived and carried Tange and the burned Nirad away. Tange was moaning softly, but his wound didn't look fatal. The other burned Nirad didn't move.

Emily sat in stunned silence at her loss of control. She was grateful Joel was still unconscious and hadn't witnessed the horror of it all. When her eyes finally settled on Chrysaor, she realized he, like the Nirad child, was dead because of her.

She watched Pegasus drop his head and paw the ground. Despite their constant fighting, the stallion had loved his brother and was grieving his death.

"I'm so sorry, Pegs," she muttered softly. Emily looked at the smooth, unblemished skin of her hands and realized that despite the damage she had just caused, she was lucky not to have burned Pegasus or the pink Nirad. This time it had been much worse than what had happened at the temple. Her powers were growing stronger, but her control was worsening.

In that moment Emily vowed never to use her powers again.

"Now will you give me your gold brace, or must we do this all again?" Stheno demanded, holding out her bronze hand. She seemed not to notice or even care what had just happened.

Emily sat beside Joel and undid the straps to the complicated golden device. She tossed it to the door of the cage, unable to look at the evil Gorgon. "Take it!"

"You are learning, Flame," Stheno said, collecting the leg brace. "Jupiter will have his proof that we possess you. He will have no choice now but to surrender to us."

The two Gorgons came together and held up the gold brace. "First we kill Jupiter; then Olympus is ours!"

ONCE THE GORGONS HAD THE GOLD LEG
brace, they cackled with laughter and left the throne
room. Emily concentrated on Joel. His face was
bruised and covered with dried blood. His nose was
broken badly, and his eyes were swollen shut. As she
gently stroked his forehead, her healing powers started
to work on him, and the bruises began to fade.

His eyes fluttered open.

"It's all right, Joel," Emily said softly. "You're safe."

"Em," Joel muttered. "What happened—" His
eyes shot open, and he sat up. "Nirads!" he cried.
"Emily, the Nirads are awake."

"Joel, be quiet!" Emily slammed her hand over his
mouth. Her nervous eyes looked toward the doors

the Gorgons had disappeared through. She helped him sit up and watched his reaction as he took in his surroundings. "What happened?" he asked in a whisper. "Where are we?"

"The Nirad world."

Emily explained how she and Pegasus had been attacked at the Red Apple and brought here. Then she told him what she knew about the Nirads and how it was the Gorgons who were behind the attacks on Olympus and not the Nirads themselves.

Joel shook his head in disbelief. "The Gorgons? Really? There's not much written about Medusa's sisters. Just that Medusa was mortal while they were immortal. And they were as bad as she was and could also turn people to stone."

"They're the most terrifying and hideous creatures I've ever seen," Emily said. "Much worse than the Nirads when we first saw them. Their heads really are topped with hissing snakes, and they're covered in scales."

"Just like in the myths," Joel said.

"Joel, this isn't a myth!" Emily shot back. "The Gorgons have enslaved the Nirads and are killing their children to keep them under control. When I wouldn't give them my leg brace, they turned that poor Nirad child to stone right in front of me!" Emily dropped her head. "She died because of me. Then they said they'll do the same to you and Pegasus if I don't do what they tell me to."

"What's that?" Joel asked.

"They want me to kill Jupiter."

"What?" Joel cried.

Emily wouldn't have thought it possible for Joel to look any more shocked. But when she told him the Gorgons' plans, his eyes grew as big as saucers. "You can't do it!" he insisted. "No matter what they do to Pegasus or me, you just can't do it!"

"I won't," Emily said. "I won't use my powers again. They're too dangerous. You should have seen what happened at the Red Apple and here right before you woke up. They got away from me. Joel, my powers are growing and I can't control them. I think I just killed a Nirad, and I know for sure I hurt Tange."

"Tange?"

Emily explained to Joel about the large orange Nirad and the damage she did in the throne room.

She pointed at the big burned spot in front of their cage. "It could have been even worse."

Joel tried to comfort her, but Emily was almost as frightened of her own powers as she was of the Gorgons. She was terrified that eventually she wouldn't be able to stop them, and her nightmares of burning up the whole world would come true.

"Emily, I'm sure Tange is fine. The Nirads have skin as tough as stone."

"You didn't see it, Joel. It was like a firestorm I just couldn't stop."

"But you did stop it," Joel said.

"Barely," she answered. "But what about the next time?"

"I'm sure your dad, Paelen, and Cupid will get us out of here before then—"

"My dad?" Emily cried excitedly. "Joel, you've seen my dad? How is he? Did you get him out of the CRU facility? Does he know about me and what happened at Olympus? Did you tell him how much we wanted to get back to him?"

Joel caught hold of her hands. "Emily, calm down. Your dad is fine." He filled her in on what had happened at the CRU facility. "The Nirad caught me, but I'm sure the others got away safely."

Emily sat back against the cage bars. This was the best news she'd heard in a very long time. She was glad her father had been freed from the CRU, but still worried that he might have been hurt by the Nirads. "So they brought you here alone?"

Joel shrugged. "I guess so. The Nirad hit me, and I passed out. I woke up with you here."

Emily and Joel sat together holding hands. Having him there made her feel much better. When Tange returned to the throne room, Emily tried to see how badly she'd hurt him. Tange first approached the pink Nirad's cage and then walked slowly back to his post.

His chest was covered in a thick dark-green paste, but there were exposed burn marks around the edges showing where her flames had touched him.

"I'm so sorry, Tange," Emily called. "Please forgive me. I swear I didn't mean to hurt you or that other guard. The power ran away from me. I don't have any control."

Tange didn't react to her words and stood stone-still at his post.

"Tange, please," Emily begged. "I swear I would never hurt you or your people. It was an accident!"

Across the throne room, Pegasus was pacing the confines of his cage. His head was down and he was whining softly, stopping occasionally to lunge at the bars, trying to break out.

"What happened to Pegasus?" Joel asked, seeing the burns covering his body.

"I'm what happened to him," Emily said miserably. "He was hurt in the fire I started at the Red Apple. And then the Gorgons killed his brother." Her eyes went over to Chrysaor. In his final, agonized moments, she had seen the change in him. He'd realized his mistake in siding with his aunts. That regret was now permanently etched on his stone face. She crawled over to the bars closest to Chrysaor. Joel joined her and looked at the boar.

"That's his brother?" he said in shock. "I'd read that Pegasus had a twin brother, but most of the stories say he was a giant. I didn't know he was a winged boar."

Emily nodded and reached out to stroke the boar's cold stone snout. "Chrysaor led the Nirads to the Red

Apple." She looked at the statue. "I wish you hadn't done this, Chrysaor. If you hadn't betrayed Olympus, we could have been friends."

Beneath her fingers, Emily felt the stone snout of the boar warm up. She pulled her hand back. Had she imagined it? She looked and could see the stone was fading as brown rose to the surface.

"Em, did you see that!" Joel cried. "Touch him again!"

Pegasus stopped pacing and stood watching her. He bobbed his head up and down and snorted as Emily reached her hand through the bars and stroked Chrysaor's face. Once again the stone beneath her hand grew warm.

Suddenly, from the front of the room, the pink Nirad the Gorgons called Segan made a single sound.

They both looked up as Tange left his post and approached their cage. Joel moved forward to protect Emily. "Stay back!" he cried, bravely preparing to fight the huge Nirad. "Emily told you she was sorry and didn't mean to hurt you."

Tange shook his head, grunted a few soft words, and pointed at the stone child in their cage.

"What's he want?" Joel asked.

"I think I know."

Emily crawled closer to the statue of the Nirad child and touched one of its marble arms. Instantly the stone started to warm and color rose to the surface. She released the child and looked up at the orange Nirad.

Tange's eyes went wide, and he let out an excited cry that was repeated by the three other orange guards in the room. He turned back to Segan and called out to her.

Pegasus was jumping in his cage as Emily's heart went wild with hope. "Tange, I can save the children!" she cried. She looked at Joel. "They're not dead! All those poor children can live again. If we defeat the Gorgons, I can heal everybody!"

As Emily reached for the child again, Segan made another strange sound. Tange reached into the cage and caught hold of Emily's hand. He shook his head and pointed to the doors by the thrones.

"Em, they're coming back," Joel said. He helped her move to the rear of the cage, while Tange returned to his post as if he'd never moved.

Emily sat against the bars and clutched Joel's hand. She stole a peek at Chrysaor and saw her hand marks still on his face. If the Gorgons were to look, there would be no way they could miss it.

"It is done," Stheno said. "The message has been sent. It is only a matter of time before Jupiter surrenders to us."

"We must prepare," said Euryale. She turned to the pink Nirad. "Order your men to clean this area. We have a very special guest coming, and we do not want to give him any clue as to what is happening." The Gorgon's eyes trailed over to their cage and settled on Joel.

Emily's heart nearly stopped, and she felt Joel's hand tighten on hers.

"You are awake," said Stheno as she drew near. "What is your name, boy?"

Emily could feel Joel's hand trembling as the Gorgon concentrated on him. The snakes on her head hissed and spat at him. "Joel," he answered softly, staring at the grotesque creature.

"Well, Joel," the Gorgon continued. "We brought you here because we know the Flame of Olympus cares for you. As long as she cooperates with us, you will be perfectly safe. But if she tries to use her powers against us, you will be the first to suffer." Her vicious eyes settled on Emily. "You would be wise to remember this. We used to feed on the flesh of young humans like Joel. It has been too long since I have savored such a sweet, tempting morsel as him. Mind your manners, child, or you will see horrors beyond your imagination!" As Stheno walked away, she stepped up to Tange and looked him up and down. She touched his burn and sniffed the dark green paste. Then she pointed to the stone Chrysaor. "Have that thing removed."

Tange grunted once and came forward. As he hoisted the heavy statue in his four arms, he looked at Emily and Joel and gave them a quick, almost imperceptible nod.

All around them, Nirads started to clear the room. Several moved forward to carefully lift the stone children around the dais.

"No," Euryale ordered. "Leave them here. We must ensure that your new queen understands the penalties of defiance." She looked back at the pink

Nirad. "Segan, you know how many of your children we possess. Do not make us destroy them all."

"Queen!" Joel whispered as his eyes went up to the pink Nirad. "She's their queen."

The final piece of the puzzle fell into place. Just like colonies of bees or ants, the queen controls her people—and by threatening violence against their children, the Gorgons controlled the queen. As she watched, Segan dropped her head and nodded.

Emily and Joel sat back against the bars of the cage, holding hands as the huge Nirads tidied the room. The four primary orange guards, including Tange, went about gently picking up the pieces of broken stone statues. Emily wondered, if the pieces were put back together, would she be able to heal the broken children?

Discovering that she had the power to free those turned to stone gave her some degree of hope. Somehow, they had to find a way to escape.

And when they did, they would fight to free the enslaved Nirads and face down the Gorgons once and for all.

23

TIME STOOD STILL AS EMILY AND JOEL SAT IN the cage. Across from them, Pegasus paced and kicked at his cage door. He whinnied loudly to the two Gorgons seated on their thrones.

"We will release you when Jupiter is dead," said Euryale as she rose from her throne and flew down from the dais. "But not a moment before. I will not have you trying to warn him."

Pegasus whinnied furiously. Euryale flew closer to his cage and held up a hand. "I grow tired of your constant complaints. Be silent or you shall join your brother in the stone garden."

But the stallion did not stop. As her irritation increased, the Gorgon fluttered her tiny gold wings and flew over to Emily. "For reasons beyond my comprehension, Pegasus is loyal to you. I would suggest you tell him to keep silent or I will turn him to stone."

Emily's eyes returned to the stallion. "Please, Pegs," she begged. "She'll do it. Please stop—I couldn't bear to lose you."

"Listen to the Flame, Pegasus," Euryale warned. "You know me—I will do it."

Finally, Pegasus fell silent. He looked over at Emily and snorted lightly.

"I believe I have underestimated your power over my nephew. I have never seen Pegasus surrender to anyone."

Joel stood and defiantly faced the hideous Gorgon. "It's not power that connects them. It's something you'll never understand. They care for each other."

"Foolish words." Euryale waved her hand dismissively. She flew back to her sister on the throne. "We have much to prepare. It is time we rested."

Stheno rose from her throne and turned to approach the Nirad queen. Her hand hovered threateningly before the delicate gold bars of the cage.

"Take this warning, Queen. If any of these prisoners are not in this room in the morning, we will kill you and destroy what is left of your disgusting world. Make sure they do not escape."

Segan lowered her head.

"Come, sister. The time of our exile is swiftly drawing to a close. Soon we will be free to rule."

When they were gone, Emily sat back, sighed heavily, and dropped her head. "I'm really sorry, Joel."

"Sorry for what?" he frowned.

She was unable to face him. "Sorry I got you involved in all of this. If I hadn't come to your brownstone when Pegasus first crashed on my roof, you wouldn't be here."

Joel put his arm around her and pulled her closer. "Don't be silly. You saved me that day. If it weren't for you, I probably would have ended up in prison! And even if we die here, which I know we won't, I would never regret a single moment of any of this. Don't you know what you mean to me?"

Emily looked up into his warm brown eyes.

"Emily, you're the sister I never had. Don't you

know I'd do anything for you? I'd fight those Gorgons bare-handed if I had to."

Emily felt tears rising to her eyes.

He gave her a light squeeze. "Now dry those tears before you blow us all up and ruin my plans for escape."

Emily sniffed and dabbed away her tears with Neptune's handkerchief. She looked over at Pegasus and realized Joel was right. She didn't regret a moment of her life since the stallion had entered it. She just wished she could have seen her father again. Was he safe? Was Paelen still with him? Did he know how much she really loved and missed him? Those questions haunted her as she slowly drifted off to sleep.

A short time later Emily awoke. Joel was snoring softly with his arm wrapped protectively around her. Pegasus was leaning against the bars of his cage and dozing lightly. The queen was curled in her chair, sound asleep in the gold cage. Emily looked at Tange and the other throne room guards. They were still standing at their posts. They never seemed to leave or sleep. They just kept watch over their queen.

Just as Emily was about to settle back against Joel, sounds of roaring shattered the stillness of the throne room.

Tange and the three guards stood at full attention. The guard closest to the door called out into the hall. A quick, short answer was barked back.

Up in the golden cage, Segan awoke instantly and sat up in her chair. She lifted her head and closed her eyes. To Emily, it looked like she was concentrating very hard on listening.

Joel startled and looked around wildly. "What is it?"

"I don't know," Emily said. "Something is up."

"Maybe Jupiter is here."

Pegasus nickered to the queen, who responded with a soft answer. Emily saw the stallion's reaction. He began to pace in the tight cage and paw at the floor. Whatever she had said to him upset him greatly.

"What is it, Pegs?" Emily called. "Is it Jupiter? Is he here?"

Pegasus stopped pacing and stared at her. He shook his head and snorted.

"Not Jupiter," Joel remarked. "What, then?"

The sound of the screeching Gorgons silenced Emily and everyone else in the throne room. But it didn't keep Pegasus from pacing in his cage.

The Gorgons entered and flew over to the queen. "Segan, command your men to deliver the prisoners to us at once!"

"Prisoners?" Joel said.

Emily's mind instantly flashed to her father, Paelen, and Cupid. Had they managed to find the Nirad world and been captured?

Moments ticked by slowly as they waited to see whom the Nirads had caught. Finally there were sounds in the hall outside the throne room. Emily and Joel held their breath. Their hearts sank when they saw the twins Diana and Apollo being dragged into the throne room by several gray Nirads. Deep cuts and bruises covered their arms and faces, signs of a terrible fight.

Diana's eyes flew wide when she spotted them. "Emily, Joel, what are you doing here? Are you all right?"

"They are quite unharmed," said Euryale. "Do you think we would harm children?"

"Do not tempt me to answer you, Euryale!" Diana spat as her furious eyes landed on the Gorgon. "I know all about your hideous appetites."

Apollo struggled to pull free of the Nirads holding him. "Release us, Gorgon, before I lose my temper!"

"You are not in Olympus now, Apollo," said Stheno as she flapped her tiny golden wings and flew off the dais. She landed before the Olympians. "You cannot order us around ever again. This is our world now. We rule here. Not you, not your twin sister, nor Jupiter himself! If we say bow, you will bow to us. You have no power here."

"Nor can you do anything to stop us," Euryale added. "We have waited a very long time for our vengeance. Jupiter will know our wrath for what Perseus did to our beloved sister, Medusa—"

"And for what all of you have done to us throughout the ages," Stheno finished.

"Anything we have done, you have deserved!" Apollo shouted. "You are vile, filthy creatures who have destroyed countless lives. You bring death and misery with you wherever you go. It is only through our father's generosity that you have been allowed to continue to live. But when he learns what you have done to this world and its people, there will be no escape for you."

Stheno cackled loudly. "No escape? Foolish boy! When Jupiter arrives here, he will die. Then all Olympus will be ours!"

"You cannot defeat us, Gorgons," Diana spat furiously. "That was Medusa's arrogance and fatal mistake. She tried to take us on and underestimated Jupiter's power. Remember what happened to her! You have no powers against our father."

Stheno hissed at Diana. "Your father is a coward. He did not have the courage to face Medusa himself! So he sent Perseus to murder her."

"He sent Perseus to offer Medusa a choice," Diana responded. "She refused to listen and received the justice she so richly deserved."

"The only justice will be when Jupiter dies."

"You cannot kill our father," Apollo spat. "You do not have the power."

"True," Euryale acknowledged as she stalked over to Emily's cage. "But I am not going to be the one who kills him." She pointed at Emily. "She is. It has taken us time and great effort to draw out the Flame of Olympus. But now she is ours. Emily has more than enough power to destroy Jupiter. She will do the deed, and then she will hand Olympus over to us."

Emily felt sick. How could the Gorgons expect her to kill Jupiter? They were insane. There was no way she would ever do it.

"Enough chatter! I do not care what you say—Jupiter is going to die!" Euryale screeched.

"We will stop you," Apollo challenged, struggling against the Nirads. "You will not destroy Olympus."

Euryale moved toward him. Her eyes glowed a brilliant gold. "We will do whatever we please, Apollo. Our Nirad warriors are much stronger than Olympians. However, you may rejoice in the knowledge that you and your sister will be the first of Jupiter's children to decorate our new stone garden."

Emily watched in horror as Apollo began to turn to stone. The Nirads released him and stood back as Apollo screamed in agony. In moments the spreading stone had cut off his screams and an expression of agony sealed his smooth marble face.

"Apollo!" Diana howled. She turned desperately to

the second Gorgon. "Stheno, stop your sister before it is too late."

Stheno cackled with laughter. "Too late for what, Diana? You cannot stop us. However, if you care so much for your twin brother, you will join him!"

Emily and Joel screamed helplessly as the Gorgons turned their deadly powers against Diana. Pegasus was going mad in his cage. He reared and kicked at the door again. When it was over, the Gorgons' eyes returned to normal, and they roared with laughter as they inspected the two new stone statues.

"You there," Stheno screeched as she pointed to Tange. "Have your people set these two up beside our thrones. When Jupiter gets here, I want him to see what we have done to his children."

Emily collapsed to the floor of her cage as heaving sobs escaped her. "I'll never do it," she cried. "I won't kill Jupiter and give you Olympus."

"Oh yes, you will!" Euryale shouted as she stormed up to the cage. "If you wish to keep Pegasus and Joel alive, you will. The choice is simple. You will kill Jupiter and serve us, and they will live. But if you refuse, we will kill them both and then you. With the Flame of Olympus extinguished, Jupiter will lose his powers anyway. He will be easy prey for us then. We will feast on the bones of Olympus and then your world."

"If you doubt our words, child, believe this!" Stheno crossed over to Pegasus's cage. Her eyes glowed golden as she focused her attention on the stallion's hind end.

Pegasus started screaming as his lower hind leg changed from glowing white to a cold stone marble.

"Stop it!" Emily shouted, banging her fists against the bars of her cage.

Joel was at her side. "Kill me if you must, but leave Pegasus alone!"

Stheno released Pegasus. The stallion had one marble back leg. Every time he tried to put it down it caused him so much pain, he was forced to lift the heavy stone limb in the air again. His deep whines of misery cut through Emily like a knife.

"Each time you defy us, more of your precious Pegasus will be turned to stone." Euryale laughed.

"You're sick!" Emily cried.

"No," Euryale said. "We are Gorgons!"

As soon as the Gorgons left the throne room, Emily fell to the floor, weak and defeated. She missed her father more than ever and wished he were there to guide her. They were in so much danger she just didn't know what to do.

Joel paced. "We can't let them do it. We've got to get out of here and warn them."

"How?" Emily asked. "Even if Tange lets us out, the moment the Gorgons discover we're gone they'll kill the queen."

"Then we'll take the queen with us. We'll get her back to Olympus, where we can protect her."

Tange left his post and approached them. He pointed to the lock on the door, then up to Segan's cage, and shook his head.

"There is no lock on her door?" Joel asked as he peered up to the queen's cage.

Tange nodded.

"Then all we have to do is break her out of there," Emily said.

Once again Tange shook his head. He used his large, monstrous hands to explain that the bars of the cage were very weak. Then he clapped his hands together. With all the gold weight on the top roof, it would take very little for the thin bars to collapse and the massive weight to come crushing down on their queen.

"Then we can't take her with us," Emily stated. "But we've got to do something." Emily was certain the Gorgons would kill the queen even if Emily did as they ordered and killed Jupiter. They were far too conniving to let any of them live.

In her cage, Segan started to make strange sounds. Pegasus whinnied painfully and nodded his head. The queen seemed to reply.

"Pegasus, can you really understand her?" Joel asked.

The stallion nodded and then whinnied in pain again as he moved his stone leg.

Hearing his suffering plunged a dagger into Emily's heart. "I wish I could help you, Pegs," she called softly.

As the queen continued to make soft sounds, Tange left the throne room.

Joel helped Emily settle back against the bars of the cage. "Em, we've got to ask Tange to let us out.

You can't be here when Jupiter arrives. The Gorgons will force you to kill him."

"I won't use my powers again," Emily said firmly. "No matter what they do to any of us. The next time I try, I may not be able to stop it."

When Tange returned, he was carrying the stone body of Chrysaor. He placed the statue before their cage, unlocked the door, and motioned for Joel to help Emily get out.

From his cage, Pegasus neighed to Emily. She glanced from Pegasus to Tange and then to the queen. They were all looking at her hopefully, and she understood exactly what they wanted. They needed to reach Jupiter. Chrysaor was their only hope. But after everything he had done, could they trust him?

Joel saw her hesitation and shrugged. "Em, we don't have much choice. Do it."

He helped Emily settle on the floor beside the stone Chrysaor. She reached up and rested her hand on his snout. Beneath her fingers the temperature began to rise. Moment by moment the stone melted away, and the dark brown hair and feathers of the winged boar returned.

Soon the brown spread over his entire body. She jumped when she saw one of Chrysaor's whiskers start to twitch. After a few minutes the color poured back into his dark brown eyes. The boar suddenly took a very deep, unsteady breath and woke up.

Chrysaor jumped when he saw Emily sitting beside him. He gazed around the throne room in confusion. Behind him, Pegasus started to neigh, and Chrysaor trotted over to him. The stallion lowered his head and poked as much of his face through the bars as he could to touch him.

Watching their reunion nearly brought tears to Emily's eyes as she remembered how they had tried to kill each other back at the Red Apple. Now it appeared Chrysaor had changed and everything was forgiven. Chrysaor squealed lightly and trotted over to Emily. She looked into the boar's large brown eyes and saw so much of Pegasus there. She only hoped he had changed enough to share in his brother's compassion and sympathy for others.

"We desperately need your help, Chrysaor," she explained softly. "We can't let the Gorgons kill

Jupiter. Look at what they've done to the Nirads and what they did to you. Do you really think they won't do that to everyone else? All they want is power and destruction. They don't care who they kill to attain it."

She reached out her hand and lightly stroked the coarse hairs on Chrysaor's snout. "The Gorgons are asleep. You've got to fly back to Olympus and find Jupiter. Warn him that they are planning to make me kill him. Explain to him how they've imprisoned the Nirad queen in a fragile cage of Olympian gold. Any attempt to rescue her will kill her. And tell him how they're killing Nirad children to control her. Please, Chrysaor, you are our only hope. You must tell Jupiter to bring all his warriors here to fight the Gorgons."

Chrysaor shook his head.

"Look at him, Em, he won't do it," Joel said. "Even after you saved him, he won't help us!"

Chrysaor looked at Tange and squealed softly. Obeying him, Tange suddenly wrapped his four arms around Joel and hoisted him in the air.

"Tange, no!" Emily cried. "Let him go!"

Across from them, Pegasus whinnied softly. He was bobbing his head up and down.

"Please, Tange," Emily begged, "please don't hurt him."

The huge Nirad lifted Joel higher and grunted. Chrysaor moved and stood beneath Joel's dangling legs and opened his wings so that Tange could lower Joel onto his bare back.

It was Emily who understood first. "Joel, wait, they want you to go with them."

"What?" Joel said. "No, they don't—" Tange released him and took a step back. Joel was now seated on Chrysaor, with his legs hanging down under the boar's brown wings. When he looked back up at the huge Nirad, Tange pointed to him, then the boar, and finally to the entrance.

"Yes, he does," Emily said. "And they're right. You must go."

"There's no way I'm leaving you!" Joel tried to climb off, but Chrysaor clamped his wings tightly over Joel's legs, pinning him in place.

"You must!" Emily insisted. "Chrysaor betrayed Olympus. They won't believe him. But they'll believe you. Tell them everything you've seen here. Tell them about Diana and Apollo, and how they expect me to kill Jupiter."

"I can't leave you here," Joel said. "If the Gorgons find out, they'll kill you and the queen!"

"They'll never know. It's still early. If you go now, you can be back before they return. Just do this as fast as you can and get back here before dawn."

Joel looked uncertain. But Tange and Pegasus were nodding in encouragement. Up in the cage, the pink queen also nodded her head. "See?" Emily said. "Everyone agrees. I'll be all right. Pegasus is here, so is Tange." Emily struggled to get to her feet. Tange helped her up and led her over to Joel. She gave him a fierce hug. "Please be careful. My dad should be in Olympus by now. Find him. Tell him what's happened and that I'm waiting for him."

"I will," Joel said. "And I'll be right back—I promise."

Emily reached forward and lightly stroked the boar's head. "Please take good care of him, Chrysaor, and come back quick."

Now that she was out of the cage, Emily looked

over to Pegasus and was tempted to heal his leg but knew that she couldn't. Leaving him in pain was one of the hardest things she'd had to do, but it would be too dangerous to leave any evidence that she'd been outside. Tange carried her back into her prison and locked the door. With a final wave good-bye, she watched as the large orange Nirad escorted Joel and Chrysaor safely out of the throne room to help them escape from the palace.

OLYMPUS WAS FAR TOO QUIET. PAELEN KNEW instantly something was terribly wrong. Flying down into the back gardens of Jupiter's palace, he heard and saw no one. There were birds, small animals, and insects, but not one Olympian.

The palace itself was standing silent and untouched. If the Nirads had conquered Olympus, he felt certain there would have been more signs of damage. But he searched and saw no traces of Nirads at all.

Olympus was completely empty.

Ordering the sandals to take him in the air, Paelen flew over the top of the palace and looked around. Nothing moved, and he could hear no sound.

"Hello!" Paelen shouted. "Is anyone here? Please answer me!"

The gentle breeze was all he heard. As panic started to settle in on him, Paelen ordered the sandals to search for any Olympians in the area. They carried him higher. For the first time, they seemed uncertain of where to go.

But then they seemed to catch the scent of something. They turned sharply and darted forward. Paelen strained his eyes, searching for movement below. Every building, theater, and roadway was eerily quiet and empty.

The sandals carried him away from the palace and toward the Temple of the Flame. As he approached, Paelen caught movement on the ground beneath him. His eyes shot open when he saw who was there.

"Chrysaor!" Paelen shouted as he flew at the winged boar. "Where is she?" he demanded. "What have you done with Emily?"

Paelen's anger took over as he attacked the winged boar. Chrysaor was more than twice his weight, and much larger than him, but Paelen didn't care.

Chrysaor had sided with the Nirads and taken Emily and Pegasus away.

"Where are they?" he demanded as he struck the boar. Wrapping his arms around its thick neck, he fought to tackle the large animal to the ground. But despite his best efforts, Paelen was no match for Chrysaor's strength. He couldn't move him. Instead he jumped on his back, punched down on his wings, his head, and his face.

Yet despite the pounding, Chrysaor did nothing to defend himself. He stood perfectly still and let Paelen do his worst.

"Paelen, stop!" Arms wrapped around his waist and hauled him off the boar's back. "Stop it, please!"

That voice!

"Joel!" Paelen turned and screamed when he saw Joel trying to hold him back. Tears rushed to his eyes at the sight of his best friend. He threw his arms around the boy and gave him a ferocious hug. "I thought you were dead!"

"Can't breathe . . . ," Joel gasped. "Paelen, stop. . . . Can't breathe!"

Paelen released him quickly. He was shaking all

over and could hardly believe what he was seeing. "How?" he rasped. "That Nirad killed you!"

Regaining his breath, Joel rubbed his crushed ribs. "No, he just knocked me out. But listen—I can't stay here long. I've got to get back to Emily. Where are Jupiter and the others?"

"I do not know. I just arrived here."

"So did we," Joel said. "Emily's in terrible danger. We came here to raise an army, but everyone is gone."

"Where is she?" Paelen asked. "What happened? Is Pegasus with her?" Finally his eyes settled back on the winged boar, and his rage resurfaced. He pointed an accusing finger at Chrysaor. "And what are you doing with *him*? He betrayed us!"

"Yes he did, at first," Joel explained. "Now he's helping us. But we don't have a lot of time. If the Gorgons find out I'm gone, they'll kill the Nirad queen and all their children."

"Gorgons?" Paelen asked. "Are they involved in this?"

"It was never the Nirads. It is the Gorgons who are waging war on Olympus." Joel explained how the Nirads had been enslaved by the Gorgons. How they had turned Diana and Apollo to stone, but how Emily had discovered her ability to restore those turned to stone by the Gorgons.

"Why are they doing this?" Paelen asked.

"They say it's revenge for Medusa's death, but I think it's more than that. They're after power. Their plan is to force Emily to kill Jupiter. When she does, they'll take over." Joel started to walk away. "C'mon. We've got to find everyone so we can tell them what's happened."

"Joel, stop. There is no one here," Paelen insisted. "I asked the sandals to find any Olympians, and they only took me to you. The others must be using the Solar Stream to search all the other worlds for Emily."

"Then it's just us," Joel said. "We've got to stop the Gorgons." He paused and looked around. "Where are Steve and Cupid?"

"Cupid!" Paelen cried. "I almost forgot! He is still in your world and has been badly wounded. I need to take ambrosia and nectar to him and to Emily's father and Earl!"

Together they flew back to Jupiter's palace. The banquet table was still laid with untouched bowls of ambrosia, golden plates heaving with ambrosia cakes, and urns filled with nectar. They gathered as much as they could carry and raced into the back gardens of the palace.

"I will deliver this to the cabin and then meet you in the Nirad world," Paelen said.

Joel shook his head. "No, I'm going with you."

"You must not," Paelen insisted. "Joel, you must get back to Emily before the Gorgons awaken. There is no telling what they will do if they discover you have gone. Go back to her, and I will take ambrosia to Cupid and then find you."

"How will you find the Nirad world?" Joel asked. "Can your sandals track us through the Solar Stream?"

Paelen paused. "I am uncertain."

Joel caught him by the arm. "Then let's not waste any more precious time. We'll get Cupid and Steve, and then we can all go to the Nirad world together."

Paelen surrendered. "All right. If we move quickly, we may still get you back before you are missed."

They arrived at the cottage. Agent T had bandaged Cupid's wounds, but the winged Olympian was dangerously pale and still unconscious.

Within minutes of nectar being poured into his mouth, Cupid started to come around. When his eyes fluttered open, Paelen and Agent T helped him to eat the ambrosia. He feasted as though he'd never eaten before. With each bite, Cupid's strength returned.

Joel helped feed nectar to Steve and Earl. The effect was slower for the humans, but it worked. Soon Steve awoke and was able to move. Before long, he was able to sit up and feed himself. It took longer for Earl to react to the healing properties of the nectar and ambrosia, but finally his breathing steadied and his burns started to fade; he was still very weak.

"Wow, this is powerful stuff," Joel said in awe. "The myths say if mortals eats ambrosia, they become immortal. I don't know if that's true, but it's sure working wonders on Steve and Earl."

Cupid rose slowly from the coffee table. His eyes settled on Joel in shock. "I thought you were dead!"

"I could say the same about you," Joel said as he stepped closer. The Olympian was covered in bandages.

Agent T was fussing around Cupid and handed him another ambrosia cake. Cupid took a big bite and then a long drink of nectar. He held the glass up to Paelen. "You brought this?"

Paelen nodded. "It was the only way to help you. Unfortunately, we do not have time to set your wing properly, because we must get moving."

While Cupid, Steve, and Earl continued to eat, Paelen and Joel brought them up to date with everything that had happened. "The Gorgons have Emily in the Nirad world and will force her to kill Jupiter when he arrives."

Paelen saw a flash of fear on the winged Olympian's face. Cupid was still terrified at the mention of Nirads.

"Surely you are not suggesting I go with you to the Nirad world?" Cupid cried.

"You don't have to come, but I've got to go," Joel insisted. "The Nirads are on our side. It was the Gorgons who forced them to attack. It's not their fault. They want to help."

"And what if the Gorgons order them to kill us?" Cupid challenged.

"I don't think the Nirads would do it," Joel said. "They now know that Emily can restore their dead, so they won't do anything against us. And it was a Nirad called Tange who helped Chrysaor and me escape to warn Jupiter. But Olympus is empty." Joel reached for a coat. "Now, you can stay here if you want. But I've got to get back to Emily before I'm missed."

As he moved to the door, Chrysaor moved with him. He squealed lightly, and Paelen translated. "He says climb on his back. He will take you to the Nirad world."

"Wait—" Steve rose stiffly from the sofa and reached for a shirt. "Can he carry two of us? I'm going with you."

Paelen saw the look of fierce determination on Emily's father's face. He'd seen that same determination in Emily enough times to know there would be no talking him out of it, despite his wounds. "Chrysaor says he can take you both. But we must go now."

Just as they were about to leave, Cupid stepped forward. "Chrysaor is going to have to carry three of us. If you are planning to fight the Gorgons, I am going with you."

"But there are Nirads," Joel warned. "Millions of them."

"Then you had better not have lied to me, Joel. You say the Nirads are on our side? I will trust you."

"Cupid, no!" Agent T howled. "Your wing is broken, and you aren't well enough! You can't go to the Nirads, not without me!"

Cupid dropped his head and swayed on his feet. "Agent T," he said slowly, "come with me." He escorted the CRU agent over to Earl. Cupid closed his eyes and turned on his charm. Power flowed out of him, toward Agent T. "You want nothing more than to stay here and help Earl. He means more to you than I do, more than anyone. Use your CRU skills to keep him safe. Do this for me and do it for him."

Cupid turned toward Paelen. "I have never tried that before. I hope it works."

Agent T stood beside Earl's stretcher. He was looking down on Earl and stroking his hair gently. His eyes shone with brotherly love for the wounded man.

"That was kind of you, Cupid," Joel said.

"Kindness has nothing to do with it," Cupid said gruffly. "I could not have him trying to follow us and raising the alarm. At least now Earl should be safe while he recovers. So, can we please go before I change my mind?"

ON THE OTHER SIDE OF THE SOLAR STREAM, they found themselves in a cave filled with huge orange Nirads. Despite Joel's assurances, Paelen still had doubts, and Cupid was noticeably terrified.

"It's all right," Joel assured them as he, Steve, and Cupid climbed off Chrysaor. "They've been waiting for us."

The Nirads parted, and a strange creature stepped forward. He looked like a Nirad but was smaller than the others, with intelligent gray eyes and features that were fine and sharp. His skin tone was dark pink with a black marbling effect that made him stand out even more from the orange Nirads in the cave.

Chrysaor approached the pink Nirad and started

to squeal. When the pink Nirad responded, Paelen was shocked to discover he understood.

"I am Paelen," he said as he bowed to the pink Nirad.

"Who is he?" Joel asked, coming forward. "He's the same color as the queen."

"That is because he is her brother," Paelen explained. "This is Prince Toban. His sister sent him and these royal guards to help us defeat the Gorgons."

The prince closed his eyes and lifted his head. He looked back at Paelen and made several strange sounds.

"He can speak with his sister silently, just as the queen can communicate with all her people through the power of thought," Paelen explained. "That is what makes her queen. Segan says the Gorgons are still asleep but does not know for how much longer. Joel must return quickly."

Joel approached Chrysaor. "Will you take me back to the palace?"

The boar opened his wings and invited Joel to climb onto his back. "I'll tell Emily you're here," Joel told Steve. "That'll calm her down."

Steve patted Joel on the back. "Be careful. Don't

let them catch you. Tell Emily I'll be there as soon as I can and that I love her."

"I will," Joel promised. He looked over at Paelen. "Stay safe and watch out for the Gorgons. They have killer eyes!"

"You also," Paelen said as he watched Chrysaor carry his best friend to the front of the cave, spread his wings, and take off into the dull night sky.

Paelen walked out of the cave and into the dark, arid world. In the distance he could make out stone structures. There was a glow of green coming out of most of the windows, but very few Nirads were walking around the area.

Cupid emerged from the cave with an expression of doubt on his face. He looked at Toban and then at the huge Nirads surrounding them. "If you are siding with us, why did you hand over Diana and Apollo to the Gorgons? They could have helped us defeat them."

The prince sighed before he spoke. Both Paelen and Cupid nodded.

"Well?" Steve asked.

Paelen translated, shaking his head sadly. "Toban

says it was Diana's fault, not the Nirads'. When she and Apollo emerged from this cave, they started to attack the Nirads in the village. The villagers were not given a chance to explain the situation and were forced to defend themselves. The fight caused such a stir that the Gorgons were alerted. The queen had no choice but to order their capture or the Gorgons would have killed more of their people."

"Do you believe him?" Steve asked.

"With Diana's temper?" Paelen asked. "Absolutely. You have met her. She is not one for negotiating or waiting to hear details. Apollo will follow his sister in everything. Had they paused for a moment, they would not have been captured and would have been here with us."

The prince spoke again and Paelen translated. "Toban has offered to take us to a safe place until we are ready to go after the Gorgons. We cannot remain near this cave—the Gorgons have been checking it regularly since Diana and Apollo's arrival." He looked at Emily's father. "You need to rest."

"I'm all right," Steve said. "Besides, if Jupiter is coming, we should wait here to warn him."

But Paelen could see that he was far from all right. Though the ambrosia had helped greatly, Steve was still very weak and was swaying lightly on his feet. He needed more time to heal.

The prince shook his head and spoke urgently. "Toban says the Gorgons have made a fatal mistake," Cupid translated. "They are unaware of how powerful or intelligent Queen Segan really is. Once she realized Emily's abilities and that she could heal their dead, Segan called across the Solar Stream to her warriors. They have already alerted Jupiter to the danger he is facing and from whom. The Nirads are no longer bringing him here as their prisoner. Jupiter is leading them."

PAELEN WAS SEATED ON A SMOOTH ROCK IN a Nirad home, deep inside the village close to the cave. The furnishings were sparse and all made of carved, black stone. There were pots of moss scattered throughout the small room. The moss was giving off the bright, greenish glow that was the room's only light source and had been what he'd seen from the cave. In his hands was a stone bowl of foul-smelling, slimy black goo, but he couldn't bring himself to eat it.

Across from him, Steve lay on a marble slab. A different type of dark green moss was growing on the surface and worked as a kind of living mattress. A large female Nirad was applying a very smelly paste to Steve's bullet wound and tying clean bandages around his chest.

When she finished with Steve, she approached Paelen. She forced the bowl of black goo up his mouth and grunted loudly, showing a wide row of sharp, pointed teeth.

"I think you should do as she says and eat," Cupid warned as he leaned against a wall. His wing had been set and bandaged, and most of his wounds were healed.

"I am not hungry."

"It is actually not bad," Cupid said as he shoveled handfuls of the black food into his mouth. When his bowl was empty, he crossed to where a large stone barrel was stored. He refilled his bowl and continued eating.

After he downed his second helping, Cupid said, "It would not be wise to offend our host in her home. She has two children being held at the palace, and her nerves are raw with fear. It will not take much to enrage her. If she wants you to eat, you must eat."

Paelen knew the female Nirad was upset. But so was he. His two best friends were in the palace as prisoners of the murderous Gorgons, and there was no obvious way to help them. Reluctantly, he lifted the bowl to his lips and tasted the food. As she watched him, he was forced to swallow the sticky black goo. Cupid was right. Despite how bad it smelled, it really was quite good.

"Delicious," he said, smiling up at the huge female Nirad. "Thank you."

That seemed to satisfy her, as she nodded and lumbered out of the room.

When they were alone, Steve sat up slowly. "All right, everyone. Jupiter is on his way here. But Emily and Joel don't know that he's been warned. We've got to get in there to let them know. Emily must not use her powers against him."

"She would not," Paelen said. "She would never hurt Jupiter."

"Can you be so sure?" Steve asked seriously. "Paelen, you know my daughter. Answer me truthfully. Who does Emily care more for, Pegasus and Joel, or Jupiter? Who would she save if it came down to a choice?"

Paelen paused and thought back to everything he knew about Emily. She cared for Jupiter. But in truth, if their lives were at stake, there was no question who she would choose. Paelen quickly stood. "We must get in there before Emily kills Jupiter!"

"So, we are agreed?" Steve asked. "We let the Nirads capture us and take us into the throne room."

"I do not like this plan," Cupid said. "It will get us all turned to stone."

"Perhaps," Paelen said. "But we have no choice. Toban says there is only one way in and out of the palace. We must get into that throne room. If you two distract the Gorgons, I can sneak in and get the message to Emily and Joel. We must let Emily know Jupiter has been warned and that he is coming to fight the Gorgons."

"Yes, it's risky," Steve agreed. "But we don't have much choice." He stepped up to the young prince. "Toban, your sister knows the plan, right?" When the prince nodded his pink head, Steve continued. "Good. Tell her to let the Gorgons know you have just captured two more people at the cave and are bringing us in."

The prince closed his eyes. A moment later he nodded and grunted.

"Okay, boys, let's get moving."

EMILY COULDN'T KEEP HER EYES OFF THE
marble statues of Diana and Apollo standing at either
side of the thrones. The pain of transformation was
carved into their stone faces, reminding her of the
horrors yet to come.

She looked over at Pegasus, and her heart constricted. Her beloved stallion was leaning against the
bars of his cage. His heavy stone leg was still raised
in the air. Every few minutes he cried out as the stone
hoof grazed the floor.

"It won't be long now, Pegs," she promised softly.
"You'll see. Joel will let everyone know what's hap-
pening. Jupiter and the others will be here soon. Then
I can heal you." Emily said the words as much to

reassure herself as to help Pegasus. It seemed like ages since Joel had left. She prayed that Chrysaor hadn't betrayed them again and hurt Joel or even handed him over to the Gorgons.

Just when she thought she would go insane from waiting, Tange moved from his post. He came forward and opened the door to Emily's cage.

"What is it? Is Joel back?"

Tange nodded. He looked back to the entrance of the throne room. Emily followed his eyes and heard the sound of running footsteps. In the front cage the queen sat up and made several urgent calls.

Joel finally appeared. He dashed toward the cage. Tange held open the door and locked it after him, then returned quickly to his post.

Emily threw her arms around him as he collapsed to the floor beside her. "I was so scared," she said. "I thought Chrysaor might have betrayed you."

Joel was panting heavily and covered in a light film of sweat. "No, he didn't," he gasped. "But when we got back here, we heard the Gorgons coming down the stairs. So Chrysaor had to leave me to find my own way in here. We couldn't risk him being seen."

"Did you reach Olympus?"

Joel nodded and wiped down his face. "But everyone was gone. Olympus is deserted, and we don't know where Jupiter is." As he caught his breath, Joel quickly explained what had happened.

"So my dad is actually here in this world?" Emily asked. "Is he all right?"

"He's fine," Joel said. "He won't be running any marathons this year, but he's up and moving. So is Cupid, though his wing is still broken."

Emily sat back against the cage bars, stunned. She had always feared that her policeman father would get shot in the line of duty one day. But to hear he'd been hurt fighting the Nirads . . . It terrified her to think what could have happened to him. Now they were in the same world and facing the Gorgons.

Before she could find out more, the Gorgons flew into the throne room. Their expressions were darker and even more threatening than the day before. Their tempers were up, and they were ready to blow.

"Where are your warriors with Jupiter?" Stheno demanded as she flew over to the golden cage. "They should have been here by now!"

The queen looked up at Stheno and spoke softly.

"I do not care what he does!" Stheno spat. "Tell them to strike him. Knock him out! Tear his arms off if they must. Just get him here. This is why we chose you to fight our battles—because Jupiter's powers are useless against you."

Euryale moved closer to the braided gold bars of the queen's cage. Her bronze hands hovered threateningly before them. "Segan, you will command your warriors to get moving, or I will have more children brought in here. You will watch their suffering as we slowly turn them to stone!"

Dark tears trailed down the queen's pink cheeks. She closed her eyes and raised her head. After a time, she opened them again and spoke softly.

Stheno smiled in satisfaction. Her tiny gold wings flapped as she flew off the dais and landed before Emily and Joel's cage. "It will not be long now, Flame of Olympus. Jupiter has just entered the Solar Stream."

The tension in the throne room was intense. The Gorgons paced impatiently in front of the dais. "What is taking so long?" Euryale demanded of the queen.

"One Olympian against all your warriors should be easy to contain. What is happening?"

The queen grunted softly and held up her four arms.

"Excuses! Always excuses!" Euryale roared. "Tell them to hurry or you will feel my wrath!"

The queen closed her eyes and raised her head.

"Calm, sister," Stheno said. "Our time is nearly here. Soon Jupiter will be dead and we will rule Olympus and all the worlds along the Solar Stream. The murderers of our beloved sister will know our pain and rage. Medusa will be avenged."

"Perhaps I should go to the cave to wait," Euryale suggested.

"No, do not. I do not wish to be denied the pleasure of seeing Jupiter's face when he realizes it is we who have waged war on him. Patience, my sister, we can wait a bit longer."

As time ticked slowly by, there was a stirring in the hall outside the throne room. Soon another small pink Nirad entered. Emily could see that it was male. Was he royalty too? His sad eyes looked up at the queen in the cage before he approached the two Gorgons and bowed deeply.

"Who's that?" Emily whispered. "He looks just like the queen."

"That's her brother, Toban," Joel explained. "He was waiting in the cave for us."

The prince continued speaking with the Gorgons. Finally he lowered his head and barked out orders. All eyes in the throne room turned to the entrance. Several huge Nirads entered, escorting two people.

"Dad!" Emily cried, before she could hold it back. She struggled up to her good leg and hopped over to the bars of the cage.

"Emily!" Her father tore away from his guards and ran over to the cage. He put his arms through the bars and hugged her.

Emily clung to her father, grateful that he was alive. Suddenly everything was better. As long as he was there, she could face almost anything. But their reunion was cut short when Euryale flew forward and wrenched him away.

"More intruders!" she howled, and tossed Steve across the room. She stormed over to Cupid. "How many more Olympians are here?" she demanded. "How do you all keep finding this world? First there were Diana and Apollo and now you. How many more are coming?"

"It is just us," Cupid answered as he stood defiantly before the raging Gorgon. "Emily's father was desperate to reach her. So we followed the Nirads here."

Euryale turned furious, lethal eyes to Tange. "They followed your men! We told you to be careful! You have failed us, Nirad!"

Stheno came forward. "Sister, calm down. We ordered the Nirads to bring the Flame's father here. That he came by choice makes no difference. With Pegasus, Joel, and her father's life at stake, the Flame will have no choice but to obey us! This is a day to celebrate!"

Emily's eyes were locked on her father as Cupid helped him slowly to his feet. He was unshaven, and his hair had grown long and wild. But he'd never looked so good to her in all her life. In that moment Emily pledged that no one, not even the Gorgons, would ever separate them again.

Joel stepped up beside her and whispered tightly. "Em, look over by the entrance."

Emily reluctantly drew her eyes away from her father and nearly gasped when she saw Paelen slide into the throne room. His body was long and thin, like a large python. He was slipping past the Nirad guards, who must have known he was there but gave no warning. With the Gorgons' attention on Cupid and her father, Paelen was able to slither to the front of the room and hide behind the cage containing the queen.

"So, human," Euryale challenged as she advanced on Steve, "you wanted to see your precious daughter? There she is. Caged and defeated. Soon she will destroy Jupiter and Olympus will be ours."

"She'll never do it," Steve said. He looked over to Emily. "Don't do it, Em. Not for Pegasus, and not even for me. Do you hear me? Don't do it!"

Euryale flew into another rage and struck Steve with a crushing blow that smashed him against the bars of Pegasus's cage. The stallion screamed and started whinnying loudly.

"Dad!" Emily screeched as her father fell to the floor unconscious. "Leave him alone!" She could feel the flame starting to rumble in the pit of her stomach.

"Stop it," she cried as she raised her hands, "or the Flame will rise, and you know I can't control it!"

"Silence, Flame!" Euryale spat. She approached Steve with her hands held out and fingers bent like claws. Her eyes were glowing gold as the snakes on her head spit and hissed in anticipation. "Foolish human, now you will understand our power!"

"Sister, no!" Stheno shouted. She flew over to Euryale and placed herself in front of Emily's father. "This is what he wants! With him dead we will have no control over the Flame. Look at her—her powers are barely contained! If you kill her father now, she will lose control and destroy us all. We must not harm him yet."

"We still have Pegasus, Cupid, and the boy," Euryale challenged as her eyes continued to glow. "If she moves against us, we will kill them all."

"But this is her father!" Stheno argued. She forced her sister to look back at Emily and her raised hands. "We will not harm him—for now. Lower your hands, Flame, and contain your powers, or none of us will survive this day."

Emily was quaking with fear and rage as the

Gorgons hovered above her prone father. Finally she lowered her hands and took a deep, steadying breath. "Just don't touch him again," she warned, "or I swear I'll do it. I'll unleash it all!"

Stheno ordered Tange to move Emily's unconscious father into the cage with Pegasus. "Keep him quiet, Pegasus," she warned the stallion. "We will not hesitate to turn him to stone if we must."

Joel put a comforting arm around Emily. "Em, you've got to calm down," he whispered. "I can feel the heat coming off you. But this isn't the time to make our move."

Together they watched Tange gently carry her father into Pegasus's cage and lower him to the floor. The stallion leaned down and checked on him. He turned back to Emily, nickering softly, and nodded his head.

"Take good care of him, Pegasus," she said sadly. Emily looked up into Joel's warm brown eyes. "Maybe this is the time, Joel," she whispered. "Maybe now is the only time we'll ever have to move against them. Right now, before Jupiter arrives and I'm forced to kill him."

Her eyes trailed around the room, up to the queen in her cage, over to Cupid, who was being held by Nirads. Then they came to rest on Pegasus and her father in the cage opposite. No matter how hard she tried, she couldn't see a way out of this. With all the Olympians missing, who would come to challenge the Gorgons?

Tears rose in her eyes as hope slipped away. She automatically reached into her pocket and pulled out the green handkerchief to wipe away the tears before they could trail down her cheeks and fall to the ground. She watched as the hidden fold in the beautiful silk fabric opened and caught the volatile drops in its secret pocket.

It felt as if she had cried an ocean's worth since she had arrived in the Nirad world. She looked at the hidden pocket and pried it gently open. Deep inside was a small pool of water. These were the tears of the Flame of Olympus that contained the power of the sun.

"We'll get out of this somehow," Joel said softly.

"How?" she asked miserably. "Joel, look around you. They've got my dad, Cupid, Pegasus, and you. They'll turn you all to stone if I don't do as they tell me."

"Then you can turn them all right back again," called a high, willowy voice.

Emily turned around and saw that Paelen had crawled through the throne room and made it to the back of their cage.

Joel and Emily moved to the rear of the cage and sat down side by side to block their friend from the Gorgons' view.

"Listen to me," Paelen continued urgently. "Toban told us his sister has already warned Jupiter. Once she realized you could heal her people, she knew the Gorgons must be stopped. Jupiter knows it is them and not the Nirads who are waging war on Olympus. He is coming to face them. The Nirads will help."

"So what's the plan?" Joel asked. "What did you guys decide?"

There was a long silence.

"Paelen? Did you hear Joel?" Emily asked out of the side of her mouth. "What's the plan? What are we going to do?"

Paelen sighed. "There is no plan."

"What?" Emily whispered.

"Our plan was for your father and Cupid to distract

the Gorgons long enough for me to get in here to tell you that Jupiter has been warned about them. And to say you must not kill him."

"I wasn't going to," Emily said. "No matter what they do to me."

"Oh."

"That's it?" Joel said. "All you can say is 'Oh'? Jupiter is on his way here right now. The Gorgons are going to expect Emily to kill him. Surely Jupiter has a plan."

"If he has, he did not let the queen know," Paelen said. "All we can do now is wait."

EMILY SAT BESIDE JOEL, CLUTCHING HIS HAND as they awaited Jupiter's arrival. Paelen remained safely hidden behind them. He had made himself as small as possible. In the cage opposite, her father was standing beside Pegasus, stroking the stallion's thick neck. After strict warnings from the Gorgons, he did not try to speak to Emily again.

Emily was tormented. She was so grateful to actually see her father again and know that he was alive. But another part of her was terrified for him and wished he were still back on Earth. The Gorgons wouldn't hesitate to kill him if she didn't cooperate. Would she have the strength to defy them, with everyone she loved doomed to suffer if she did?

She had never faced such a terrible choice before. Whatever decision she made, someone would suffer. She was too young to have such a heavy responsibility thrust upon her. She should be at home in New York, her biggest worry being what to wear to school the next day or if a boy in her class liked her. Not whether she should kill the leader of Olympus in order to save those she loved or defy the Gorgons and possibly lose everyone she cared for.

The decision was too big. She wasn't up to it. Emily wished more than ever that the choice would be taken away from her. But, like it or not, she was the Flame of Olympus, and she faced a decision that would change the very existence of worlds.

After what seemed an eternity, the queen started to speak. The Gorgons were instantly on the dais and rubbed their bronze hands together excitedly. "Have your warriors bring him here immediately!" They roared in celebration.

Stheno flew to the center of the throne room and threw back her head in a screeching howl. "Jupiter, your reign is about to end!"

Emily studied the Gorgons as they awaited Jupiter's arrival. Her dread grew. She didn't have a clue what they were going to do or how this would turn out. She reached into her pocket and felt for the reassuring presence of her handkerchief. She pulled it out and checked the hidden pocket again to make sure her tears were still there. If her other powers failed, at least she had these.

"You are not planning to use those, are you?" Paelen asked softly as he reached into the cage and poked her softly in the back.

"I don't want to, but if I have to, I will," Emily whispered. "We can't let the Gorgons win."

"It wouldn't be much of a victory if we are all killed by your tears," Joel added. "But I guess it's better than letting them get control of Olympus and the Solar Stream."

Emily fell silent. They were right. Her tears would have to be the last resort. But if things got too far out of hand, she would have no choice but to use them. Outside the throne room heavy footsteps drew closer.

Emily felt Joel's hand tighten in hers. "This is it," he said softly.

As the sound increased, Emily heard heavy chains rattling and dragging on the marble floor. Soon a stream of large, gray Nirads filed into the throne room, followed by several orange-marbled Nirads. Emily spotted Jupiter at the center of them.

"Oh my God!" Joel cried. "What did they do to him?"

The leader of Olympus was wrapped in heavy chains that bowed his back and trailed along the floor. His hands were bound behind him, and he wore a heavy metal collar around his neck, with another thick chain attached to it. The lead Nirad was dragging him around like a dog on a leash.

Emily gasped. His face was badly bruised, and there was fresh blood on one eyebrow. His once-white tunic was filthy and shredded. Blood streamed down his exposed arms and legs—the result of what must have been a terrible fight.

The majestic leader of Olympus had been reduced to a bruised and battered prisoner. Had all this been a Nirad trick? Were the Nirads really on their side? Looking at Jupiter, it didn't appear so. Was this just a ploy to get her to remain in her cage and keep her from using her powers against them?

"Jupiter!" Emily called.

The leader of Olympus glanced slowly back at her with vacant eyes and appeared not to know her. After a moment he lowered his head again and was dragged forward. Pegasus also called out to Jupiter, but if he heard, he gave no indication.

"What happened to him?" Joel asked. "The Nirads are supposed to be on our side, but look what they did. They beat him up!"

"It is not possible," Paelen uttered. "I have never seen Jupiter look so defeated."

"We don't know what the Nirads did to him before the queen reached them. Maybe they really are stronger than Jupiter?" Emily suggested.

"Or maybe the Nirads really aren't on our side at all," Joel whispered.

"They must be," Paelen insisted. "We cannot defeat the Gorgons without them."

Joel turned back to Paelen. "I sure hope you're right."

Emily sat back as she watched the parade of Nirads approaching the thrones. She needed desperately to believe that the Nirads were on their side. But looking at what they did to Jupiter, she was not convinced.

When they reached the dais, Jupiter was dragged forward. The tall Nirad pushed down on Jupiter's hunched shoulders until the leader of Olympus was kneeling, defeated, before the vile Gorgons.

"Not so mighty now, are you, Jupiter," Stheno challenged.

Jupiter slowly raised his head. He gasped when his eyes fell on the stone Diana and Apollo standing on the dais beside the thrones.

"Oh, do you like them?" Euryale teased. "They shall make nice additions to our collection. I wish you could join them in our garden, but unfortunately our powers do not work on you. We do, however, have other forms of entertainment planned for you."

"What do you want, Gorgon?" Jupiter asked coldly. "Why have you waged war on Olympus?"

Jupiter may have looked defeated, but his voice was as powerful and commanding as ever. For an instant, fear rose on the Gorgons' faces. It was quickly replaced by anger.

"From you," Euryale finally spat, "we want nothing, unless you care to bring our beloved sister back to us."

"Medusa died long ago," Jupiter said. "No one can change that. Not even me. But even if I could, I would not. Medusa got what she deserved."

"Medusa did not deserve to die!" Euryale screeched. "Your son had no right to kill her!"

"Medusa was insane," Jupiter continued. "No one, not even you, could control her bloodlust. She murdered without thought. You know she had to be stopped."

"We know no such thing," Euryale replied angrily. "She was our sister. She did not deserve the punishment your son levied on her. Perseus had no right to take her head. She could have been reasoned with."

"Reason?" Jupiter responded. "What do you Gorgons know of reason? I have seen the devastation you have wrought upon this and every other world you have poisoned with your presence. You are as mad as Medusa. You must be stopped!"

Both Gorgons laughed their horrible, screeching laughs. Euryale stood and climbed down from the dais. "Stopped? You fool. We are only just getting started. You should be grateful you will not live to see our truth wrath."

She turned to one of the Nirads. "Bring Cupid over here. We shall show Jupiter what we have planned for all the people of Olympus."

Emily and Joel stood and crossed to the bars of their cage as the orange guard approached Cupid. Emily could see the terror rising on the winged Olympian's face. His worst nightmare was being realized. He was being attacked by the Nirads. As others held him in place, the orange guard caught him by the arm and hauled him forward.

"No!" Cupid screeched. "Let me go!"

"Cupid!" Emily howled.

"Emily!" Cupid cried as he opened his wings and flapped them in wild panic, desperately trying to break free of the guard's grip. But he was no match for the strength of the powerful Nirad. "Help me, please!"

"There is no one to help you, Cupid," Euryale said as Cupid was dragged forward to stand before her. The Gorgon turned to Jupiter. "Watch, Jupiter. Watch as we turn the son of Venus to stone!"

In his cage Pegasus was going mad, whinnying furiously and kicking the heavy bars with his front hoof. Emily's father stood back as the stallion raged.

"Silence, Pegasus," Stheno shouted, "or you will follow him!"

"No!" Emily howled. "Please, don't do it. Let Cupid go!"

"And you, Flame," Stheno shouted back at her, "be silent, or I will do the same to Joel and then your father."

"Em, please," Joel whispered at her side. "Calm down. You can turn Cupid back later."

"How?" Emily asked desperately. "Look at Jupiter. He can't fight them."

"Then we will," Joel insisted. "We just have to get out of this cage."

Emily and Joel gazed back to the front of the room as Cupid started to scream. Euryale's eyes were blazing gold. The snakes on her head squirmed and hissed with excitement as the Gorgon concentrated her full attention on the winged god.

"Emily, help me!" Cupid howled as the terror on his face was replaced by pain. The feathers on his open wings were the first to turn to stone. They were followed by his arms and then legs as the marble crept through his body. Finally his torso and face were frozen in a stance of pure agony.

Emily's heart constricted in pain as she saw the statue of Cupid standing at the front of the dais. He had fought for her, done everything she ever asked of him, and this is how he was to be repaid—by being tortured and turned to stone. "I'm so sorry, Cupid," she mourned softly.

Her eyes trailed over to Jupiter. She saw no reaction from the leader of Olympus. He was still on his knees looking at the floor, not at the Gorgons or Cupid. "He doesn't care," Emily muttered in haunted shock. "Look at him, Joel. Jupiter doesn't care about Cupid!"

"You are wrong," Paelen called from the floor at the back of the cage. "Jupiter cares about all of us."

"Then why doesn't he do something?" Emily challenged.

At the front of the room, Euryale screeched with delight. "Do you see, Jupiter? See the destiny awaiting all the children of Olympus?"

Stheno came forward and approached Jupiter on the floor. She slapped him violently across the face with her bronze hand. "First we will watch Olympus fall. Then we will move through the Solar Stream like a raging storm until every world knows our names and worships us!"

Jupiter looked up at the Gorgon. Finally he spoke. "And if they do not?"

"Then we will turn their worlds to stone as well!" Stheno screeched. "But you need not worry for those worlds, Jupiter. All that is will become Gorgon!"

Euryale stood before the kneeling Jupiter and caught hold of his long beard. She wrenched his head back. "You are taking your final breaths, Jupiter. Savor these moments, for the hourglass of your life runs short."

"You cannot destroy me, Euryale, and you know it," Jupiter said. "No weapon can kill me, and not even your strongest Nirad is capable of my destruction. Surrender now and I shall spare your lives."

Emily listened to the cackling laughter of the two Gorgons as they stood before the defeated leader of Olympus. They stroked his head and tugged on his beard, teasing him. "Are you so certain we cannot destroy you? If so, you are in for a big surprise."

"We've got to do something—" Emily looked back to Paelen, but he wasn't there. He was slithering behind her cage, toward the front of the throne room.

"Paelen, no," she whispered tightly. "Come back."

"Paelen," Joel added softly. "Stop, they'll kill you."

Paelen paused. "No one else is coming. It must be us who save him. Trust me: I have an idea."

Emily wanted to call to him again but feared exposing him. Instead she split her attention between him and Jupiter in the center of the throne room. She was certain the Gorgons would see him. But for now they were concentrating solely on Jupiter. Emily's eyes then went up to the queen. She was following Paelen, fear etched across her young face.

Across the room, Pegasus and her father also watched. Pegasus started to whinny, ensuring his aunt's attention was kept away from Paelen.

"Not now, Pegasus," Euryale said irritably. "Be patient. You will be out of there soon enough."

But Pegasus would not stop. He kept whinnying and pounding the floor of his cage.

"I said stop!" Euryale stormed as she flew over to Pegasus's cage. "Do not make me destroy you so close to our victory!"

"Leave him be," Stheno called to her sister. "I grow weary of all this chatter." She fluttered her tiny gold wings and flew across the room to Emily and Joel's cage. She looked at Tange. "Open the door. It is time for the Flame of Olympus to end this."

Tange looked at Emily as he unlocked and opened the door to her cage. "Child, you cannot fight your destiny," Stheno said.

Emily hopped to the back of the cage and shook her head. "I won't do it. You can't make me kill Jupiter."

"Leave her alone!" Joel moved to block Emily from the Gorgons and Tange. "Just leave her alone."

Stheno waved her hand at Tange dismissively. "Kill the boy and bring Emily out of there."

Tange stooped down and entered the cage. His mouth was working hard to try to form the word "please." There was desperation in his face.

"No! Tange, please, don't hurt Joel!" Emily begged.

"Then stop fighting us," Stheno said, "and the boy will live."

"Em, don't do it," Joel said to her. "Forget about me. Whatever happens, don't kill Jupiter!"

Emily looked at Joel, fearing it was for the last time. They had been through so much together, but now their time was at an end. This was the point where she had to make her choice, a choice where there could be no winners. She gave him a fierce hug and hoped he didn't feel her trembling.

"It'll be all right, Joel," she whispered softly, knowing full well that she was lying. She kissed his cheek, then gave him a final hug before turning to face Tange. "I'm ready."

Tange lifted her gently into the air. He carried her past Joel and out of the cage. Emily saw that Tange hadn't locked the door after her. Joel was free to leave the cage anytime he wanted. Joel had noticed this too. He moved to the door and waited.

"Please let him run when he gets the chance," she prayed silently.

Emily looked up and saw the queen sit bolt upright in her chair, anxiously. She, too, knew the end was drawing near.

When they stood in front of the thrones and faced

the kneeling Jupiter, Tange put Emily down on her good leg and helped to steady her. He wrapped one thick arm around her shoulders for support.

"Jupiter," Emily begged, "help me, please. I don't want to do this."

The leader of Olympus raised his bruised and bloodied face to her. She could see the pain and defeat in his dark eyes. Jupiter suddenly looked very old and frail. He was too tired to fight. "You will do what you must for the good of Olympus, Emily."

"That is sound advice," Stheno agreed as she moved up beside Emily. "The time has come. Your choice is simple. Summon up the power of the Flame and destroy Jupiter, or my sister over there will turn your beloved Pegasus and father to stone."

Emily glanced over at the cage. The stallion was shaking his head and snorting loudly, while her father mouthed the word "no" to her.

She looked again at Jupiter. Then back at Pegasus and her father. Her eyes trailed over to Joel, who was also frantically shaking his head no. Finally they returned to Jupiter. But the leader of Olympus had lowered his head and would not face her. Was he doing this to make the decision easier? It wasn't working. Every instinct in her body told her not to do it. But then her emotions exploded. What about her father? Pegasus and Joel? The Gorgons would kill them if she refused.

"Do not try my patience, child," Stheno warned. Emily was close enough to hear the snakes on her head hissing in wild anticipation of the violence yet to come.

In his cage Pegasus continued whinnying frantically and waving his head back and forth. She didn't need to understand him to know what he was saying. Pegasus was begging her not to do it.

"Silence, Pegasus," Euryale ordered. "You cannot tell her what to do!" The Gorgon looked at Emily. "Must I turn another of his legs to stone to prove I will not hesitate to kill him?" she asked. "How would your father look with stone legs?"

"No, please don't!" Emily cried.

"Then use your powers!" Stheno ordered. "Kill Jupiter!"

"Emily, no!" Joel shouted.

"I-I—" Emily stuttered as she faced Jupiter.

The leader of Olympus raised his head. "You know what you must do, Emily. I understand."

Emily looked around in wild desperation. She had hoped and prayed for a miracle. That somehow all the Olympians would burst into the throne room at the very last minute and rescue them. She could no longer see Paelen in the room and had no idea where he was or what he was planning. But if the others were trying to get into the palace, they were too late. The moment had come. Right or wrong, her decision was made.

Emily took a deep, unsteady breath. She closed her eyes and felt the tingling of the Flame's powers deep within. Her emotions were fanning the barely contained flames. They wanted out with or without her permission. The power was alive, rumbling and growing, moving steadily from the pit of her stomach to along her arms.

"Forgive me," she muttered as she raised her hands to Jupiter and released her power.

PAELEN WAS HIDING BEHIND ONE OF THE Nirads. The huge creature knew he was there but gave no alarm. Instead he opened his thick arms farther to offer him more protective cover.

He watched as Emily stood before Jupiter, wrestling with her decision. There was only one she could make, but did she have the strength to make it?

Paelen held his breath. She wouldn't do it. Would she? Would Emily really kill Jupiter to save the others? He watched her raise her arms. He heard her soft plea for forgiveness. He saw her let the flames go. . . .

Two sharp beams of deadly light flew past Jupiter's head and burned the lock on Pegasus's cage door. The laserlike flames shot past Pegasus and through the cage, the wall behind it, and the outer walls of the marble palace, then continued out over the land of the Nirads.

"I won't do it!" Emily shouted as her fury stopped the deadly flames before they flew out of control. She turned toward Stheno. "I won't kill Jupiter!"

Paelen cheered Emily's defiance. He saw her father burst through the melted cage door and run at Euryale, howling in fury. Whinnying in anger, Pegasus limped behind him, flapping his burned wings and dragging his heavy stone leg.

Euryale spun around, her eyes turning brilliant gold. Emily's father's agonized scream was cut short as he and the stallion turned instantly to white marble. Only then did everyone in the room understand. The Gorgons could choose how long it took for their victims to turn to stone.

"Dad, no!" Emily howled.

Emily's father was frozen beside the marble Pegasus. In the center of the room, Emily's pain-filled howls turned to roars of rage. She raised her hands to fire at Euryale.

Beside her, Stheno's eyes blazed gold as she faced Emily. "If you will not kill Jupiter, I will extinguish the Flame of Olympus myself!"

"Emily, watch out!" Paelen shouted as he burst from his cover and lunged at the Gorgon. He launched himself into the air and landed on Stheno's back.

"For Olympus!" he shouted as he wrapped his arms around the Gorgon's head and slapped both his hands over her deadly eyes. Paelen ignored the countless snakes biting painfully into his face and arms as he clung to the enraged Gorgon. Stheno screeched and howled. She spun around madly, trying to dislodge him.

"Shoot them!" Paelen called to Emily. "Do it now: Stop the Gorgons!"

Paelen clung to Stheno and felt his hands grow cold. They were becoming stiff and difficult to move. His feet and legs were frozen and unresponsive as he tried to jump away from the enraged Gorgon. Finally, his vision started to fade as his muscles seized up.

"No!" he howled.

The Gorgon beneath him screeched and screamed in fury. "You will die in agony, boy!"

Paelen suddenly realized his terrible mistake. The Gorgon's eyes did not need to be open to be deadly. The freezing in his hands spread throughout his whole body. Already he could feel his blood slowing as each cell in his body turned to stone. Paelen experienced pain he'd never known before. It was like he was freezing and burning at the same time. He could no longer move. All he knew was pain and then . . . black nothingness.

30

EMILY SCREAMED AS PAELEN TURNED TO stone. He was curled around Stheno's head like a grotesque hat. On his marble face was the pain of transformation. Stheno lifted him and screeched in rage as she tossed him aside.

Just before Emily's best friend hit the ground and shattered into a thousand pieces, Tange released Emily and dove to catch Paelen. He lowered the coiled Paelen statue safely to the floor. When he rose, Tange threw back his head and roared loud enough to shake the whole palace.

At Tange's command, the throne room erupted in fighting as the large Nirads attacked the Gorgons. But the Gorgon's deadly eyes were faster and much more powerful. No Nirad could get close without being turned to stone instantly. The throne room quickly filled with marble Nirads.

"Jupiter!" Emily cried. She hopped over to the kneeling Olympian and tried to undo the heavy chains binding him. "Please help us."

"Not yet," Jupiter replied as his wild eyes scanned the room, but he remained motionless before the thrones. "This is not the time."

"The time for what?" Emily demanded. "For all of us to die?"

"Emily!" Joel cried as he ran out of the cage.

"Go to him, child," Jupiter warned. "Leave me here and do what you must. Remember, you are the Flame of Olympus!"

Emily saw Chrysaor running into the throne room and toward Joel. The pink prince darted around the Nirad statues to join them. More warriors flooded into the throne room and joined the fight. The sound of their furious roaring was deafening, but not nearly as bad as the howls of pain that filled the room when the warriors were turned to stone by the Gorgons.

Emily reluctantly left Jupiter and joined the others as they crouched down behind a wall of stone Nirads.

"Why don't you use your powers?" Joel demanded. "You're the only one who can stop them."

"I can't," Emily cried. "Joel, you know I don't have any control. I could kill everyone in here, including Jupiter!"

Toban started to growl and pointed up to his sister locked in her cage. He caught Joel by the arm and tried to lead him up to it.

"We must save the queen!" Joel insisted. He turned frightened eyes to Emily. "It doesn't matter how much control you've got. It's the only way."

"But what if I can't? What if I kill you?"

"We're as good as dead anyway. You know we can't let them leave here to destroy other worlds!"

"But—"

"Em, look around you!" he shouted. "The Nirads can't stop the Gorgons. You're the only one who can! Look, just stay here, take a few deep breaths, and calm down. Concentrate on what you need to do. You can do it, Emily, I know you can. I'll see if we can get the queen's cage open. But be prepared to use your powers."

Emily watched Joel, the prince, and Chrysaor darting between the large stone Nirads. The room was growing crowded with statues as every Nirad who tried failed to get close enough to attack the Gorgons.

In the center of the room, Jupiter remained still. Nirad statues were falling all around him, but he refused to move. *What are you waiting for?* Emily thought. *Please, Jupiter, help us!*

Joel and the prince reached the thrones. They jumped onto the dais and moved to climb the stairs up to the queen's cage. In their determination, they did not see Stheno turn her deadly golden gaze in their direction.

But Emily did. "Joel, look out, she's right behind you! Get down!"

Joel and the prince cried out in agony as they turned instantly to stone. Halfway up the stairs to the cage, Joel was caught off balance, with one foot still raised in the air.

"Joel! No!" Emily howled as her friend teetered on the edge of the steps. Then, as if in slow motion, he fell forward and smashed into the fine braided gold bars of the queen's cage.

Beneath his heavy stone weight, the gold bars bent and crumpled. Joel tumbled, rolling down the stairs until he finally slipped off the dais and crashed to the marble floor below. On impact, his right arm exploded into hundreds of tiny stone pieces.

Emily dashed forward. But moments before she reached Joel, all the surviving Nirads in the room roared and turned toward their queen. Segan was looking up at the roof in terror as the gold bars to her cage trembled. Unable to withstand the roof's weight after the impact of the stone Joel, the top of the cage began to come down.

"No!" Emily screamed. Jupiter moved.

He rose from the floor and easily tore away all the chains wrapped around him. In three short strides, the leader of Olympus reached Segan's cage. He pushed inside and lifted the small queen from her prison chair. Jupiter wrapped his arms and powerful body around her just as the heavy gold roof collapsed down upon the two.

"Jupiter!" Emily cried.

Tange howled mournfully as he and the three other large orange throne-room Nirads charged forward. They leaped up to the dais and, each taking a corner, started to lift the heavy gold roof off Jupiter and their queen. Beneath the roof, Jupiter rose, with the queen still alive and safe within his arms.

Tange and the others howled in agony and strained to use their four arms to lift and support the gold roof. Down on the floor, Stheno raced forward. "You will all die!" she screeched.

The Gorgon directed her deadly gaze at the four Nirads and Jupiter. Tange's cries grew unbearably loud as he and the others continued to support the roof while their bodies turned to stone.

Inside the cage, Jupiter remained unaffected by the Gorgon's deadly stare. With the pink queen still wrapped in his protective embrace, he glanced over his shoulder at Stheno. "You and your sister have failed, Gorgon. You should have surrendered when you had the chance. There will be no mercy for you now."

Beside Emily, Chrysaor squealed in pain as he was turned to stone for the second time in as many days.

"You should have joined us, child," Euryale screeched as she stalked toward Emily with murder in her eyes. "We would have embraced you as our daughter."

"I had a mother," Emily cried defiantly, "and I loved her. She was enough. I would never join you."

"Then you are a fool!" Euryale shouted. "You could have ruled with us. All the worlds of the Solar Stream could have been your playground. You would have been an empress! But you made your choice. It was the wrong one!"

Euryale raised her hands as her terrible eyes blazed the brightest gold Emily had ever seen. "It is over, Flame of Olympus. You . . . are . . . extinguished!"

Emily felt searing pain in every part of her body as she stiffened. She couldn't move. Couldn't scream and couldn't breathe. Her eyes faded as the room around her blurred and turned to black. An instant later she was solid stone.

EMILY WAS AWARE. SHE COULD NOT HEAR, she could not see, and she could not feel. But she remained completely aware.

Was this what it was like for everyone else? Was her father conscious but trapped in a casing of stone? Was she alive or dead? Did her heart still pump blood through her marble body? Was this it? Was she facing an eternity as an unmoving statue while remaining fully conscious? Panic settled in as Emily struggled to move her fingers. But nothing happened. She was frozen stone.

No! Her mind raged. Emily thought of all the others she loved who were suffering the same fate around her. Was her father calling silently to be freed? But there was no one left alive to hear him. Was Pegasus suffering? Was he still feeling the pain of his burns? Emily was the only one who could heal them all. But how could she when she, too, was stone?

As Emily thought and worried for the others, her concern fed the Flame. It began to bubble within her. But trapped inside the stone casing, unable to move her arms, it had nowhere to go. For an instant, Emily feared the Flame would turn in on itself, consuming her body like a Phoenix that died in the ashes of its own fire. But she had already been burned up once. Could it happen again?

"Don't think about it, Em," she ordered. "Think only of Dad. Think of beautiful Pegasus and the pain on his face when he was turned to marble. Think of sweet Paelen, brave Joel, and handsome Cupid. Think of how they fought and suffered beside you."

Emily felt her panic subside as she thought of those she loved. Fear for her own life faded, and anger at Stheno and Euryale grew. The thought of those two vile creatures being responsible for so much pain and suffering was unbearable.

As more faces of the dead flashed in her mind,

Emily's anger boiled. No way would she let them get away with it. They could not be allowed to rule Olympus and all the other worlds along the Solar Stream. She would fight them. If it took every last bit of energy, if she had to burn herself out to stop them, she would not let the Gorgons succeed!

She concentrated on the Flame. Already boiling with her fear, she let her anger stoke the fires. If she was the Flame, so be it. Emily would finally become THE FLAME OF OLYMPUS!

A silent roar started deep within her core as Emily summoned all the powers she had been fighting so long to suppress. She fed them, called them forth, and commanded them to melt the stone shell keeping her imprisoned.

She could feel the heat rising. It was just as Vesta had told her it would be. The full power of the sun! But Emily felt no pain, only growing strength and control. As the Flame rose from her center, she was able to move again. At first just a finger, but soon more.

Her hearing returned. Emily heard the sound of the two Gorgons cackling and shouting at Jupiter.

They were taunting him and celebrating his defeat. Euryale's voice was closest. The Gorgon was standing directly beside her.

"It is over, Jupiter. See how your great Flame is nothing now but dead, cold stone. When our Nirads return to Olympus and extinguish what is left of the Flame at the temple, you will truly know defeat. Medusa is finally avenged!"

Emily felt the pressure of Euryale's bronze hand resting on her stone arm. The Gorgon was unaware of the changes raging deep inside her, oblivious to the danger standing at her side. Emily summoned up the Flame, and her hand burst free of its marble prison. Before the Gorgon could utter a word, Emily caught hold of her bronze hand and held it in a fierce grip.

"What—" Euryale cried. "Let me go!"

Emily unleashed her powers. She was a living volcano about to erupt. The stone encasing her seemed to melt and flow away from her like lava. Her temperature climbed impossibly high, yet she did not feel the heat.

Euryale, however, did. The Gorgon screeched and screamed as the bronze of her hand melted and dripped to the floor. The snakes on her foul head hissed and spat as they slowly roasted and shriveled in the intense heat.

Emily turned her head slowly and saw the Gorgon's face start to smoke and then burst into flame. Euryale's eyes went brilliant gold as she tried to fight back. But Emily did not return to stone. She was a raging inferno, untouched by the Gorgon's lethal power.

Stheno screamed in fury when she saw her sister burning. She directed her deadly golden eyes at Emily, but they had no effect. When Euryale collapsed to the floor in a melted, smoldering heap, Stheno ran over to Steve. She put her hands on his shoulders and threatened to topple him over.

"Stop now, Flame, or I will destroy your father!" she wailed.

Emily's fury renewed. She raised her hands, summoned all the power she possessed, and fired at Stheno. Unlike Euryale, who had burned, Stheno simply disappeared in a soft, soundless puff. Black ash filled the air and rained down where the Gorgon had been standing.

The Gorgons were gone.

"Emily," Jupiter called softly. "It is over, child. Call it back."

Through flaming eyes, Emily looked up at Jupiter. He was still in the cage with the queen. He lifted her lightly in the air and carried her between the bent gold bars, careful not to let the gold graze her delicate pink skin. He lowered her onto the dais and walked closer to Emily.

Jupiter raised his hands against her blazing heat. His whole body was starting to smolder. "Pull it back, Emily," he said, sounding strangely calm. "You can do it now. The powers are yours to command. Pull the Flame back."

Emily closed her eyes and concentrated on pulling the Flame back into herself. She imagined she was a giant vacuum cleaner sucking up a pile of flour from the floor. Only this wasn't flour she was collecting, but the raging power of the sun. As she concentrated harder, she felt the Flame obeying her commands. Her core temperature was dropping. The Flame was growing smaller and easier to contain. Finally it stopped completely, and Emily was herself again.

She looked around at the devastation of the room: not a living soul moved except for Jupiter and the Nirad queen. Everyone else was stone. "Jupiter?" she called softly.

Jupiter swooped in and closed his strong arms around her. He lifted her off the floor and gave Emily the biggest, most powerful hug she had ever had in her life.

"I am so very proud of you!" he cried as he kissed her cheeks. "You were magnificent!"

"I don't—don't understand," she stammered. "Jupiter, what happened?" Then she remembered how he had done nothing when the Gorgons started to attack. "Why wouldn't you help us?" she demanded. "You just knelt there while the Gorgons turned every-one to stone. They turned *me* to stone! Why didn't you stop them?"

Jupiter put her down and knelt on one knee before her. He took both her hands in his. "Forgive me, but I could not. When I came in here, my only concern was for the Nirad queen. I knew you would be safe. And anyone who was turned to stone could be healed by you. But if the queen had died in her cage, this entire Nirad society would have been destroyed."

"But, but—"

"Child, listen to me," Jupiter said softly. "This is the price I must pay as leader. Making these difficult decisions is never easy. But I could not help you no matter how much I wanted to. You had to learn to help yourself. Until this moment, you have feared and dreaded your powers. Because of that, you could not control them. It made you a danger to yourself and everyone in Olympus. But here, today, you finally embraced them. You have faced your destiny and become the Flame's master. Emily, you saved everyone and defeated the Gorgons because you are finally the Flame of Olympus. It was more than I could ever have achieved."

Emily sucked in her breath. "But—but you're Jupiter," she protested. "There's nothing you can't do."

Jupiter chuckled and rose. He kissed her on the forehead. "I appreciate your faith in me, child. But I am nothing without the power of the Flame of Olympus behind me." He reached out his hand. "May I see the handkerchief Neptune gave you? I need to check something."

Emily handed over the green fabric with the white Pegasus embroidered on it. She watched him open the hidden pocket and peer inside.

"It worked perfectly," he muttered. "I must tell my brother."

"Tell him what?"

Jupiter handed back the handkerchief. "Look inside: Your tears are gone."

Emily saw he was right. The small pocket was empty. "Where did they go?"

"Back into you—they added fuel to your fire. When Neptune had his Sirens weave this for you, he made certain that when you needed your tears back, the fabric would return them. It appears it did." Jupiter wrapped his arm around her to support her weight. "Now, Emily, I would like to properly introduce you to Segan, the queen of the Nirads."

Emily put the handkerchief back in her pocket and looked at the young queen she had spent so much time with. She bowed her head. "Your Majesty."

The queen smiled. She wrapped her four arms around Emily and embraced her tightly. She growled softly in her ear.

"Segan says thank you for your bravery and for freeing her people from the terror of the Gorgons," Jupiter explained.

Emily smiled back. "You're welcome." She looked around the room at the countless stone statues. "But you're not really free yet. We've got a lot of work ahead of us to free everyone."

Segan stepped over to the stone statue of her brother and grunted a few soft words to Jupiter. "She has asked a favor. Would you be kind enough to free her brother first?"

Emily nodded and was helped over to the pink Nirad. "I really hope this works," she said nervously as she reached out her hand and touched the prince's stone arm.

The change started immediately. Where her hand grasped the Nirad's arm, pink returned to the surface. It spread along his whole body, until he took in a deep, unsteady breath and staggered on his feet. Segan reached out to support him. Recovered, he looked at his sister and howled in joy.

Emily felt her throat constrict as she watched their noisy reunion. The queen turned to her and spoke softly.

"Segan would like you to meet her brother, Toban," Jupiter explained.

Before Emily could speak, the young prince threw his four arms around her and embraced her while growling enthusiastically in her ear.

"You're very welcome," Emily choked out when he finally released her. Leaving the pink Nirads free to continue their reunion, she looked up at Jupiter. "Will you help me get to my dad and Pegasus?"

"With pleasure," Jupiter said as he lifted her easily in his arms and carried her carefully between the marble Nirad fighters and over to the stone statues of her father and Pegasus. Emily felt a biting pain in her chest as she stared into the expressions on both of their faces.

Jupiter lowered her to the floor. Emily put her arms around her father and stood on tiptoes to kiss his stone cheek. "Come back to me, Dad."

Holding him close, Emily could feel the life flowing back into her father as the stone faded and his flesh returned. After a moment her father opened his eyes and found her in his arms.

"Em!" he cried, hoisting her in the air and giving

her a hug equaling Jupiter's. Tears rushed to his eyes, and he buried his face in her long, dark hair. "My Em, my beautiful Em!"

"Daddy!" Emily squealed, suddenly sounding like a child again. She stood, clinging to her father. It had been the longest journey of her life to get to this moment, and she didn't want it to end.

Her father put her down and looked around the room. He wiped his teary eyes. "What happened in here?"

Jupiter offered his hand. "Your daughter saved all of us. You should be very proud."

"I am," he said.

With her father at her side, Emily hopped over to Pegasus. Agony was etched on the stallion's marble face and revealed in his half-opened wings. Emily put her arms around his cold stone neck and pressed her cheek to the white marble. "Forgive me, Pegs," she whispered softly, "but I couldn't kill Jupiter to save you. Please, please forgive me. Come back. I need you."

Beneath her cheek, Emily felt the stone react. "That's it," she coaxed, "keep coming."

Soon the marble stallion warmed and became flesh again. His burns were healed, and the feathers on his wings were restored. With one heaving breath, his eyes opened and he finished the screaming whinny he'd started when Euryale had turned him and her father to stone.

"It's all right, Pegs," Emily soothed as she stroked his quivering neck. "It's over now. You're all right!"

Pegasus jumped when he saw Emily standing beside him. She started to laugh at the confused expression on his face. Pegasus looked around at all the statues in the throne room. His frightened eyes went up to the queen's cage, and he neighed loudly to Jupiter.

"The Gorgons are gone, Pegasus," Jupiter said. "Queen Segan is safe. She is with her brother, over there." He pointed at the two pink Nirads. "Soon we will heal the wounds of this world and return to Olympus."

The confused expression remained as he nickered softly. She put her arms around his neck and hugged him tightly. "I couldn't have done it without you, Pegs," she said softly.

When Pegasus neighed, Jupiter smiled and stroked his soft muzzle. "Emily did more than even I could ever have imagined. I am sure she will tell you all about it in time. For now, come, my nephew, we have a lot of work ahead of us."

With Pegasus on one side and her father on the other, Emily hopped carefully through the throne room filled with statues. She would never admit it to Jupiter, but she was frightened she wouldn't have enough power to heal everyone. But Pegasus understood. He helped her over to her best friends first.

Her father helped her down to the floor in front of Paelen. Emily stroked his head and kissed him lightly on the cheek. "Thanks for trying to save me from Stheno, Paelen," she whispered softly.

The stone beneath her lips began to warm as life quickly returned to Paelen. After a moment he took in a deep breath and screamed.

"It's all right," Emily said as she wrapped her arms tightly around him. "Paelen, you're safe. Calm down!"

Paelen looked wildly around the room and rose,

preparing to fight again. "Where are they? What happened?"

"Gone," Emily's father said as he helped her rise to her good leg.

"Gone where?"

"Well," Emily said awkwardly, "Euryale sort of melted. As for Stheno, she just evaporated. That's what is left of her, over there." Emily pointed at the dark ashes littering the floor and blowing around the throne room.

Paelen looked from the ashes back to Emily. "Did you do that?"

She shrugged. "Kinda. They turned me to stone too, and that made me really angry."

Paelen looked at her in wonder. "They made you angry, so you turned them to dust?" When Emily nodded, he whistled lightly, and his crooked grin appeared. He stepped up to Pegasus. "Pegasus, please warn me if you ever see me start to make Emily angry!"

Emily laughed and punched him lightly on the arm. "He will. Now c'mon. We've got to help Joel."

Jupiter and her father were gathering pieces of

Joel's broken stone arm at the base of the dais. The leader of Olympus looked up at her, grim faced. "I fear this may not work. Please, take this. We must see what happens." He handed Emily a small piece of stone.

The smile dropped from Emily's face when she looked and saw it was one of Joel's fingers. She enclosed it in her hand. Nothing happened. It remained a cold piece of marble. "What does this mean?"

Jupiter rose. "I am uncertain. But it may mean that once someone has been broken, not even your powers can restore them."

"Are you saying that Emily can't heal Joel?" her father asked.

Behind them, Pegasus whinnied loudly and pounded the floor. He snorted and shook his head.

"No," Emily cried. "Not Joel. I will heal him!"

Before Jupiter could stop her, Emily knelt down and touched Joel's face. It was then she noticed that part of his right ear was missing as well. "Please," she prayed as she closed her eyes. "Please, Joel, wake up! I can't go on without you here."

Finally the stone beneath her hand started to warm. "It's working!"

Paelen knelt down beside her, and Pegasus pressed in closer. Together they focused on the jagged edge of the break in the stone of his right arm.

"Come on," Paelen urged. "Grow back!"

Joel was gradually coming back to himself. His flesh returned, but they watched as the rough edge of the break folded in on itself. The wound closed and covered with healed skin. But there was no new growth. They realized that his right ear and arm were not going to grow back.

"Joel?" Emily said softly.

"Em?" Joel said as he opened his eyes. Just like Paelen, he looked wildly around the room. "The queen?" he cried as he looked back up to the cage. The four stone guardians were still holding up the roof, but the cage was empty.

"She is safe," Jupiter calmed, "thanks to your bravery."

"Joel, we've got something to tell you," Emily said.

Before she could warn him, Joel sat up and immediately noticed the change in himself. "Where's my arm?" he asked in confusion. Fear rose on his face. His left hand reached up and felt the healed stump at his right shoulder. "Emily, where's my arm?"

He looked desperately at Paelen, and his eyes flew around the room. "Tell me. Where's my arm?"

Emily quickly embraced him. "I'm so sorry," she cried as tears filled her eyes. "The Gorgons turned you to stone. You fell over, and your arm broke. I tried to fix it, but it wouldn't work. It's gone, Joel."

"Gone?" Joel said in a haunted whisper. "Gone where?"

Emily sniffed and let him go. She reached for her handkerchief to collect her tears. As she wiped them away, she watched Paelen hand over the stone finger to Joel.

"It shattered," Paelen said. "Emily tried, but—"

Joel took it in his left hand. "Is this really mine?"

Paelen nodded. "Do not worry, Joel. I promise you, Vulcan can make you a new arm, and I will help. It will be a better one. Look at the legs he built for himself."

"And my brace," Emily added. "He can do it, Joel. I know he can."

Emily's heart broke as Joel's haunted eyes lingered on his stump. He was in deep shock. "It doesn't hurt a bit," he muttered softly. "It should, but it doesn't."

"Emily's powers have healed you as much as they possibly could," Jupiter said. "I, too, am sorry she could not restore your arm. You have my word, Joel: Vulcan will have everything he needs to build you a new one."

Joel climbed awkwardly to his feet. His eyes scanned all the statues in the room. Several had been knocked over and broken in the battle. He saw a couple of Nirad statues without their heads. "What about them?" he asked.

Jupiter inhaled deeply and let it out slowly. "I am sorry to say, but most of the broken ones are dead. Perhaps some of those with lesser breaks may survive, but if Emily could not restore your arm, it is doubtful she can do anything for those who have suffered major breaks to their bodies or heads. We must all grieve their loss."

"Joel, are you all right?" Emily asked softly as she reached out to him.

He looked down at her. Tears were rimming his

eyes, but he refused to let them fall. He shook his head. "Not really." He embraced her tightly and whispered in her ear. "But I will be."

Next Emily approached Diana and Apollo. She felt a great sense of relief at the joyful and heated reunion between the twins and their father. Seeing their shining faces lightened the mood as Diana cursed and complained at not being the one to destroy the Gorgons. While his sister ranted, Apollo took Joel quietly aside and promised to teach him to fight one-armed.

The throne room was still crowded with statues. Emily's father lifted her onto Pegasus, who took her around to heal the Nirads one by one. The queen and prince were at her side, ready to reassure all the Nirads as they came back to themselves.

"Hey, do not forget fly boy over here," Paelen called as he stood beside the Cupid statue. "Personally, I believe he looks good just as he is. But Venus may not be too pleased if we leave him like this."

Emily leaned forward on Pegasus. "Pegs, I forgot all about him!"

Pegasus turned his head back to her and nickered

softly. There was a twinkle in his big brown eyes. Emily was certain the stallion was laughing at her.

"It's not funny, Pegs. How could I forget about Cupid? Please don't tell him. He'll never forgive me!"

Pegasus carried Emily over to Cupid. She reached down and touched the top of the winged Olympian's head. As Cupid returned to flesh, he panicked and cried out.

"Calm down!" Paelen said. "You are safe. Emily saved you, and the Gorgons are dust."

Cupid looked up at Emily on Pegasus. He gave the room a final check to be certain, then cleared his throat, fluttered his healed wings, and adjusted his tunic in embarrassment. "I was not panicking, Paelen," he corrected abruptly. "I was concerned that the Flame might be in danger."

Paelen started to laugh and slapped Cupid playfully on his wings. "Do not worry about my Emily. She can take care of herself!"

THE TASK OF RESTORING THE STONE NIRADS
in the throne room seemed to take forever.

"Come on, Pegs," Emily said softly. "Let's go get
Tange and the others back." She went to move toward
Tange and the three others supporting the top of the
gold cage. Segan and Toban were standing beside
Tange, their heads lowered. The queen was lightly
stroking Tange's back.

"Emily, stop," Jupiter called. He was standing with
Diana, Apollo, and several large Nirads.

"I'm just going up to help Tange."

"You cannot help him," Jupiter said. "Leave him
be, as he is."

Emily frowned and slid off Pegasus's back. She

clung to his wing as she hopped over to Jupiter. "But I can bring him back. If you and a few Nirads support the cage, no one should get hurt."

Jupiter sadly shook his head. "You must not do it."

Emily's heart started to race. "Why? Tange was the first Nirad to be kind to me! He showed me there was more to them than the monsters I thought they were. Please, Jupiter, I've got to help him!"

Diana stepped closer and put her arm around Emily. "Listen to Father, Emily. He knows what he is talking about."

Emily shook her head and pulled away. "No, he doesn't." She looked at Jupiter. "Tange is good—he really helped us. Why won't you let me help him?"

"I am not forbidding you to help him," Jupiter said kindly. "I am asking you not to. Let me explain—I think you will agree with me."

Jupiter moved closer to Emily and started to support her. With Pegasus on one side and her father on the other, he led her up to the dais. "Take a good look up there and tell me what you see."

"I see Tange," Emily said, looking up at the stone statue of the Nirad.

"Yes, and what is Tange holding?"

"The top of the cage."

"That is correct," Jupiter said patiently. "What is the cage made of?"

"Gold."

"Not just any gold," Diana added. "That is the same gold as your leg brace and our weapons."

"Olympian gold!" Paelen cried, suddenly understanding. He climbed up to the cage and pointed at the roof. "Emily, look—Tange and the others are holding the gold roof with their four bare hands. It is poisoning them."

"That is correct," Jupiter said sadly. "If you were to touch Tange or any of the others, you would certainly bring them back to life. But even your powers cannot stop the gold's poison from coursing through their systems. They will die in agony. Believe me, child, the kindest thing you can do for them now is to leave them as they are."

Emily was too stunned to speak. She looked up at Tange and saw that the marble of his four hands was black with the poison from the gold. Pain was etched on his orange marble face. That expression was there long before the Gorgons turned him to stone. Tange had known he was dying.

"They knew it would kill them, but they lifted the roof anyway," she said.

"What father would not do the same for his daughter?" Jupiter asked.

"Daughter?"

Jupiter nodded. "Tange was Segan's father. He sacrificed himself for her. The three other Nirads with him are his brothers. They were devoted to their niece. They refused to leave the throne room after Tange was ordered to travel to your world to get you."

Emily felt her throat constrict as she looked up at the four stone guardians. "Tange is really . . . dead?" she whispered. She looked at her own father. "Dad?"

Her father pulled her into a tight embrace and kissed her on the top of her head. "I'd do the same for you, Em, any day."

Segan and Toban left their father and came off the dais. Emily saw dark tears flowing down the queen's young face. She approached Emily and uttered a few soft words.

Diana stroked Emily's hair. "Tange told her how

much you reminded him of her. You share the same spirit and bravery. She says he would have died to protect you, too." Emily felt her heart breaking. As deep sobs wracked her, the pink Nirad queen put her arms around her and held her tight. Standing together, the two shared their grief.

It took several long and exhausting days to restore the lives of several thousand stone Nirads throughout the land. The Gorgon attack had been brutal and extended far beyond the palace limits.

Though still very quiet, Joel was slowly getting used to life with one arm. As Emily rode on Pegasus's back, she watched him, her father, Paelen, and Chrysaor playing a form of soccer with a group of Nirad children and Prince Toban. Chrysaor and Joel were on opposite sides, and Chrysaor snuck up behind Joel and tackled him down to the ground. The winged boar invited all the Nirad children on his team to join in the pile-on. Emily smiled as she heard Joel's shouts and, finally, laughter coming from the bottom of the pile.

"He'll be fine, Pegs," Emily said softly as she patted his neck and got back to work restoring more Nirads to life.

Jupiter, Diana, Apollo, and Cupid entered the Solar Stream to gather the other Olympians home. With so many worlds to search, they knew it would take some time to get everyone back to Olympus.

At the end of yet another seemingly endless day, Emily was relieved to restore the last Nirad. She slipped off Pegasus's back and hopped up to the lilac Nirad. With the queen at her side, she reached out and touched this final victim.

With the knowledge that this was the last statue, exhaustion pressed down on her. She had lost track of just how many there were, but it was more than she had imagined possible. She was grateful that her power to heal had been enough. As the last statue began to warm, she knew that every Nirad that could be saved had been. A sharp stab of pain pierced through her when she thought of Tange. Like the loss of her mother, his death was a pain she knew she would carry with her for the rest of her life.

The final Nirad came back to life screaming. After Segan spoke reassuringly to him, he bowed his head and knelt before his queen. Emily shared the Nirad's joy when his young children came rushing up to him and threw their tiny arms around him.

Queen Segan looked at Emily and nodded. They didn't need to speak the same language to understand. It was done. Emily smiled back. She hopped up to Pegasus's head and kissed him on the muzzle.

"We did it, Pegs," she said softly.

Emily stroked the stallion's face and looked at the strange land around her. The Nirad world was slowly coming back to life. The skies were still as dark and cloudy as ever, with the strange batlike creatures circling high overhead. There was still no plant life in sight. The earth was as black and dusty as the day she arrived. And yet, to Emily, it was beautiful.

"Em!" Joel called.

Emily looked up and saw Joel and Toban riding Chrysaor. Joel was holding on to the boar's ear with his left hand, and he was smiling. Paelen was flying beside them using his winged sandals. They touched down beside her.

"Emily, you and the queen must come back to the palace immediately," Paelen said.

"What's happening?" Emily asked.

Joel's smile grew. That alone was enough to make the day perfect for Emily. Her friend was going to be all right in the end. "Come back and see for yourselves," he said, laughing.

Emily looked over at Segan. "There's room on Pegasus for the both of us."

When Pegasus took off into the sky, the queen cried out in fear mixed with roaring excitement. Her four arms nearly squeezed the breath out of Emily as she clung to her for dear life. They flew over the bustling village and heard the calls and saw the waving of the Nirads on the ground. Finally they touched down outside the palace.

"It's in the throne room," Paelen said excitedly as he dashed up the steps into the palace. "Hurry up!"

"What is?" Emily asked.

"C'mon," Joel cried anxiously as he and Toban climbed off Chrysaor and they followed Paelen in.

Emily looked back at the queen and shrugged. "Let's go see."

Pegasus carried Emily and Segan up the steps of the palace. She hadn't been back here since the horrific battle. The scene of so much suffering and loss still disturbed her, and she hadn't been able to return. As Pegasus's golden hooves clopped on the marble floor, Emily heard voices. Lots and lots of voices.

"Hurry up, you slowpokes," her father called as he appeared at the entrance to the throne room. He was clean shaven again, and his hair had been neatly trimmed. But best of all, a broad smile spread across his face.

Emily's eyes grew large as Pegasus trotted into the throne room. The room was filled with Olympians and Nirads gathered around long banquet tables. Ambrosia and the black Nirad food sat side by side at the tables. Laughter rang out as the great celebration started.

The Gorgon thrones had gone, and there was no dais. Emily looked back at Segan. They both noticed the same thing. The golden cage with Tange and his three brothers was also missing.

At the huge head table sat Jupiter; his wife, Juno; and his brothers, Neptune and Pluto. Diana and Apollo sat at their mother's side, while several chairs remained empty between Jupiter and Pluto.

When Jupiter saw Emily, Segan, and Pegasus standing at the entrance, he stood and called the room to order. Everyone turned to face the leader of Olympus.

"Olympians and Nirads, we have gathered together to celebrate the peace between our two worlds." Jupiter held up his goblet of Nectar. "And together we mourn the loss of family and friends. We all honor our dead!"

Cheers rang out around the room as everyone raised their goblets in salute to the fallen.

Jupiter raised his cup a second time and called the room back to silence. "We are also here to thank someone very special." As he spoke, Jupiter was looking directly at Emily.

She felt her face flushing and her heart pounding. Pegasus turned his head back to her. He nodded and nickered loudly in agreement, while Segan, with her arms still around Emily's waist, gave her a light embrace and spoke softly. Paelen approached on one side of her and rested his hand on her leg; Joel and Chrysaor approached from the other. Her father reached up and took her hand and gave it a reassuring squeeze.

"None of us would be here today," Jupiter continued, "were it not for the bravery and strength of Emily Jacobs and Pegasus. My family—Olympians and Nirads—I give you the Flame of Olympus!"

Epilogue

EMILY AND PEGASUS COULDN'T HAVE BEEN
any happier.

Since their return to Olympus, trade between
Olympians and the Nirads had started. Nirads could
often be seen walking the Olympian streets.

It wasn't long after their return that Joel had a new
arm fashioned by Vulcan and his best armorers. He
was proud to show it off to anyone who cared to look
at it. It gave him remarkable strength, and for the
first time since they met, he was able to beat Paelen
at arm wrestling. Like Emily's new leg brace, it was
made entirely of Olympian silver. Vulcan abandoned
the use of gold because of the danger it posed to all
the Nirads.

But what made Emily's life complete was having her father with her and her friends there in Olympus. She now had everything she could have dreamed of.

"Hi, Dad," she said, a smile rising to her lips as she greeted him.

"What are you smiling at?" He laughed, his dimples pinching in his cheeks.

"Nothing," Emily said. He was a sight to see in his white tunic and sandals—a far cry from his New York City Police Department uniform. He had settled in easily. "I'm just so glad to see you again."

"Me too," he said as he reached up to take her hand. "It's been a very long road for both of us, kiddo. But we've made it. Your mother would be so proud of you." His bright smile returned. "I need you and Pegasus to come with me for a moment—we have something to show you. The Nirads just delivered it."

"What is it?"

"A monument," he said. "It represents the union between the two worlds. But Jupiter says he won't have it in his garden without your approval."

"Why does Jupiter need my approval?"

"Come along, and I think you'll understand."

They moved through the beautiful, fragrant gardens at Jupiter's palace. Paelen and Joel came running up to her. "They have just finished setting it up."

Ahead of them, Emily saw a newly constructed rock garden. Huge black stones were set up to form a circle, and the ground was covered with black Nirad soil. As Pegasus approached, the crowds of Olympians and Nirads parted to let them through. Emily sucked in her breath when she saw what was at the center of the circle.

"Tange," she hushed.

Ahead of her stood the stone Tange and his three brothers. There were chains of the most beautiful Olympian flowers woven around their necks. Although pain was still etched on their faces, they no longer supported the gold roof of the queen's cage. They now held a black marble slab that supported a throne. Seated on the throne was the statue of an older pink female Nirad also surrounded by fragrant flowers.

"She was the original queen," Paelen explained softly. "When the Gorgons arrived in the Nirad world, the first thing they did was turn her to stone and smash her to bits. That was how Segan came to power. Since the Nirads do not grieve their dead the same way we do, they put the broken pieces of their queen back together and offered this to us as a way to remember the struggle that brought our two worlds together."

Beside the statue, Jupiter and Juno stood with Queen Segan and Prince Toban. They acknowledged Emily with waves and friendly nods. Jupiter stepped forward and reached up to help her climb off the stallion. Together they walked up to the monument.

"Emily, the queen and prince have given us their parents to safeguard. They want to show us their gratitude for what you did for their people. However, I explained that seeing Tange every day may cause you pain, knowing that you must never touch him or his brothers."

Emily looked at the statue of Tange, then over to Segan. She could see the anxious expression on her face. She felt her own father's reassuring presence behind her and was grateful to have everyone she cared about here, including Tange.

She walked up to the queen. "Thank you so much

for trusting us. I promise you, we will take care of your family. You and all your people are welcome to come visit them anytime." She looked over at Jupiter. "Right?"

"Of course," he agreed as he nodded. "Queen Segan, you have my word that from this day forward, Nirads will always be welcome in Olympus."

As the cheers rose and a new celebration started, Emily made her way back to Pegasus. She climbed onto the stallion's back and sat in silent contentment, watching the gathering around her. A large banquet was planned for later that evening. But for the moment, she was happy just to stay where she was.

She noticed Paelen, Joel, Toban, and Chrysaor huddled together. Paelen looked up at her and waved as a crooked grin rose to his face. Something about his expression told her they were up to more mischief, and she knew that before long, she would be invited to join in the fun with her friends.

Beside Tange's statue, her father, Diana, and the Nirad queen were speaking quietly. She smiled as her father wrapped his arm protectively around Segan's shoulders.

While he lived, Tange had treated her like his own child. He had protected her and risked his life for her. She hoped that, somehow, Tange knew her father would do the same for his daughter.

Not far away, Cupid stood with his mother, Venus. The feathers on his wings were neatly groomed, and his hair was combed perfectly into place. He was wearing a new tunic and looked impossibly handsome. She wondered if he had ever told his mother what he had done to the CRU agents at the Red Apple. Emily doubted it. After a moment Cupid felt her eyes on him, and he looked at her. He nodded his head and smiled his most radiant smile. Emily smiled back and waved. Cupid had surprised her. He had overcome his fears of the Nirads and come through for them. She was grateful to call him her friend.

Pegasus nickered and looked up at her.

"Don't worry, Pegs," she said softly, stroking the new feathers on his wings. "Cupid was just a silly crush. I'm over him." As she spoke, her eyes trailed over to Paelen and Joel, and her smile increased. She doubted if even Pegasus knew who really held her heart.

Emily looked down into the stallion's beautiful white face and laughed. "What do you say we go for a quick flight before the party gets started?"

Pegasus whinnied and turned from the crowd. He trotted into a full gallop, opened his wings, and carried Emily up into the sky.

THE ADVENTURE CONTINUES
IN BOOK 3:
The New Olympians

THE ROAR OF THE CROWD WAS DEAFENING. Olympians sprang to their feet cheering on the very first inter-Olympian soccer match. The Solar Streamers were playing Hercules's Heroes, but this was no ordinary soccer match. The scene on the field was as impressive and extraordinary as you would expect on Olympus.

When Joel first proposed the event, he was amazed by how many Olympians wanted to get involved. Now, with a full stadium of spectators cheering him on, Joel, captain of the Solar Streamers, expertly maneuvered the ball down the pitch and between the legs of a charging satyr. The half goat, half boy turned and charged after him as if his very life depended on it.

Joel broke through the defense line and passed the black-and-white ball to his Olympian teammate and friend Paelen, who dashed forward to get into position. The winged boar, Chrysaor, caught up with Joel and drove away the Hercules's Heroes defenders, Mercury and Minerva, while Pegasus flew across the field over a line of centaurs and giants and called to Paelen to pass the ball. With a quick kick, the ball was in the winged stallion's possession.

Emily sat on the sidelines beside Jupiter. She marveled at how adept Pegasus was at a sport he and the other Olympians had only just learned. Pegasus was able to keep moving forward while the ball remained in play between his four hooves.

Suddenly a satyr ducked beneath Pegasus and stole the ball away. Moving swiftly on his goat legs, he kicked it back to his teammates. But no sooner did the opposing team have the ball than a young female centaur on Joel's team made a move that caused the crowd to cheer even louder. Leaping gracefully into the air, she blocked a high kick with her brown equine body. As the ball touched down on the ground, she expertly kicked it forward to Joel.

Running toward the goal line, Joel and Paelen kept the soccer ball moving between them. Finally Joel moved into position to shoot it at the goal.

"Go for it, Joel!" Emily shouted from her seat. "Shoot!"

The opposing side's goalkeeper was a terrifying sight. The Sphinx reared on her lion's haunches, spread her arms and eagle's wings wide, and prepared to block Joel's shot.

With one quick dart away from a young Nirad defender, Joel kicked the ball. It flew in the air and then seemed to arch as if it had a life all its own. It caught the upper bar of the goalposts and flew into the net above the head of the Sphinx.

When the goalkeeper saw the ball enter her goal, she roared in fury and sprang forward, tackling Joel to the ground.

Emily's heart nearly stopped. The Sphinx had Joel pinned down with her large lion paws. She threw back her head, roaring a second time, and raised a fearsome paw in the air, as if to tear into him with her sharpened claws.

"Jupiter, stop her!" Emily cried to the leader of

Olympus standing beside her. "The Sphinx will tear him apart!"

But instead of moving to stop the attack, Jupiter cheered louder and started to applaud. He leaned closer to her. "My dear child, Alexis may be short-tempered, but she knows this is just a game. Joel is perfectly safe." Jupiter paused and looked at all the men in the stands raising their hands and cheering. "I am certain that Joel is the subject of many Olympians' envy."

Out on the field, the players on Joel's team continued to celebrate the goal, unconcerned by the goalkeeper's assault on their star player. Finally the Sphinx brushed back the hair from Joel's eyes, leaned forward, and kissed him full and long on the lips.

"Foul!" shouted Emily as she ran furiously onto the field. Pushing between the players, she shoved the goalkeeper. "Get off him!"

As the Sphinx climbed slowly off Joel, her serpent's tail swished playfully in the air. She narrowed her green eyes and smiled mischievously at Emily. "Is the Flame of Olympus jealous?"

The Sphinx may have looked ferocious and dangerous with her lion's body, eagle's wings, and serpent's tail, but she had the head and upper body of a young woman. In fact, she was breathtakingly beautiful.

Emily paused and looked from Alexis to Joel. Seeing him on the ground with his beaming smile, warm brown eyes, and handsome face, Emily was stunned to realize that she was very jealous.

"Of course not!" she shot back. "But kissing the opposing players isn't part of the game."

The smile never left the Sphinx's face as she padded lithely back to her position in front of the goal. She looked playfully over her shoulder, flicking her long raven hair. "Pity. It should be."

Paelen reached forward and, with Emily's help, lifted the stunned Joel to his feet. As they brushed him off, Paelen stole a look back at Alexis. "Wow!" he breathed. "That was some kiss. You are so lucky!"

The color in Joel's cheeks brightened further as Alexis called, "I will see you later, Joel."

"Don't count on it," Emily fired back. She ignored the soft chuckles coming from the Sphinx and returned her attention to Joel. During his time in Olympus, he had grown taller and more muscular from all the physical work in Vulcan's workshop. Joel's growth spurt was the cause of much complaint from Vulcan, as he constantly had to enlarge the silver mechanical right arm that replaced the one Joel had lost in the fight against the gorgons.

"Did Alexis hurt you?" Emily asked.

Joel looked back at the Sphinx curiously and then shook his head. "Not at all."

Paelen smiled his crooked grin, then pursed his lips in an exaggerated kiss. "Perhaps bruise your tender lips?"

"What?" Joel cried. He shoved Paelen away as his cheeks reddened deeper. "Stop that. I'm fine! Can we please get back to the match?"

As the players returned to their positions, Pegasus escorted Emily to her seat on the sidelines. The stallion nickered softly, and Emily saw an extra sparkle in his beautiful dark eyes. Pegasus was laughing.

"What are you laughing at?" she challenged.

Emily's teacher, Vesta, approached, overhearing the conversation. "Pegasus believes the Sphinx was correct. You are jealous of her."

"Jealous of Alexis? That's crazy," Emily said. "For

one, she's just an overgrown, green-eyed, flying house cat. And for two, Joel and I are friends. That's all."

The smile on Vesta's face grew. "Of course you are, dear. . . ."

"We're friends," Emily insisted as she returned to her seat. "That's all! Now, Pegs, your team is waiting for you; you'd better get back."

Pegasus let out a loud, laughing whinny before trotting back to the field of play to take his position on Joel's team.

As the match progressed, the score remained tied. While the Sphinx was the Hercules's Heroes goalkeeper, Joel's team had a huge orange Nirad called Tirk guarding their end. With his four arms, he proved a capable goalie and rarely allowed the ball into the net.

"That's quite a match going on out there. But I'm not too sure if flying up and down the field is in the rulebook."

Emily jumped at the sound of her father's voice. "Dad!" She threw her arms around his neck. "I've missed you."

He had been away from Olympus with Diana and

Apollo for what felt like ages. They were leading a small team back to Earth to determine if Jupiter's ban on visits should be lifted. The Olympians had heard about human advancements and were curious to learn more. Her father went as an adviser and guide.

When Emily released her father, she welcomed Diana with a firm hug. "I've missed you both. When did you get back?"

"Not long ago," her father said. "We went to the palace first and were told about the big match."

He looked at the pitch and whistled in amazement. "When you told me you and Joel were teaching some of the Olympians to play soccer, it never dawned on me who or what would be playing. I've never seen a more fantastic sight."

Emily looked over at the satyrs, harpies, centaurs, giants and some of the Muses out on the field playing alongside winged creatures never mentioned or even imagined in the ancient myths.

"We tried to teach Cerberus to play, but it didn't work," Emily continued. "His three heads kept fighting over the ball and tearing it to shreds. It was the same with the Cyclops. With only one eye, he kept missing the ball and got really frustrated. He even tore down the goal in a rage. Jupiter finally had to ask him to keep score. You can see him over there." She pointed to the end of the field, where the giant Cyclops was updating the scoreboard with each goal. "But most of the other Olympians seem to enjoy the game."

Their eyes were drawn back to the field, where a satyr had broken free of the giant guard and was rushing with the ball toward Joel's team's goal. As she neared the net, Paelen appeared from the left to block the kick. But the satyr was faster and ducked away from him. With a second quick dart, she kicked the ball between the Nirad's four arms, and it entered the net.

The crowd exploded with excitement and stood cheering. Emily looked around and smiled ruefully at the Olympians. She glanced back to her father. "I don't think they fully understand the concept of supporting one side or the other. Everyone celebrates when there is a goal—it doesn't matter which team made it."

Her father nodded. "Maybe they've got the right

idea. We could use more sportsmanship like that back in our world." He focused on Emily again. "You love soccer. Even with your leg brace, you can move just as well as before your leg was hurt. Why aren't you out there playing?"

Emily hesitated before answering. "I didn't feel like playing today. I wanted to watch with Jupiter so I could explain the rules. Not that anyone actually follows them."

Emily watched her father's face, relieved that he accepted her explanation without question. Emily wanted very much to play, but she couldn't. She couldn't because she couldn't trust herself.

Since her return from the Nirad world, where they'd defeated the gorgons, Emily had mastered the power of the Flame that lived deep within her. She could now control it fully. But recently more powers had surfaced. Powers that went beyond the Flame. Where objects moved by themselves, or sometimes, if she became very frustrated or upset, vanished completely. Vesta hadn't mentioned more powers. Emily wondered if her teacher even realized there were others. But too many things were happening around her. Until Emily could better understand and control them, she wasn't going to risk hurting her friends.

The match ended with Joel's team losing by one goal. A celebratory banquet was planned for later that evening. Emily walked with her father and Pegasus back to the apartment they shared with Joel and Paelen in Jupiter's palace.

"I am going to tell Jupiter that I don't think it's a good idea for Olympians to visit Earth. There are just too many dangers. Our world has changed far too much for them now. They had no idea how different or advanced it is."

"But after everything they've heard from us, they're all so anxious to visit," Emily insisted.

"I know," he agreed. "The big problem is that Olympians aren't human. Very few of them look even remotely human. Can you imagine what would happen if a centaur or even the Cyclops were to visit our world? In the past, they were accepted as gods, but today . . ." He paused and looked back to Pegasus. "Look what happened to him in New York."

Pegasus snorted and nickered loudly. Emily reached over and stroked the stallion's neck. Memories flashed to the surface of her mind. Pegasus had been shot by the secret government agency the Central Research Unit, and taken to their hidden facility on Governors Island. The sight of her beloved stallion lying prone on the floor and struggling for each breath caused a stab of pain in her heart, even now.

Emily looked back at her father and nodded. "It wasn't just Pegasus who was hurt. Look what the CRU did to Cupid. Their helicopters nearly killed him, despite Olympians being immortal. If they stop eating ambrosia, they become vulnerable, and it's too easy for them to get hurt."

"Or captured," her father added. "Personally, I don't think it's a good idea at all. I'm going to tell Jupiter this. Olympians are an amazing people, and I don't want to see anything happen to them."

As they continued to walk down the tranquil, cobbled road, the clopping sound of Pegasus's golden hooves was the only thing to disturb the calm of Olympus. After a long silence, Emily's father spoke again.

"Your aunt Maureen sends her love."

"You saw her?"

He shook his head. "There were CRU agents posted around her building; we couldn't get near her. But I did call and tell her we are fine. She asked a lot of questions, but I'm sure her line is bugged. So I told her we're in hiding but together and safe."

"I wish we could see her again," Emily said wistfully.

"Me too," her father agreed. "Maybe one day soon we can go back for a real visit. Just you and me."

Emily brightened. "That would be wonderful."

When they arrived at their apartment, Emily's eyes flew wide at the assortment of gifts her father and Diana had brought back for her, Joel, and Paelen: clothes, music, and some of Emily's favorite snacks, like salted peanuts and her real weakness, marshmallows. There was even an assortment of chocolate bars just for Paelen.

Emily noticed a stack of newspapers. She had never been interested in the news when she lived in New York, but now that she was living in Olympus permanently, she craved to learn what was happening in her city.

Top of the pile was the New York Times. A photograph on the front page caught her attention.

Was that Pegasus?

Emily immediately snatched it up, curious.

Yes, it was definitely Pegasus—but without wings!

She read the caption under the photograph.

RECORD BREAKER! TORNADO WARNING
WINS TRIPLE CROWN WITH GREATEST TIME
AND DISTANCE EVER RECORDED.

"Tornado Warning?" Emily muttered aloud as she read the article about the winning horse breaking every record in the history of horse racing.

"Look at that face," her father said lightly. "He looks just like Pegasus, doesn't he? His body and legs are darker gray, but if he were all white, it could have been Pegasus. Tornado Warning is everywhere and causing quite a stir. They haven't had a Triple Crown winner like him since Secretariat—and Tornado's even broken his records!"

Emily barely heard the knocking on the door. As her father went to answer it, she continued to scan the article.

"Pegs, you've got to see this." Emily held up the

newspaper for the stallion. "Look at his face. He really does look like you. I mean, you two could be twins!"

When Pegasus looked at the photographs, Emily could sense he was greatly disturbed. Apart from the color, Tornado Warning was identical. His size and shape were the same. All that was missing were the wings and golden hooves. Emily looked at the stallion. "How is this possible?"

"So you have seen the newspapers." Diana had entered the living room and approached Pegasus. "Is there something you wish to tell me? Did you get up to some mischief while you were in Emily's world?"

Pegasus snorted angrily and stamped a golden hoof.

Emily frowned and then shook her head. "That's not possible. Tornado couldn't be his son. Look here, the paper says Tornado Warning is three years old. But Pegasus only came to our world last year."

"But he does look just like you, my friend," Diana said softly as she stroked Pegasus's face. "What else could it be?"

Emily's father, Steve, shrugged. "Maybe he's just a

very handsome horse who happens to look a lot like Pegasus."

Emily studied her father's face and realized he didn't see Pegasus the same way she and the other Olympians did. On the surface, Pegasus could look mostly like a horse, but there was a big difference. It was something that she could plainly see, but her father couldn't. Pegasus was more than a horse, much greater than one. It was in his intelligent eyes and the way he held himself, that created the aura surrounding him that said, "I am not a mere horse."

Olympus had many horses and some, like Pegasus, had wings. But none of them were remotely like Pegasus. He was unique—until now.

"You're wrong, Dad," Emily insisted. "Tornado Warning doesn't just look like Pegasus, he's identical to him."

Diana put her arm around Emily and gave her a light squeeze. "Well, whatever it is, that horse, Tornado Warning, is in your world while we are all here in Olympus." Diana abruptly changed the subject. "Now, would you like to try on some of the new clothes that your father and I chose for you?"

Emily looked at Diana and saw there was something the tall woman was not saying aloud. A secret message that said they would speak later. She nodded. "You're right. Let's forget Tornado Warning. I want to see what you've brought back."

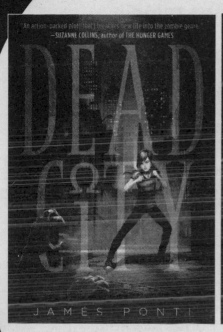

Molly Bigelow is NOT your average girl. She's one of an elite crew assigned the task of policing and protecting the zombie population of New York. *The Hunger Games* author Suzanne Collins says *Dead City* "breathes new life into the zombie genre."

From Aladdin • KIDS.SimonandSchuster.com

EBOOK EDITIONS
ALSO AVAILABLE